The Pirate Prince

The Paladin Princess Series Book 4

Also by Samaire Wynne:

Mad World: EPIDEMIC

Mad World: SANCTUARY

Mad World: DESPERATION

ROMANOV

The Paladin Princess series:

#1: The Pirates of Moonlit Bay

#2: The Pirate Queen

#3: The Lost Treasure

#4: The Pirate Prince

#5: The Death of the Queen (Fall 2020)

#6: The Fountain of Youth (Fall 2020)

#7: Magellan's Tears (Fall 2020)

The Pirate Prince

The Paladin Princess Series Book 4

Samaire Wynne

Black Raven Books

This is a work of fiction. All of the geography, characters, organizations, and events portrayed in this novel are either products of the author's imagination or are used fictitiously.

Black Raven Books

The text was set in 12-point Californian FB

ISBN-13: 9781948594165

First Edition: September 2019

10 9 8 7 6 5 4 3 2 1

Dedicated to my cat Tyrion, who brings me comfort when I get melancholy.

The Pirate Prince

From a story idea by Stephen Provost

Chapter One

Of Storms and Nightmares

"No! NO! AIEEEEEEE!"

The screams were so loud in my ears they made my head ring.

Who on earth is screaming?

I groaned in my sleep and turned over.

I saw a black cloud approaching fast as I stood at the deck of my ship, *Pride of the Sea.*

Why aren't I flinching?

The cloud was moving unnaturally fast, and I couldn't take my eyes off it, couldn't even blink.

"Charlotte, we need to take cover. Babe? Come on!" Tam was pulling at my arm, trying to get me to go below decks, but I refused to budge.

I was captivated by the sight of the massive, roiling black cloud that was almost upon us.

"Come on!"

"Is she coming?"

"No."

"Well, she has to."

"Well, she's not. I'll just stay with her."

"Then you'll both be swept overboard."

"Tam, just grab her."

"I tried. She won't let go."

"Here, let me."

I felt myself grasped from beneath, and two strong blue-green-purple arms lifted me into the air a foot and turned.

"Hey! No, wait!" I exclaimed.

"No, Charlotte. We have to get below decks. That's a massive storm, and we'll be lucky if the ship doesn't sink," the djinn said quietly but firmly. "Anyone left on deck will be lost. Now stop struggling."

Was I struggling? I didn't think so.

I looked down and saw my hands were pulling at his arms and my feet were kicking.

I flipped over in his arms and struggled to get free.

"Charlotte, Babe, stop! You've got to stop!" That was Tam, holding on to my arm, pleading with me to be still.

The djinn reached the doorway to my cabin and tried to go through it while holding me. Even on a good day, without a pitching deck, without a crazed woman in his arms struggling to get free, the djinn had a hard time fitting through that door. At nearly ten feet tall, and heavily muscled, he had to crouch and fold himself a bit just to get through the passage.

"I'm going to have to set her down," he said.

"Uh oh."

"Wait."

"Okay, I'll hold her arms," said Tam. He gripped both my arms tightly.

The djinn set me down.

I immediately turned, wiggling free of their grasps, and ran back to the deck railing.

The wind blew so hard my head was snapped back, and I struggled to keep my eyes open.

"CHARLOTTE!" Tam screamed, struggling to join me at the railing.

The wind howled, and the rain stung my face.

I watched the storm, unblinkingly.

I saw a waterspout approach and zip over the ship.

I felt myself lifted from the deck by the wind.

"CHARLOTTE!"

"AAAHHHHHHH!" I heard myself scream as I was pitched overboard into the sea.

I sat up, drenched in sweat.

"Oh, God." I murmured.

Tam opened the door and walked into the room, Khepri right behind him.

"She was screaming in her sleep again," said Tam. "I couldn't wake her."

"Here, Charlotte, why don't you sit up?" Khepri said.

"Oh my God, that was intense," I said, holding my head, which was pounding.

I allowed them to pull me up in the bed, and tuck pillows around me.

Khepri busied herself brewing her medicinal tea, dribbling a large handful of dried flakes into the pot of water she set to boil.

Tam sat beside me and took my hand.

"Babe, what was it this time?" he asked.

I took a deep breath, blinking rapidly, trying to bring myself back to the present.

"Uh," I took another deep breath, "it ... it was a storm, a really bad storm. You all were trying to get me to go below decks, but I fought you." I blinked and met his concerned gaze. "I fought everyone, trying to stay on deck."

Tam rubbed my arm in sympathy.

"I ... I was swept overboard," I said faintly. I still felt so dazed.

"Here you go, sweetums." Khepri brought a steaming mug to me, and held it as I slowly brought both hands to grip the sturdy sides. A fragrant scent wafted into my face, and I closed my eyes and inhaled deeply.

Mmmmm

I took a sip.

Warmth and a slight bitterness flooded my mouth. I grimaced, but swallowed, familiar with the flavor of Khepri's tinctures.

"Mmm, thanks." I smiled up at her.

A wave of dizziness washed over me, and I blinked.

"Careful." With one hand, Tam gripped my hands wrapped around the mug, his other hand going over my shoulder to steady me.

"Dizzy again?" asked Khepri.

"Yes. I don't know why," I murmured.

"The tea will help with that as well," said Khepri, letting herself out the door, "But so will lots of rest." She smiled at us and shut the door behind herself.

"Yeah, but I get nightmares when I sleep," I murmured to myself.

"Charlotte, I think you should drink the tea before you sleep, from now on," Tam said, kissing my forehead. "Besides, you can't get a good night's sleep if you're always having nightmares, can you?"

"I don't expect so," I said.

I sighed.

My stomach roiled.

"Here," he handed me a small piece of crusty bread with an opaque gel spread on it.

I took a bite.

"Mmmm, it's warm," I said around the bread in my mouth.

"Caroline baked it just this morning," Tam said.

I took another bite, licking the gel from the edge. "Mmmm, is this bacon grease?"

Tam chuckled. "Christianne says we're going to call it 'bacon butter' – and yes, it is. Caroline is slow-cooking the boar they brought on board yesterday."

"Ohhh, that will be delicious." I glanced out the porthole on the side. "Have we made much progress?"

"Yes. We've sailed about fifty or so leagues since we left the isle."

I thought back to the small island we'd encountered the previous evening. It hadn't been on any nautical chart, although it was a dozen miles wide. It had been teeming with life, and Tam guessed that ships had stopped there frequently and had accidentally let animals off.

There'd been a freshwater spring, and an abundance of trees and game, as well as an old shipwreck on the lee shore. Tam had taken a small hunting group out, eager to try out the new bow he'd been carving the month before.

They'd come back with several wild hogs, and Caroline had set about cutting up and smoking some of the meat. Salted, dried meat was a staple aboard our ship, but it was most often fish, or poultry.

I'd been so happy with the boars. I loved pork.

"Here, I'll take that." Tam picked up the mug I'd drained and had been holding on my lap.

"I'm sorry, I was daydreaming." I shook my head. "Ugh, I hate being abed. I'm getting up."

I jumped off the bed as Tam moved to carry the mug back to the kitchen.

"Just don't fall over again," he said.

"I won't."

Lord, I hate being treated like an invalid.

I was soon dressed and out the door, bouncing on deck with and extra energy I didn't really feel. I wanted to appear strong and energetic to the crew.

"Okay, what's the report today, sailor?" I asked the mariner nearby.

"Smooth sailing all night, Captain. Nothing but calm swells," she answered.

I peered at the port horizon.

"And what about those dark clouds?" I asked.

"They just appeared in the last half hour. The crow's nest reports glassy seas all around, though," the sailor said.

"Well, you can't be too careful," I said, remembering my nightmare. "Glassy seas can herald an approaching storm. Keep an eye on that cloud cover, and give me reports every hour." I nodded at her.

"Aye, aye, Captain." She saluted and was gone, barking orders to her subordinates.

I sighed and looked out to sea, leaning on the ship railing, enjoying the feel of the sea breeze that whipped back my hair.

I studied the dark clouds on the horizon, remembering my nightmare.

Was it an omen of things to come? I had no way of knowing.

The sound of laughter came to me, and I turned to look at what the commotion was.

Kym had transformed into her chimera form and had Caroline's daughter Greta on her back, and she was trotting back and forth on the fo'c'sle deck above me. Greta was laughing in delight, hanging on to the chimera's lion's mane.

"Hey, you two! Do I get to ride, too?" I called up to them, grinning. Greta waved and laughed again as the chimera pivoted to look at me. She had a fierce, proud, serious look on her leonine face, and she held her head still for a moment, then gave me a nod and pirouetted back to trot along the deck again.

I smiled.

Such an amazing troupe.

We'd been sailing north from a long journey down to the southern tip of Alkebulan, a curiosity I'd been wanting to settle for some time now.

An exploration of the southern waters had yielded some amazing results, meticulously cataloged by Khepri and Christianne, and I'd beheld the sea monster.

It had been far off, which was good. I had watched it for hours, until my face bore a green ring around my eye from holding my brass sight up to my brow for extended periods. I rubbed my eye socket, smiling and remembering how it had taken several days for the green to fade.

Totally worth it.

Three hours later I was below decks consulting with Khepri and Christianne on their progress with *The Book of Mysteries* when the sailor I'd spoken to that morning came and found me.

"Captain," she saluted and snapped her heels together, and waited for my acknowledgement.

She's so military. I have got to have a talk with her.

"Yes?" I asked.

"You asked to be informed if the dark clouds approached and became a concern."

Uh oh.

"Have they gotten closer?" I asked.

"Closer, and they've grown, Captain. They now cover half the horizon."

What?

Without a word, I turned and ran out the door and up to the deck.

Reaching for my brass sight, a constant presence in the holster at my belt, I brought it up to my eye.

I stood at the deck watching the storm approach, while the others gathered near me.

"That looks bad," Caroline said.

"Charlotte, can I have a look, too?" Kym asked, at my other side. I glanced down at her. She was small, and appeared as a six-year-old little girl.

That was her human form.

Her chimera form was massive, imposing, and majestic as anything I'd ever beheld in years.

I handed her the brass sight.

She brought it up to her eye and looked.

Tam walked up behind me and put his arms around me, and I leaned back, enjoying the warmth of his chest.

We'd been a mated couple ever since we'd left the old continent of Iq Ameq'el. Ever since we'd kissed.

Ever since he'd died and been brought back to me.

I shuddered internally, remembering.

Closing my eyes, I turned and, lifting myself up on tiptoes, kissed him deeply.

He brought his arms up to hold me, one reaching around the small of my back, the other higher up, around my shoulders.

He didn't say a thing. He understood.

I'd told him, in detail, what had happened, and what I had seen: the cyclops who'd attacked us and run off with him, seated at a campfire, and roasting Tam's arm over the flames.

I shuddered again.

Great gobs of dragon dung, that had been an awful sight. One I hoped would eventually leave my memory.

Tam held me tighter and kissed the top of my head.

I opened my eyes, trying to get the scene out of my head. I stared off to the side, Tam's sleeve against my face, and inhaled the scent of him.

I will never get tired of this.

I could see several sailors rushing about off to the side, and I was brought back to the present.

The storm.

"Hey," Kym exclaimed, "What is that?"

My head came up and I turned.

"What is what?" I asked.

"That," Kym pointed.

I leaned out and squinted. I saw the black clouds, reaching from left to right across the horizon. They were overtaking us fast.

"Tam, we need to make for shore. Fast." I said.

He nodded and turned and began giving direction. His smart, deep voice was loud, snapping orders right and left.

The crew scurried to obey.

As first mate, Tam was in charge of the ship, right below me. And he was very good at his job.

I watched as he climbed up to the crow's nest. He preferred to see things for himself.

"Charlotte." Kym tapped my arm, handing me the brass sight.

I took it and brought it up to my eye and looked.

What the heck is that?

A black speck, darker than the clouds it was racing, was flying fast toward the ship. It wings strained as it flapped, trying to beat the storm in a race it couldn't win.

Or could it?

"Jim?" I turned, calling out.

The big man was there at my elbow in a second.

"Yes?"

"See that bird?" I pointed out across the sea, which had begun to toss waves into the air.

Jim looked, then gestured for the brass sight. Putting it to his eye, he focused.

"Oh, dear," he said. "He's not going to make it."

"Can you go get him?" I asked. "I can't think of any reason why a raven would be this far out at sea, unless it was delivering a message."

Jim looked again. "Yes, I do think I see something tied to his leg."

He handed the sight back to me. Then he shimmered and concentrated, and was suddenly the massive djinn, ten feet tall, green-blue-purple, deeply muscled, and up in the air in the blink of an eye.

We watched as the magical djinn zipped out across the sea so fast he was a blur.

He moved so swiftly it made me dizzy watching him.

"Ohhh," I gripped the ship's railing.

"Uh oh, here we go," Khepri said from behind me. "Tam, grab her."

But Tam was already wrapping his arms around me and lifting me up in his arms. He moved a few steps back from the edge, and stood against one of the ship's wooden masts.

My eyes were glued on the point the djinn had disappeared.

I handed my brass sight to Kym, who brought it to her face and looked.

"He's already headed back."

Sure enough, the djinn appeared, the large raven in his arms. Luckily, the bird was accustomed to being held.

The djinn transformed the second his feet hit the deck, and walked up to me, cradling the raven.

My eyebrows shot up.

I could see the distinctive blue-and-golden seal around the parchment tied to the raven's leg.

Tam untied the message, and Jim walked off with the bird, cooing to it and muttering about a "nice bit of fresh fish for you," as he walked.

Tam examined the scroll in his hands. It was about two inches long, and half an inch in diameter, and tightly sealed with the royal crest. He shrugged and handed it to me.

I broke the seal, the wax falling from my hands in glittering shower. I unrolled the message and studied it.

My face blanched.

"Trouble?" asked Tam.

"Yes. Swerighe is in the throes of a crisis." I looked down and read it again, trying to read between the lines. "Freak storms and floods have beset my homeland. Indeed, the whole of the Northlands." I studied the message, reading it again and again.

My throat felt tight, and my stomach hurt with worry.

The wind whipped around us suddenly, and I looked up to see the dark storm clouds were almost upon us, even as our ship racing away toward the shore.

Within moments, they had unleashed a downpour upon the ship, torrents of water falling so hard that the drops bounced when they hit the deck, casting spray upward.

The memory of my nightmare came flooding back into my mind, and I felt a desperation born of foreboding.

"We've all got to get below decks. Batten down the hatches! Secure all sails! Steer the giant manta rays toward shore with all haste! Double speed!" I called out to everyone, the troupe, the sailors, the very essence of my ship.

We all rushed toward the door to safety. I stopped at the hatch, leaned against the wall, and gestured for the others to hurry down.

Tam stopped next to me.

"You aren't going to do something like 'ride it out' or 'sit low in the crow's nest' or something like that, are you, Charlotte?"

I looked up at him, his beard and long hair wet with the rain that was slanting toward us and stinging our faces.

I thought about the nightmare.

"No way!" I pushed through the door, and Tam followed, close behind.

We'd ride this one out below decks, thanks.

Chapter Two
Handfasting

The storm thrashed the ship all day and into the night, but the mantas continued to pull hard for the coastline. We'd been sailing north alongside it for a week, but we'd veered out to sea a bit more every day, until we were a day's travel from the coast.

The ship tossed and turned and didn't fall apart, although right before I fell asleep, I worried that it might.

I woke up to a calm cabin. Tam was asleep beside me, snoring softly. I heard a ruffle of feathers and looked over by the door and saw someone had brought the raven in sometime after I'd fallen asleep.

The huge black bird shifted position, stretching his wings out sideways, one by one. The perch he sat on was the old parrot perch that had been in the cabin from the beginning of my time here, and it consisted of a wooden bar, a flat base, and two wooden cups. I could see one of them had water, and the second had remnants of fish stuck to the edges. I smiled.

If I knew Jim, he had made sure the raven had been fed to bursting.

I stretched and noticed the ship was calm and not storm-tossed, as it had been the night before. Closing my eyes, I sensed we were going about fifteen or twenty knots.

I quietly dressed and left the cabin without waking Tam.

Patting my stomach, I was glad to be feeling fine this morning.

And no nightmares last night, thank goodness.

Although if I remember correctly, it had been an alarming evening, the ship tossed and bouncing on the storm waves in almost animal action.

Now Charlotte, the ship is not alive. Don't go down that road.

I passed by the gallery and grabbed an apple. It was still very early. I was glad I'd worn my coat.

I emerged on deck and found it was barely dawn. The wind whipped my hair, but the rain and storm had stopped. I looked to the starboard side and thought I saw a sliver of land in the distance.

The shimmer-whirring of someone descending a rope filled the air, and I saw that the sailor on night watch was coming down from the crow's nest. Another sailor was climbing over the edge of the nest to take her place.

"Captain." The sailor nodded, tipping her hat. I saw it was the same mariner from the morning before, and I smiled.

"Don't you ever sleep, mate?" I asked, laughing.

"Not if I can help it, Captain."

I grinned and patted her shoulder as she passed. "Good night, sailor."

"Good night, Captain."

And I was alone on deck.

There were a few sailors on the fo'c'sle, and a few more up at the quarterdeck, but otherwise, I was solo on the main deck.

I leaned out over the ship railing and scanned the horizon for any sign of bad weather. The sky was an expanse of light grey, smooth and unmoving, looking almost ashamed of the fuss it had put us through the day before.

I watched the sun begin to rise, the wind whistling passed my ears, making me tie my scarf tighter.

Caroline appeared beside me and handed me a mug of steaming tea.

I took it gratefully.

"Couldn't sleep, Carrie?" I asked.

"No, Miss, I slept well, just woke early. I was studying the note your mother sent with the raven, and I found it odd," she said.

"Mmmm, you and me both." I took a sip of tea. It was delicious.

"It looks like the storm is over, Miss. And the shoreline is coming up, I believe," Caroline said.

"Thank goodness, Carrie."

Later that day, as we sailed north along the shore of Alkebulan, we all sat in a circle in my cabin, all nine of us. We even squeezed Akim in, his slim thirteen-year-old frame sat on the shelf above my bed, his knees drawn up to his chest, his arms around his legs, hoping no one would notice him.

I pretended to not look at him, but I did see Greta glance at him a few times. At eight years old, she was a curious, inquisitive girl whose light brown curls streaked with gold, and huge green eyes, hinted at the beauty of the woman she would one day become.

"Okay, everyone," Khepri said, holding court, "I've got at least five to six percent of the book translated and figured out, and this first part is incredibly helpful. It deals with cures and solutions to illnesses we had no idea how to treat."

"Well, at least some of them," Christianne muttered.

Khepri nodded at her. "Yes, Chrissy is correct. We *did* know the direction a few of the cures would take, but the book showed us how to focus and purify the remedies we'd considered. This should hasten the resolution of many human, and even animal ailments." Khepri smiled.

I lifted my glass, "Here, here, Khepri!"

The others followed suit, and a chorus of "here-here's" filled the cabin.

"The ship came through the storm better than expected," Tam began at the nod of my head. "The mantas, of course, were nearly unaffected. They are tired from the strong run to the coast, but since we rested them and fed them a double breakfast, they seem to have recovered all their strength." He nodded toward Jim, who nodded back.

Jim was usually the one who went into the sea to check the mantas, the five massive beasts had fifteen-foot-long wingspans and were used to the djinn the most. I'd noticed Jim was a huge animal lover, probably the strongest one on board, although Kym was a close second.

Both magical beings, both of extreme longevity, both dear, dear friends.

"Okay. Thank you, Jim, for keeping a close eye on the mantas. I don't know what we'd do without them, to be honest." I paused and took a deep breath, then continued. "About the raven's message from Swerighe ..." Everyone leaned forward, and I held up my hand. "I have no information other than yesterday's note from my mother, the queen. But Khepri, Caroline and I have been talking and consulting the sea charts, and we've decided that, although the situation in Swerighe seems odd and troubling, it does not really require our return – at least not right away."

Jim shifted in his seat. I nodded to him.

"What we did receive, late this morning, was a message from Tupu," I said.

"Oh!"

"Tupu! Oh I miss her!"

"How is she?"

"How is her baby?"

"I hope she's all right?"

"Oh, Tupu!"

"She's such a great warrior!"

"Yes," I held up my hand for silence. "Okay, so, you may have noticed," I nodded my head toward the perch in the corner, "that there are now two ravens in the cabin. We received Tupu's message late this morning, a few hours ago. In fact that's why I called you all together."

"Are the ravens okay? That one's feathers look off," Kym pointed.

"Yes, they're okay. They just need rest and good food. They'll be ready to fly off tomorrow, most likely. Now..." I paused, looking around for anyone else who wanted to comment.

The troupe looked back at me expectantly.

"We've decided to return to the Mare Nostrum and the twin islands," I said. "Tupu will be meeting us there, and she will be rejoining us."

"YAY!"

"WOO HOO!"

"WHOOP!"

"TUPU!"

"Oh! I'm so pleased, Miss!"

"I did miss her."

"Jim, you must be happy?"

"Yes, I am very happy," Jim said, turning scarlet.

I grinned.

Jim spoke again, "You know," he mused, "I miss her so much, I think I can smell her."

Khepri looked at him sharply.

"So can I," Kym said.

"Well," I stood up, "Who's ready for a handfasting?"

"Miss, we are all ready."

"I'm sure ready," Tam squeezed my hand.

Tam and I stood on deck, the sun setting behind us. I wore a white shift, a huge departure from my normal black outfit, and I had a flower crown on my head that Kym and Greta had woven for me. The white shift was borrowed from Caroline. It was actually her mother's: She carried it with her wherever she traveled, and it was beautiful.

It was a simple white dress that fit me well, and was comfy. Which is important to me. I guess I'm not really a girly-girl.

Tam looked wonderful; he actually combed his hair!

I had forgotten the flowers I was to hold, and Christianne rushed to get them; her wings whirred behind her as she ran across the deck, making her go so fast she was a blur. But she was back in less than a minute. I couldn't stop giggling.

Khepri performed the handfasting, and I was in tears by the time the ribbon she'd borrowed from Greta was wrapped around our hands.

Caroline slipped me a handkerchief so I could wipe my eyes. Which was a good thing, because I didn't want to trip when we jumped over the broom.

The ceremony was short, and then came the celebration.

The party aboard *Pride of the Sea* was huge and loud. The rum flowed freely. Caroline and Christianne had prepared a feast of wild boar and wild carrots and onions, and Khepri had created several delicacies, some of which I had never heard of. Everything was so delicious, and I ate far too much.

Then Tam had me up and dancing a jig with him, a few of the sailors in the background playing a flute, a mandolin, and an instrument I could not identify but which produced such a sweet sound it tugged at my heart.

Then we danced to several slow songs, and I laid my head against Tam's chest as we swayed, closing my eyes and losing myself in my love for him.

He kept murmuring sweet words in my ear all evening, and he was so gentle with me, so tender, that I knew I had fallen in love with the right man. The moon rose in the starlit sky, and I found myself swaying to a slow song and gazing into his eyes. The moon had a halo of mist around it, and Khepri pronounced it a good omen.

Every member of the troupe produced a special gift, and they were all so sweet.

Tam told me he had something for me, but he wished to give me his gift when we were in private, so after a few hours, when I was feeling tired, Tam made excuses and led me to the captain's cabin. Caroline had produced a bottle of mead from her trip to Swerighe, and this Tam carried under his arm.

When we entered my cabin, we saw they had decorated it for us. There was a new quilt on the bed – that would be from Caroline. Flowers stood colorfully in vases in three places. A glowing moonglobe hung from the ceiling, and everything had been tidied.

Tam busied himself opening the mead and pouring two cupfuls, then turned to me where I sat on the bed.

"Princess," he said quietly, handing me a cup of mead.

It was wonderful to drink the customary handfasting beverage from my country. I sipped at the mead and watched him.

He had sat on a large chair in the corner, and stared at me, a smile on his face for several minutes as we both sipped the sweet brew.

"Oh," he said suddenly, reaching under the bed for a small box. He straightened and handed it to me.

The box was brown and tied with a red ribbon, and about five inches square. I opened it eagerly, pulling the ribbon loose and lifting the lid.

Inside was a brilliant orange and red leaf encased in a clear glass. I lifted it out of the box in awe. It looked too delicate to handle. Its colors gleamed in the cabin's lantern light, and I noticed the edges sparkled with a golden hue. I looked at Tam.

"That is the leaf I picked on the southern island, two days after you'd been gone on the quest for *The Book of Mysteries*. It was the day I woke up with a pain in my chest that I realized was there because I missed you so much. I knew I had fallen in love, and I wanted something to mark the day." He gestured at the clear glass encasing the leaf. "The mermaid helped me encase it, the glass is a substance they brought up from the bottom of their grotto. They said it will never break and its light will always shine. The mermaids said the luminescence was from the feeling of love I had for you."

"The preparation to encase it took hours, and the mermaids and I worked on it all day. I had to close my eyes and think of you while holding the leaf, and they performed some kind of spell that transferred some of the energy of my love into the leaf. Here," he reached and blew out the three lanterns.

I sat, spellbound, watching the leaf I held in my hands, as the light left the cabin.

The leaf was glowing.

Chapter Three

Ancestral Magic and a Surprise

The next morning, Tam and I slept in. I had placed the leaf in a box frame on my cabin wall, removing an old pinned butterfly that had been there. It glowed while we slept, and it was gorgeous.

We finally emerged late in the morning, and Tam excused himself to go check the status of the ship.

I wandered over to Khepri and Caroline, who were deep in conversation on a corner of the fo'c'sle deck.

"Hi," I said, yawning.

"Miss! Congratulations on your handfasting! What a grand celebration!" Caroline said.

"Charlotte, how are you feeling this morning?" Khepri asked.

"Okay, I guess. A little sleepy, I don't think I got that much sleep last night." I grinned and ducked my head.

"I should hope not. Not on your wedding night," Khepri said with a wink.

"Charlotte, here you go," Christianne walked up and handed me a mug of tea. I smelled it and raised an eyebrow.

"Medicinal?" I asked.

"Of course. Can't stop a course of restorative just because someone decides to up and get handfasted," Khepri said.

Christianne laughed.

"Charlotte," called Jim, coming up the stairs from the main deck.

I turned, sipping the steaming mug of tea. "Hmmm?"

Jim walked up to me and stared. He closed his eyes and took a deep breath, then bent to lower his nose to my neck and took another few deep breaths.

"I need to talk to you," he finally said.

"In private?" I asked.

Jim glanced at Khepri, who raised an eyebrow.

I turned to her, "What do you know of this, Khepri?"

"Nothing," the healer put her hand up and turned her head. "I know nothing."

"Come, let's go below decks," Jim gestured.

We retired to my cabin, Khepri and Christianne in tow, Caroline trailing after.

"Wait outside?" Jim told them, then entered the cabin and closed the door.

He turned and sat down, looking at me with a strange expression on his face.

"Charlotte."

"Jim."

"Congratulations on your joining. Tam's a fine fellow, and I know you're both going to be happy."

"Thank you, Jim," I smiled.

"Now," he took a deep breath, held it a few seconds, then blew it out noisily. "I had my suspicions last week, but this morning I am certain."

"Certain about what?" I asked, feeling curious.

"How do I begin? You, Charlotte, have been manifesting a certain glow about you that tells me you have a magical aura. I believe you have an ancestral magic." He sat back.

"You do?" I asked.

"Yes. Your nightmares, for instance. The way you saw the storm in your mind's eye before it arrived. Nearly a day before it arrived."

"Yes, I wondered about that. I just thought it was intuition," I said.

"There are no such things as coincidences. Or magical intuition. And your aura glows with the gold sparkles that Kym and I have."

Whatttt?

"What are you saying Jim?"

"I'm saying that I believe you have an ancestral magic that allows you to see glimpses of the future. Of what is to come," Jim said quietly. "Oh, and you also smell of the quickening."

"The what?" I was befuddled.

"The quickening. It will likely manifest in the next week."

"What are you saying, Jim? Are you saying that ..." I gulped and could not produce the words.

"I'm saying that you are expecting," Jim said.

"I had a suspicion," Khepri said, holding my hand and patting it.

We sat in my cabin, and I gazed into the distance, feeling a buzz in my head.

A baby!

"Charlotte, how long has it been since we left Iq Ameq'el? Seven weeks? I know we spent some time at the southern tip of Alkebulan ...," Khepri said.

"I think it's been seven weeks," I murmured in a daze. "Seven or eight. Something like that," I said.

"And when did your first coupling with Tam occur?" Khepri asked.

"Oh. OH." My eyes focused. I looked at her. "Our first pairing was the night we returned from the mountain." My jaw dropped open.

Could it have happened that night? So soon?

Khepri nodded knowingly. "Charlotte, you are a healthy twenty-one-year-old young lady. And Tam is what? Twenty-six?"

"Twenty-five," I said.

"Well, there you go. Nature will take its course. Now, what I'm most interested in is what Jim said about the ancestral magic he could sense in you," Khepri said.

"Yes, he said my aura was glowing in a magical way," I looked at her. "Can you see auras?"

"No, that is not among the talents of ordinary humans," Khepri said.

I thought a moment. Then, "Can you get Kym? And Tam, I guess he should be told first. About the baby, I mean." My head was spinning and a warm glow of excitement was spreading in my head.

Khepri left and returned a few minutes later with both Tam and Kym.

"Kym," I took her hand. "Do I looked or smell any different? I mean, from last month or last year."

Kym looked at me quizzically. "What do you mean?"

"Jim says I smell different lately. And that my aura is glowing in a certain way."

Kym stood back a minute, her hand on her chin. It was almost comical that way she looked, a six-year-old girl acting like an ancient and wise being.

But chimeras are very wise. I knew that already. Besides, she wasn't really six years old, at least not in human years.

"Okay, this is what I sense," said Kym. "I think you have an old magic that is starting to manifest now that you're expecting a baby."

"A WHAT?!" Tam exclaimed.

Kym turned to him. "You're going to be a daddy. I smelled it last month." She turned back to me.

"You smelled it last MONTH?" I asked. "Why didn't you say anything?"

"Well, it's a private matter. I thought you knew. Don't humans know when they're expecting young?" She looked at me with a quizzical eye. "Besides, no one remarked on Tupu when she was expecting."

"That's because she was out to here!" I put my hand several inches in front of my belly.

"Well, okay then. Um, well, about the magic: it's growing stronger because of the child inside. That tends to happen in females, magical females, that is." Kym grinned.

"But, but ..." I sputtered.

Tam came over to me and gathered me in his arms and kissed the top of my head. "Oh, my. Love, you're going to have a baby. Oh, my goodness." He smiled a very goofy smile.

I felt in a daze the whole day. I kept walking around with my hand on my belly, although it was still quite flat.

Toward the evening, the sun was setting in the sky, and everyone was settling down. I decided to take second watch that night.

I was about to climb up the rope ladder to the aft crow's nest, when Tam walked over.

"Have you seen Jim?" Tam asked.

"No, not since this morning," I answered.

"Well," Tam glanced around the deck. "Keep an eye out for him, will you?"

"Of course. He's a very private individual, so he might stay out of sight if he's lost in thought," I said.

"Khepri is worried he might have been missing Tupu," Tam said.

"Ahh. Hmmm. I'll keep an eye out," I winked and turned, and climbed up to the crow's nest.

Jim was sitting cross-legged at the bottom of the basket, completely out of sight of everyone, looking miserable.

"Everyone's looking for you, my friend," I said softly.

"Oh, I'm sorry. I just felt ..." He wiped his eyes and took a deep breath, then got to his feet. "I'm fine."

I climbed into the basket with him.

"Talk to me," I said.

Jim looked off over the sea. "I'm just missing Tupu. I'm so glad we're sailing north. It's just that ..."

"You miss her, and the baby," I guessed.

"Yes." He looked down at his hands, his fingers were intertwined. "It's as simple as that. I miss her and the baby. I don't even know which name she gave him. I wish I hadn't left."

"I think you did the best you could at the time. It sounded like a no-win situation to me. Tupu had to come around, she had to be the one to realize you two belong together. And it looks like she has. I mean, she wouldn't have sent the message otherwise. Wouldn't be waiting for you on the southern island." I patted his arm.

Jim looked up. There were tears on his face, and he was smiling. "I want you to know that I am so incredibly happy you and Tam are expecting a baby."

He hugged me, then climbed down to the deck below.

Boy, he's got it bad.

"I know how I would feel if I was separated from Tam. Poor Jim," I said aloud to myself.

Poor Jim.

I stood in the crow's nest, scanning the sea. The sun was nearly down, and the sky was purple. The sea was still and calm, and the skies were clear.

No more storms for a while, I'm guessing.

I wondered if my intuition was the ancestral magic or just a sailor's wish. This foretelling the future stuff could really come in handy, but I needed to know when it was real and when it was just wishful thinking.

I sighed.

An hour passed, and it was dark. The moon was bright on the water, the nearly full globe a shining lamp in the night.

I heard a flapping sound and turned. A raven was flying into sight.

Oh, no.

Missives by raven were always an emergency or something that couldn't wait. Tupu's message had been urgent, because she was hoping to catch us before we sailed north passed the Mare Nostrum.

And because she missed Jim so much there'd been dried tears on the parchment.

I felt a twinge of guilt at looking over Jim's shoulder as he had unrolled the note and read it.

And the missive from Swerighe had certainly been an emergency, or at least the beginnings of one. Mother had written about the crisis, and had said they had things in hand, but I could read between the lines. She was worried.

Could this be another message from Swerighe?

The raven flew straight to me, landing on my shoulder. I recognized the seal of the queen immediately.

Another message.

I untied the small, rolled-up parchment and unraveled it.

Tam's head popped up over the basket's edge. "Problem?"

I jumped, then laughed.

He looked sheepish. "I spotted the raven," he gestured to the bird, who hopped to his arm.

I spread open the note and read it.

"Oh, no," I murmured. I read the note again.

Tam waited silently.

My eyes scanned the note for a third time.

"The kingdom is under attack. A new kind of magical creature has appeared – something they haven't encountered before." I dropped my hands and looked at him. "We have to make double speed."

He nodded and I heard him zip down the rope, his leg wrapped around it, his gloved hand guiding his descent.

I looked out over the sea.

Why would Swerighe be under attack?

The whole troupe gathered in the captain's cabin, and we'd passed out mugs of the last bottle of mead Caroline had brought.

"To celebrate," Caroline had said, hugging me.

You get choked up when your best friend smiles at you with tears in her eyes.

Caroline's husband had died in an accident, and now all she had left was Greta, who was on her lap now, holding on to her with both arms.

The news that Swerighe was under attack had taken them by surprise.

"The first message said they'd had some flooding. I know my mother, she would not have sent that first message just for a little light flooding; that happens every year in Swerighe. It must have been bad for her to send that first raven. But she said she was just keeping me informed, and not to worry," I said.

"But of course, you worried," Caroline said, laughing.

"Of course," I said. "You always worry when someone does something that doesn't match the situation. I mean, 'normal flooding, no emergency, no need to come,' but here's a raven to let you know? Come on."

So, I thought we were already on our way north," Christianne said.

"We are. But now we're going faster. A lot faster," Tam said.

"So fast we are giving extra food to the mantas?" Kym asked.

"Yes," Tam smiled.

"So, okay. The second message from home says they are being attacked by some new magical creature. Something they've never seen before. And now, now my mother says, 'Can you come?' This means she's worried," I said.

"Sounds like she's more than worried, actually," Caroline said.

I turned and pointed at her. "Exactly."

"Doesn't Swerighe have a large fighting force?" asked Khepri. "I remember when the sheikha of Abdü caliphate loaned us her force, what did you call them?"

"Valkyries. They reminded me of the Valkyries back in Swerighe," I said.

"So, Swerighe has a standing army of Valkyries? Why would we be needed?" Khepri asked.

"First of all, the Valkyries are human. They are extremely skilled, but they are a blunt fighting force." I looked thoughtful. "Mother must need us for specialized work." I looked at the message parchment again. "She doesn't say much, but I know the queen. She doesn't ask for help unless she desperately needs it."

"So we're going double fast, and we should sharpen our blades. We'll still picking Tupu up, aren't we?" Jim asked.

"Of course," I said. "But it's going to be fast. I think we'll stay maybe a day, rest the mantas, load up on supplies, bring Tupu on board, then make haste to the northlands."

"Will Tupu have her baby with her?" Kym asked.

"Yes. The baby cannot stay behind, he is too young. For one thing, he will still need Tupu's milk," Khepri said.

Chapter Four
Tupu and Aaaqil

We approached the Mare Nostrum two days later, just before dawn.

"Captain," came a whispered voice, accompanied by a light rap on the door. "You asked to be notified when we drew near the Mare Nostrum."

"That's the mate on call, I've got to go." I kissed Tam and stood to get dressed.

He looked at me thoughtfully in the dimmed lantern light.

"Your belly is still flat as can be, Love," he said quietly.

"Swerighe women hold our babies tightly inside until we are much further along. My mother did as well," I said, pulling on my shirt.

I tugged my pants on and regarded him.

He lay there, the covers around his waist, his arms cross behind his head, and easy smile on his face. I grinned.

"Don't take too long to join me, first mate," I said with a wink as I finished pulling my boots on, stomping the soles on the wooden floor.

"I'm right behind you," he said without moving.

I hurried on deck.

"Report," I barked out, bringing my brass sight to my eye. I sighted along the length.

"We are approaching the Mare Nostrum, Captain. We expect to be at the southern island in an hour. The mantas are pulling hard; they are doing great," the sailor saluted.

I studied her face for a moment, then nodded.

She departed, and I decided to climb up to the fore crow's nest.

I walked to the mast and gestured for the mate to come down.

We switched places, and I stood in the basket, the wind blowing my hair, whipping it back and forth.

My stomach roiled.

Not now.

I closed my eyes and took deep breaths, willing the nausea to depart. Khepri had explained to me that the beginning of the womb-hold was often a sick time for mother.

Mothers. I'm going to be a mother.

I touched my hand to my lower belly, wondering when I'd feel the quickening.

Jim said I might feel it soon.

I'd told this to Khepri who'd snorted. "And how many times has Jim been expecting a baby? How many mothers has he cared for? How many births has he attended?" she'd asked.

Jim had heard her.

"Um, well, zero to the first question," he'd said. "But twenty-seven to the second question, and fifty-three to the third." He'd looked at Khepri with a raised eyebrow.

I had laughed and laughed.

Ha ha ha!

I looked out over the sea. The sun was just pinking the horizon on the starboard side of the ship. It was looking to be a productive day.

I shivered in anticipation.

I couldn't wait to see Tupu.

Although we may not see much of her. Jim and Tupu may disappear into his cabin and not emerge for days.

I felt so happy my friends were reconciling. At least, that's what I assumed was happening. Jim hadn't let anyone see the note she's sent him, holding it to his chest and saying, "It's private," while blushing furiously.

I smiled.

Two hours later, land was spotted.

A half hour after that, the mantas had arrived at the southern island. There was a second, smaller ship already docked at the atoll.

Tupu.

I leaned over the railing and studied the second ship. It was a light color and running the colors of Moonlit Bay.

A local ship, then.

We dropped anchor in the shallow water, and prepared to depart.

We took a landing skiff over, the whole troupe wanted to visit the centaurs and mermaids. I left instructions on pampering the giant manta rays, and the sailors had gotten to work on bringing supplies on board.

"We're pushing off at dawn, so make ready," Tam had called out to the crew.

Jim stayed with the skiff as we rowed to shore. I could see he was extremely nervous.

Several people stood on the sand, waiting for us to land. I recognized Tupu, but not the other three figures.

"That's Nhalah on the right. Tupu's mother," Jim said in a low voice.

I saw Nhalah was holding a baby.

Tupu's baby.

As we approached closer I also recognized Tikiko and Pala, Tupu's cousins we'd brought back from Abü.

This should be interesting.

Tam jumped overboard as the skiff's bottom scraped against the sand. He grabbed the rope and pulled the boat closer to shore, and we all jumped out into the surf.

Tupu began running toward us. Fast.

"OOF!" Jim expelled as Tupu jumped into his arms.

Jim was caught off balance and nearly fell backwards in the surf, but at the last second he planted one foot behind him and caught the tall warrior as she leaped into his arms. I watched as she began planting kisses all over my friend's face and smiled.

Tupu did not leave Jim's arms once the whole day. He carried her for the first hour, kissing her over and over. She wrapped her arms around his neck and would not let go. There were tears running down both their faces.

Jim carried Tupu off toward a private thicket and they talked for a long time. Everyone gave them their privacy, we were all hoping for a deep reconciliation between the two. Both were a part of our family, and we had all missed Tupu deeply during our adventures in Iq Ameq'el.

Kym and Greta accompanied Christianne and Akim with the two ravens we'd brought from the ship. They fed the birds small treats so often the ravens didn't want to leave their arms. Two centaur children came up to them, and they all began to talk. I saw Akim transfer one of the ravens to the hand of the larger centaur boy, smiling.

Then I turned and saw Tupu's mother watching the pair, she held the new baby and cooed to him.

I hadn't met the baby yet, so I wandered over.

"Greetings," I bowed deeply, my hands held together. "I do not believe we have met." I held my hands out. "I am Charlotte."

"Oh! Oh, Assalamu Alaikum, Great One! Tupu has told us of her time with you!" Nhalah bowed as deeply as she could while holding a baby.

"Oh, thank you, I am very fond of Tupu." I turned my eyes to the infant in her arms. "And this is Tupu's son?"

"Yes, this is little Aaaqil," she smiled warmly down at the sleeping baby in her arms, then back to me.

"How did you fare on the journey to this island? Well, I hope?" I asked politely.

"Yes, it was a fine journey. We had a small bit of foul weather on the last day, but other than that, it was unremarkable." She looked closely at me. "Tupu tells me you are from the northlands?"

"Yes, originally from Swerighe, to be exact." I smiled at her. "I love the climate in Alkebulan, and you have the most beautiful wares at the Tambibo market. I had a very hard time not coming away with everything I admired," I said.

"Charlotte!" Tikiko ran up to me then, followed by Pala. They both hugged me tightly.

"Charlotte, thank you again for all you did for us," Pala said quietly. I remembered she was the shyer of the two. I looked into her face and saw a small smile.

"Pala," I hugged her back. "How are you doing?" I remembered how sad Pala had been when she'd told us about her lost baby.

"I am okay," she smiled.

"She is doing better than okay. She is the prize pupil at the local school, and has been fending off several young men who want to court her," laughed Tikiko.

"I want to concentrate on my studies," said Pala with a smile. "I am studying to be a healer, like Khepri."

"Pala, that's fantastic!" I beamed at her.

Tikiko hugged me tightly a second time. "Charlotte, we can never repay you, but" – Tikiko bent close and whispered in my ear – "we have been working on our mother for months, and talking with Tupu. She has agreed it is most important that Tupu follow her heart. That is why we are here." She drew back and smiled broadly, giving me a wink.

I turned and glanced at Nhalah, and saw she was cooing over Aaaqil, pretending not to notice her daughter's whispering.

I ducked my head to hide my smile, then nodded to Tikiko.

"How old is the baby now?" I asked.

"He has passed five moons," Nhalah said, happy to talk about her grandson. She glanced up at me. "Would you like to hold him?"

"Oh, I'd be honored," I said, smiling.

Nhalah handed me the bundle, and I careful transferred him to my shoulder. He melted onto my body like a flower. I inhaled deeply. He smelled of slumber and milk. It was an intoxicating scent. I grinned from ear to ear.

Kym hopped up just then. "OOH! Tupu's baby!" She jumped up, trying to get a good view.

"His name is Aaaqil," I said, bending down on my knees so she could get a better look.

"Ohhh, he's so small ..." she gently stroked his back, a look of awe on her face.

The rest of the troupe gathered 'round then, Caroline and Tam and Christianne and Greta and Akim and Khepri. There was much cooing and soft sighs. They all wanted to stroke Aaaqil's back and arms as I held him.

Nhalah smiled in approval and kept watch.

Tikiko and Pala reacquainted themselves with the troupe, and for a long time there was talk going back and forth, of friends and family being happy to see one another.

Aaaqil slept through it all.

"What a good baby," Khepri said. She nodded to Nhalah. "He looks fat and healthy," she said in approval. She stroked her finger down one of Aaaqil's chubby arms.

"Tupu is an excellent mother," Nhalah said. "She has always been so healthy, so I knew Aaaqil would have no problems."

That night, Tam and I checked on the resupply of the ship, while everyone gathered for a bonfire on the beach.

A dozen spits were erected over the long fire; each held several large, fat rabbits. The mermaids frolicked in the nearby lagoon and taught new songs to Kym, Greta and Akim.

Christianne, now sixteen years old and already a strong beauty, showed off her new wings by zipping back and forth on the beach. Kym and Akim kept trying to win races against her, but it was impossible. Christianne ran so fast she was a blur; her feet skimming over the sand and touching down every dozen feet or so, she was unbeatable.

I was finished checking the ship's stores on board *Pride of the Sea* and walked out on deck, brushing off my hands.

Tam was already leaning against the rail, watching the party on the beach. He put his arm around me as I joined him.

"We should go down and eat. I'm starving," I said as my stomach rumbled.

Tam turned to me and began nibbling on my ear and kissing my neck. "Mmmmm."

I kissed Tam's lips.

His eyes rose and turned to the beach, and they reflected the firelight in them, almost glowing.

"Do you think Tupu will be joining us, then?" He asked, his eyes still turned to the shore.

"I think so, yes. Well, I hope so." I turned to gaze at the beach. "I don't think anyone's seen them all day."

"Hmmm," Tam said.

"Hey, Charlotte, Tam, want to join us in a ride to the shore?" Jim said, walking up behind us.

I turned and saw his arm was wrapped around Tupu's waist, and they were both smiling.

"That sounds nice," I said, smiling back.

"I can bring us all over," Jim said, transforming into the djinn as he spoke.

The look on Tupu's face was one of pure admiration.

The djinn is a magnificent sight to behold, that's for sure.

"Oh, by the way," the djinn said as he held out his arms for us to hold. "There's going to be another handfasting soon."

Chapter Five
Raven's Message

The ocean breeze blew strongly as we left the inner sea of the Mare Nostrum and headed north to Swerighe.

Jim and Tupu had spent most of the first week below decks in his cabin. We'd converted Tupu's old cabin, which had been next to Jim's, into a nursery for Aaaqil. The baby was a quiet one, he spent a lot of his waking moments looking at everything and everyone with wide eyes.

He was already trying to mimic our speech, a trait Khepri informed us that heralded the learning of a language and that usually manifested in infants closer to a year old.

"That is why my tribe waits to name a baby until it is at least three moons old," Tupu explained. "It is by then that we expect their personality to begin to emerge." She smiled at Aaaqil.

The rest of us fought for time with Aaaqil, and there was no shortage of honorary aunties and uncles clamoring to hold the little babe.

"It will take at least three weeks to sail to Swerighe, if we're lucky," Tam said, looking out to see at the last sight of the mainland. I leaned over the rail on his right; Tupu stood to his left, with Jim beside her.

For the lion's share of our journey, we'd be sailing on the open ocean; the mantas could go faster in deeper water.

"I don't like the look of those clouds. Let's hope they don't approach closer," Tupu said.

"Have I told you how good it is to have you back, my friend?" I asked.

"At least three times a day," she laughed.

"Has Christianne showed you her wings yet?" Tam asked.

"Yes, the second day on board I got a really close look at them. They are amazing. They fold right into the cracks on her back," Tupu said.

"She's really grown into them, too," I said. "Spreading them and pushing her way forward like the wind has become second nature to her. She's altered all her clothes to include slits, now."

"Amazing. I feel sorry to have missed out on that adventure," Tupu said.

"You were sorely missed," Tam said.

The wind blew harder, and I wound my long hair up and tucked it into a ponytail.

"How was the weather near your village, Tupu?" I asked. "We've seen some odd patterns recently, at least at sea."

"It was okay, I guess. A few more sandstorms than usual. We lost a boy and his pony in the summer," said Tupu. "When the storm finally died down, we found them a couple hundred yards from the edge of the village, completely buried in sand. The only way we discovered them was the long rope sticking out of a dune. It was the pony's lead."

"Oh, that's sad," Jim said.

"Mmmhmm, his mother grieved for a long time. She was still in mourning when I left."

The wind began to whip up then. and I heard a noise from behind us. I turned my head and saw the sailors were scrambling about to secure the sails.

Tam jumped to join them, calling over his shoulder, "Jim, get them below decks, there's a waterspout forming off the aft bow."

The wind whipped up so quickly it was astonishing.

Jim held Tupu's arm and guided her down below to their cabin. I assured them I would be fine on deck.

"You sure, Charlotte?" Jim looked pointedly at my midsection.

"Don't coddle her, Jim. She knows herself," Tupu said, smiling.

Jim looked sheepish and went with her.

I turned to survey the ship. The mates had gotten most of the sails tied up, except one. They struggled to grab its whipping fabric.

Tam climbed up the mast rope to grab at it from above.

I leaped over and reached for a corner as it flapped past me, grabbing it at the last moment.

It pulled hard, nearly lifting me off my feet, but I pulled it over to the mast and Tam grabbed it, along with two other sailors.

"Thanks, Love," Tam winked at me. I grinned.

That wink. Those sparkling eyes!

I glanced over at the waterspout. It looked about half a league away, but it was approaching fast.

Almost as if it's alive.

We tied everything down and made sure everything was secure for the coming storm.

"Do you think we should drop anchor?" I asked Tam, raising my voice to carry over the howling of the wind.

"No, it might seem more stable, but the ship is safer riding the waves. To anchor it would just give it another force to fight against," Tam said.

I watched the waterspout approaching. "Do you think the ship can be sunk?"

Tam grimaced. "Any ship can be sunk, Love. But I think she's a good craft, sturdy and sound, and she sits low in the water. We'll be okay." He wiped his face as a particularly big wave washed onto the deck, splashing us. "Let's go below. They can handle things up here."

"I'd feel better if I stayed," I said.

"Okay. We'll stay."

The waterspout howled and howled, and the wind whipped against the ship with a fury that took my breath away.

This seems worse than it should be.

We spent another hour watching the storm from on deck. Tam was right: The crew had things in hand.

They're well trained.

We finally made our way below decks, and Khepri met us just inside the outer door.

"About time you two came in from the storm. Here, we've made a hearty stew," she gestured along the hall toward the galley.

We soon had bowls of stew in hand and were settled into our cabin.

I brought the steaming bowl to my face, enjoying the feel of the hot, moist air on my skin.

"Mmmm, they've outdone themselves," Tam said, his eyes closing in relish as he swallowed a spoonful.

The wind howled fiercely all evening and into the night.

At one point, the cabin walls shook so fiercely Tam got up and went to check on the ship.

As I lay there in bed, I pulled the blanket off and pulled my nightgown up and stared at my belly. It was still flat as the Alkebulan sand plains.

It will begin to swell at some point, and I'll have to alter my outfits.

Khepri had already explained how to do that, and I looked forward to getting used to the new way my body would be moving.

I studied my belly. It trembled slightly with every beat of my heart. I scrutinized it closely but could see no hint of any swelling.

I knew my mother and father would be excited. I purposely didn't tell them anything in a message; I wanted to see their faces when I told them in person.

The door opened, and Tam slipped through.

"Everything's okay, it was just the fo'c'sle mast. I've secured it better. No damage that I can see." He lay down on the bed beside me, gently moving so that his face was directly over my belly.

"Helloooooo," he called softly.

I grinned.

"Anybody there?" he whispered, kissing my navel.

"Careful, this child could very well be magical. It may respond to you even now," I chuckled.

"Did Khepri say it was?" Tam asked.

"Not exactly. It was Jim who told me that magic runs in families. Not many, but a few bloodlines have it," I smiled.

Tam looked back at my belly.

"Helloooooooo?" he said, then lowered his face against my skin and blew raspberries.

"Ha ha ha!" I shook with laughter, and he grinned.

There was a knock at the door.

"Come in," I called, lowering my nightgown and sitting up.

"We just thought we'd drop by before bedtime, see how everyone is enjoying this storm," said Jim, poking his head in the door.

"Come on in," Tam said, smiling.

"Someone wants to wish you a good night and sweet dreams," said Tupu, cooing at baby Aaaqil in her arms.

They settled into the chairs, and I held out my hands, asking wordlessly to hold the infant.

"I'd better get used to holding a baby, huh?" I said as Tupu passed me her son.

"It will come naturally to you, I'm betting. It did to me," Tupu said.

I held the baby and looked into his eyes. They were violet, like his mother's.

He looked at me intelligently, or so I thought. A gentle URP! and yellow liquid slid out the corner of his lips.

"Here," Tupu handed me a soft cloth.

I took it and wiped the baby's mouth.

"Aren't you just the sweetest little baby in the whole wide world?" I touched my nose to his and was rewarded with a gurgling coo as he tried to say a word.

"Say, 'Charlotte'? 'Charlotte'? 'Charrrr-lotte'?" I said.

Aaaqil screwed up his lips and said, "Rrrrrlll."

"Close enough," I smiled.

There was a firm knock at the door, and Tam rose to see who it was as I continued cooing at the baby.

"Okay. Yes. Here," Tam was reaching through the door.

He shut it and turned around to show me ...

Another raven, the message, with its seal gleaming bright gold and blue, still attached to its leg.

I sat up, instantly worried.

I handed the baby back to Tupu and waited.

Tam undid the small parchment from the wind-ruffled raven and lifted the bird to the cabin perch. It ruffled its feathers and began to preen itself.

Coming through the storm must've been hard. I felt a deep appreciation for the creature's drive and strength.

Tam tossed the missive across to me, and I caught the small scroll in both hands and stared at it.

"Oh, no," I whispered.

"What is it, Charlotte?" Jim asked.

"The seal, it's ..." I fumbled with my words.

"Here, Love, let me ..." Tam reached for the message.

"No, I'm fine, and this is actually from the regent," I choked on the word. "The colors are the same, but see here," I pointed at the wax seal. "The emblem is not the queen's. It's from my cousin, the duchess."

I broke the seal and unrolled the parchment, my brow furrowed in concentration.

They all fell silent.

I read the message a second time. Then a third. Then a fourth.

Finally, I raised my head and took a deep breath.

"This missive is from the Duchess of Västergötland. Something terrible has happened." Tears filled my eyes.

"Babe," Tam sat on the bed, one knee extended, and put his arm around me. "What is it?"

I felt a huge lump in my throat.

Tam handed me a cup of water, and I took a few sips, trying to collect my thoughts.

"The Duchess of Västergötland is reigning in my absence. The message says that the queen and prince consort have been kidnapped, and the country is in an uproar. She asks that we make haste." I let my hands holding the message fall to my lap.

Tam immediately jumped up and left to give new orders to the crew.

"What else does it say, Charlotte? Anything more?" Tupu asked softly.

I glanced back down at the parchment, reading it a fifth time. I cleared my throat.

"Apparently, the largest glacier has begun to melt at an extraordinary rate and has broken off from the mainland. The duchess suspects an unnatural force is at work, especially after the kidnapping of the queen and prince." I swallowed loudly in the silence and looked down again. I could feel tears forming in my eyes.

"Here, Sweetheart," Tupu handed me a handkerchief. I blew my nose loudly.

Tam returned shortly. "The storm is still going at full force, but the crew have their orders to make extra haste north as soon as the weather calms a bit."

I looked into his eyes.

He slid onto the bed and took my hand.

"We'll get to Swerighe as soon as humanly possible."

Chapter Six

Rescue

We arrived in the Mare Norskehavet, a half a day from the Swerighe castle, faster than I thought possible – yet not fast enough. I spent much of my time at the railing of *Pride of the Sea*, looking forward into the wind, as if I could make the ship go fast with my mind.

Jim had filled me in on some of the lore concerning ancestral magic, and Kym had added helpful bits. Although she was not nearly so well-traveled and experienced as the djinn, she had received a thorough education on the magical attributes of the denizens of Alkebulan, among other lessons.

Apparently, the magic in my genetic line had lain mostly dormant until my baby had been conceived and implanted in my womb. Such events heralded a new paradigm in a person's body; new chemicals, a new growing consciousness. This was well known. But I hadn't expected it to manifest this way. It had awakened new dormant parts of my brain. Hence, my heightened dreaming of events soon to come.

It was something I'd need to get used to. A new normal.

I didn't have much time to make sense of it all. We were all bracing ourselves for the adventure that awaited us in my home kingdom. The news out of Swerighe did not sound good.

The largest glacier there was huge: more than a hundred and fifty miles long, and fifty miles wide at the sea. I could only imagine what must have occurred when it broke away from the main continent into the Mare Balticum. Natural disasters, flooding, damage to seaports: I could envision all sorts of catastrophes, each one worse than the last.

Such thoughts did nothing but keep me awake worrying, and as Tam reminded me, I wanted to arrive home fresh and in good spirits, ready to tackle whatever problems I could.

"What do you think the magical creature attacking the kingdom is, Charlotte?" Kym asked one day when we were still a week out from arriving.

"Not sure," I thought for a minute. "They seemed to think it was destructive enough to need our help, so it must be fierce. Otherwise, the Valkyries could've handled it."

"Might be some sort of cold weather creature," Khepri mused. "It's very cold in Swerighe. Year 'round, isn't that so, Charlotte?"

"Mmmm, mostly. We're arriving in late spring, so there'll still be a lot of ice, but the snow will have started to melt from some of the lowland forests."

It went like that for weeks, and I grew tired of the theories. I just wanted to get home. Home.

I worried about what had befallen my mother and father, and at the same time, I pitied whoever had kidnapped them. They would have the whole of the kingdom of Swerighe after them, out for their blood, and we'd soon be joining the hunt.

And I was already so angry that they'd taken my parents that my mind was turning to the bloodlust. My fingers twitched for my sword, and I spent a lot of time sparring on deck, trying to get my energy out.

Whoever had kidnapped them would pay, and pay dearly.

We arrived in late afternoon, the sun low in the sky. As our ship sailed clear of a rocky promontory, we saw a small island about a mile off the coast. I could hear faint screams coming from the southern edge.

"What is that?" Christianne asked, walking to the railing to join me.

I had my brass sight out and fixed on the island. People were scrambling to get in boats, and some of the people were in the water. There was a family on the roof of their house, calling for help.

The ocean was covering the island.

"It's a flood! Tam, alter course for that island," I called. "Ready one of the skiffs. We need to mount a rescue operation."

"Altering course, Captain," Tam called from the fo'c'sle deck, his hand at the wheel of the ship.

I watched the people as we drew closer.

Oh, no.

The people in the water were floundering. I could see adults holding their children, trying to keep them above water as they dropped below the surface, then bobbed back up. I saw a dark form near them.

What is that?

I swung around, "JIM!"

"Way ahead of you, boss," the djinn flew past me, holding a looped rope. He glided over the deck railing and out across the water.

"Tam. TAM! We've got to hurry, he can't get to them all," I holstered the sight, reached for a long loop of rope, grabbed the railing, and jumped over it, onto the skiff. "Lower it when we're close."

Tam jumped in beside me, another length of rope looped around his shoulder. "Hey now! You don't get to have all the fun."

We were quickly joined by Tupu, Christianne and Caroline.

Pride of the Sea skimmed over the water, the mates bringing it close to the island.

"That's all we can give ya, Captain, it's shallow from here on in. About three fathoms of water or so," a sailor called from the rigging."

"That's fine, lower the skiff," called Tam.

The small boat was lowered into the water, jarring us as it hit the surface. We held on and didn't lose our footing.

Tam and Tupu took the oars, and we were soon gliding swiftly across the water to the children.

"There's Jim," I said, pointing. "Let's head over to the other side of the group."

The skiff was soon positioned amid the survivors in the water.

I jumped in, swimming to a man holding an infant in his arms.

"Grab the rope!" I called out, throwing a length to him.

Caroline stayed in the boat and pulled him to her.

Tam was in the water, swimming swiftly to another child.

Several dozen youngsters were floundering in the tossed sea.

Jim was scooping people out of the water and placing them in a second skiff, piloted by Kym and Khepri.

Something brushed against my leg in the water, and I looked down to see a large dark shape swim passed.

Huh?

"Something is in the water. It just touched my foot." Tam said.

I dipped my head into the water and dove down, searching the depths for a sign of what was there. There were many forms of sea life native to the Mare Balticum that were active at this time of year.

Another dark form swam passed, then circled back and bumped up against my leg.

I surfaced.

"It's a pod of Belugas," I called out.

The small whale surfaced next to me.

I pointed to a group of three teenagers in the waters, then swam toward them.

The whales seem to understand and swam alongside me. Then, they swam off toward the children and began guiding them toward me.

Soon, they were close enough to bring them aboard.

"Here! Catch!" I called out, tossing the rope to the nearest young man, who grabbed it and wound it around his wrist.

I swung around to the skiff, "Pull him in!" I called out, and the boy began his journey to the small craft.

The beluga that had been near me was now behind the second teen, nudging him toward me.

"Can you mount her?" I called out.

"I'll try," came the answer.

I swam to the third boy in the water.

The second boy was holding on to the beluga around her middle, his arms tight in panic.

"It'll be okay," I called out as they passed me.

The first boy was in the skiff, and Caroline tossed the rope end back to me.

I grabbed it and reached out for the third teen, who took my hand and the rope and wrapped himself around my shoulders.

"Careful. Don't pull me down, or we'll both be in trouble," I said, trying to remain calm.

The boy didn't answer. His eyes were wild, and his arms kept paddling and grasping.

"Hold on, let's get you this rope, okay?" I said, feeling a little worried.

The teen's frantic movements increased.

He clawed at me, bumping my head, and I went into the water.

This will not do.

I dipped further into the water a few feet, and grabbed the boy's legs, and thrust them up out of the water – which only plunged me deeper into the sea.

Remain calm, Charlotte.

I paddled to return to the surface, and one of the boy's legs kicked my head, dazing me.

I saw stars, and my arms went still for a moment.

I looked upward. The boy's legs were kicking furiously.

I bet he can't swim.

I shook my head in the water and felt my senses returning.

A beluga from the pod swam next to the boy, and he grabbed at it frantically. I saw a rope fall into the water next to him. He didn't grab it.

I kicked hard, and returned to the surface.

"Wondered where you went," Tam said, swimming toward me.

"I'm fine, but this boy needs help."

Tam grabbed the rope and I grabbed the boy's arm, and we got the rope around him, although he slapped our faces several times in his wild panic, trying to paddle out of the water.

The whale stayed still, as if sensing we needed her buoyancy for the rescue.

We finally got the boy tied to the rope, and I held on to him and the beluga as he was pulled to one of the boats.

"Here," I pushed the boy up a bit, and Caroline grabbed his arm. He still paddled his arms in panic.

"Will you please calm down? CALM! DOWN!" I said.

His arms slowed.

Uh oh.

I let go of the boy and grabbed the edge of the boat, lifting myself out of the water.

"I think he's passing out," I said, and reached down to grab his other arm.

Together, we lifted the teen into the boat and laid him flat on the bottom.

I turned him to the side and started chest compressions.

After a few minutes I was rewarded by a slew of water vomited into the boat, then coughing.

I pounded his back, and he sat up.

"Hey, you okay?" I asked, looking into his eyes.

He was skinny and tall, and looked to be about thirteen or fourteen. A great mop of dark hair was plastered down his back. He blinked rapidly, then coughed some more and vomited sea water a second time.

I patted his back. "Yeah, get all that up and out. It's no good for you."

He sat there coughing. I looked up and scanned the water. Everyone appeared to have been fished out of the sea.

"Let's take them back to *Pride*, then we can return to get the others on the houses," I called out.

"Aye, aye,"

We began rowing back to the ship.

Two rope ladders later, and all were on deck.

"I'll get blankets and hot mugs. You going back in?" Khepri said. "I want to check to make sure they're okay."

I nodded and turned back to the skiff, then turned to Khepri.

It was late afternoon, and the wind was picking up again. Everyone who'd been in the water began shivering violently.

"Get them belowdecks, Khepri. Get them warmed up."

She nodded.

I jumped back into the skiff.

In another few minutes we were gliding along the water to the few houses with people on the roofs.

An hour later, we had everyone on the ship.

"Let's get below decks," I said. "It'll be warmer."

I couldn't wait to be in front of my cabin's small fire.

It was in an iron stove, bolted to the wood, and we kept it going night and day. The burning coals made the room toasty-warm.

"Sail to the docks and drop anchor, mates," Tam called, wringing out the edge of his shirt. Water splattered onto the deck.

Once we were in our cabin, we hung our wet clothes to dry and wrapped ourselves in blankets.

There was a knock at the door.

"Hot soup?" said Kym, poking her head into the room.

"Oh, yes. Yes, yes, yes." I reached for a bowl, handed it to Tam, then reached for a second. "Thanks a million, Kym," I smiled at her, and she smiled back and shut the door.

Chapter Seven

The Duchesses

An hour later, we docked and dropped anchor and transported the flood refugees to the mainland.

I was at the front of the skiff that zipped to the harbor, my whole troupe behind me, eager for action.

"I am sure Aaaqil will be fine with his wet nurse, Kym," said Tupu. "You worry too much. She is very capable." She winked at the chimera-in-human-form.

We were met by a page and led into the castle immediately.

"Duchess," I spied my cousin, the Duchess of Västergötland, and walking with her the Duchess of Ångermanland, far off at the other end of the throne room, and could remain walking no longer. I sprinted forward and fell into Anya Västergötland's arms.

"Oh, my princess, oh thank the gods you've arrived." Anya hugged my tightly.

After a few minutes, she loosened her arms and turned to the Duchess Ångermanland. "You remember Tilde?"

"Of course, I do. Duchess, it's been a few years, hasn't it?" I embraced her, kissing her on the cheek.

"Your Highness, we've been keeping things together in the queen's absence, but it has been tense." Tilde was practically wringing her hands in nervousness.

"Anya, let's retire to the cabinet room, and you can fill me in." I turned and lift my arm to encompass my troupe. "This is Tam, my husband, and this is my troupe. We work as a team."

"Thank goodness you're here. We'll need all your help, I'm sure," Anya bowed to the troupe, then led us off to a side room with a long table.

Several guards stood at attention beside every door we passed, their eyes straight forward; their bodies snapping to attention as I passed.

"Now," Anya began once we were all settled. "We've been hit by a series of natural disasters, and I use the term 'natural' lightly. There's nothing natural about them. The glacier breaking off into the Mare Balticum was just the first. We've had flooding, the collapse of the lower dikes and levees, and we've had to evacuate whole villages. The weather has been extreme, to put it mildly. Hurricanes in the Mare Balticum. And in the Mare Norskehavet, there have been multiple waterspouts that have not only sunk fishing ships, but have come onto the land and destroyed the fishing villages along the northern shore."

"My god," I said, a cold, icy feeling creeping down my back.

"We have observed several huge monsters along the edges of the forests, magical creatures we have never seen before. They are destroying farms and stealing livestock," Tilde said.

Anya took hold of Tilde's hand and squeezed it, a frightened look in her eyes.

"Do you have maps that show where each of these things has happened?" Tam asked. "So we can plot our strategy?"

"Yes, of course." Anya signaled to a general standing at attention at the edge of the room. She nodded and slipped out a side door, then returned in a few minutes with a sheath of papers.

Tam, Jim, and Tupu rose and moved to the other end of the table to consult with the general; they spread the maps out and began to talk strategies.

"Anya, the queen. The prince. What happened?" I asked, a lump in my throat.

"We are not sure what happened, but when the maid went to tend them with her morning duties, she found the royal bedchamber empty and in ruins," Anya said.

"We sent the Valkyries to trail them, but they have not yet returned. We suspect something bad has befallen them," Tilde said.

"You sent out *all* the Valkyries?" I asked, aghast.

"No, no, of course not. We sent out the elites. Then a few days later, we sent out the royal guard. Then I sent you that missive. I didn't know what else to do," Anya said.

"Everything we have tried has failed," Tilde added. "We did not want to leave the kingdom unguarded, so we ordered the Valkyrie foot troops and the base army to stay at their posts."

"I understand." I looked at them both, then down at their joined hands. "I need to know who is actually in charge? Are you making the decisions, Anya? Or is it you, Tilde?" I raised my eyebrows.

"Well, actually, it's been a group effort, Princess," Anya said. "Tilde has acted as my closest adviser ..."

"As Tam has for me." I smiled. "When are you two going to officially jump the broom?"

"When we have a minute to breathe," Anya laughed.

"We have also been in constant consultation with the general and her military staff," Tilde said.

"I'm sure you have done as best as can be expected." I took a deep breath and rose. "We will handle this monster that is ravaging the coastal villages, and then we will go get the queen and prince."

I took a deep breath, trying to calm down.

"And I will return with the head of the person who kidnapped the queen and prince." I fixed the duchesses with a steely look.

They nodded, and smiled.

"We knew you would be able to solve this dilemma, Princess!" Anya said.

Tilde clapped her hands. "Now we're getting somewhere!"

"Now, I wish to be shown the royal bedchamber. I trust nothing has been disturbed?" I asked.

"No, we left it just as we found it, and we sealed the room," said Anya.

"Let's go then," I said, gesturing for my troupe to follow. Tam, Tupu and Jim hurried over and stepped with us.

Anya and Tilde led us, along with five guards, down several hallways and to the pair of familiar ornate doors that led to my parents' royal bedchamber.

Four guards stood sentinel on either side of the door, which was locked with a heavy black chain.

"The strongest iron," Anya said.

"Of course," I answered.

The iron would protect against human intruders – as well as magical incursion.

"Unlock the doors," I commanded.

The taller of the guards snapped to attention and pulled a key from her pocket. She turned to unlock the heavy padlock.

I turned to the other guards. "And where were you when the queen and prince were kidnapped, soldier?" I asked in a sharp, loud voice.

They all stood rigid and turned white.

"Your Highness, we were here, on guard, right where you see us now."

"Then how could the crime have occurred?" I asked, my face stony.

"We do not know, You Highness."

"HOW COULD YOU LET THIS HAPPEN?" I barked.

The guards flinched and didn't answer.

"Come, Your Highness," gestured Anya, "Let us enter."

I scowled at the guards as I passed, breathing hard in displeasure.

Their white faces began to sweat.

"In here, Highness," Tilde called.

I walked into the room and regarded the devastation. Tears sprang to my eyes.

"Oh, my God," I whispered.

The room was in shambles.

The queen's royal bed, a huge four-poster with ornate, hand-carved scenes out of our mythology, silken cloths draped overheard, and velvet comforters covering a deeply stuffed feather mattress, was destroyed. The silken cloths were trampled on the floor, and the wooden posts were broken and splintered.

The velvet comforters were ripped to shreds.

The floor was covered in debris.

It looked like an explosion had occurred.

I stepped past the bed and toward the huge bay window that overlooked the gardens.

A wide swath of ice and rock led from the bed, through the floor and to the window.

There was a deep gouge in the floor, and it looked like the foundation of the room was affected.

I bent and touched the icy path that led from bed to window. It was searing to the touch.

"This is not normal ice," murmured Khepri next to me. She withdrew an ampule from her bag and took several samples.

The swath of ice looked to be about four feet wide. It was deeply curved, with the outer edges reaching high above the floor at least a foot.

I could see splinters embedded in the frozen crystals that formed the path, which seemed to have rooted itself deep in the wood of the floor.

I put my hand to my mouth as I saw what looked like gouges made by the fingernails of someone being dragged away, and I looked up and saw more scratches on the edge of the window.

Whatever did this took my parents by force. They fought for their lives.

I rose to my feet, unshed tears in my eyes.

The only consolation was that there was not one hint of blood anywhere.

I scanned the room for any other clue, and my eyes caught the glint of a brush on the floor, half under the crumbling remains of the royal bed. I reached down and picked it up.

It was my mother's boar-bristle hairbrush. I looked at it closely. I could see strands of the queen's long, golden locks ... and something else.

"Khepri," I said, turning to the healer. "What is this?"

She came and examined the crystals in the hairbrush.

"It looks like the maid may have beat the intruder with this," I said. "She might have been brushing the queen's hair with it when the attack occurred."

I swung around, searching, then looked up at Anya. "Was there anyone else in the room when the attack occurred?"

"Yes. The body of the queen's maid was removed from the corner there." Anya pointed to the corner of the room next to the outer wall.

I crouched and examined the spot.

"We thought we should remove the body, it was starting to ... well ... you know," Tilde said quietly.

"Yes, yes, I understand." I rose and turned to them.

"It looks like whatever took the queen and prince knocked the maid aside, and she fell against this wall. See here, and here," I indicated marks on the wallpaper and floor. I gestured to the hairbrush. "It looks like she was tending to my mother's locks when this happened, and that she tried to beat at the intruder with the hairbrush."

"These are ice crystals and some kind of fiber," Khepri said. "We need these analyzed."

"I'll see to it," Anya said.

Khepri carefully handed the hairbrush to the duchess, who gestured to a guard.

"Take this to the laboratory. Tell the wizard to analyze every single speck on it."

The guard nodded and departed with the brush.

Anya turned back to me. "They feel horrible they were not able to stop the attack. They are eager to redeem themselves," she said.

"I understand." I thought a moment. "Why couldn't they stop the attack?" I asked.

"We questioned them thoroughly," Tilde said. "They heard the commotion and tried to enter the room. The doors would not budge. They threw themselves against the doors, but they remained as if a solid wall. We believe some magic was at work, holding them closed."

"I see," I said.

I took a deep breath and looked at the two duchesses. "I leave for the northeastern coast with my troupe at dawn. I will travel from there directly to follow the path the abductor took." I stepped close to them. "I want you to repair everything in this room." I gestured all around us.

"Fix everything. Replace anything that is damaged beyond repair. Get this room looking exactly as it did the day before the attack."

I looked deeply into both their eyes for a long minute.

"I intend to rescue the queen and prince, and they will be returning to the safety of the castle soon. They will require a perfect bedchamber. Do you understand?"

Anya and Tilde both nodded. I nodded back at them.

"I'm counting on you both to oversee this project. I want it perfect."

"Yes, Your Highness.

That evening, we all checked our weapons yet again, loaded up with supplies, and readied ourselves for the trip up the coast.

"It's a two-day journey by horseback," said Tam. "We've had the horses brought onto shore, and they're waiting in the stables."

I nodded. "Shêtân is so happy to be back on land. The exercises we shared on the southern island were not enough for him." I laughed.

We took the horses to land every chance we got, exercising them and running them through their combat drills, but it was never enough.

"My Taimim is so eager for this adventure. He's chomping at everything I give him. He almost got my finger last time," Kym said.

"We'll reach the villages quickly, I'm sure," Khepri said, lost in thought. She had replenished her medical supplies on the southern island.

"Did you miss anything, Khepri?" Caroline asked.

"No, no. Well, I am a bit low on Snowdrop and Dittany," Khepri said.

"I will get those for you," I said, rising and exiting the room.

I walked to the hallway and down a bit, finally finding a guard.

"Why are there no guards posted outside our rooms?" I said in a firm voice.

The guard snapped his heels and saluted. "Your Highness, yes, I will remedy that immediately." He hurried off, and I grimaced.

Security is a bit lax in the castle these days. No wonder an aggressor was able to kidnap the queen. This is inexcusable.

I motioned for a lady-in-waiting to approach.

She curtsied before me and waited for my command.

"Fetch my healer hefty bunches of Snowdrop and Dittany, and be back within the hour."

She rushed off toward the apothecary.

Chapter Eight
Håkan

It was a long night. I tossed and turned and dreamed again.

I was in a huge forest, with just a few trees. Everything was covered in ice, and the whiteness that surrounded me was blinding.

The sun was high in the sky.

That is odd.

I looked upward, and I could see two suns in the sky.

Why are there two?

I shivered and looked down at my hands. They were frozen solid, and a blue-grey color.

"What?" I said aloud. My voice echoed. I looked around. I was alone in the forest.

Why would my voice echo in a forest?

I hiked through the sparse trees, around the frozen shrubs, and out onto a barren flatland.

There was movement in the distance. I squinted my eyes and tried to see what it was, but couldn't. Several figures moved about on the horizon. I could not tell how large or small they were, whether they were human or something else.

"HELLO!" I called out, cupping my hands around my mouth.

The movement intensified. I could see the creatures were now coming toward me.

Looking closer, I saw the many figures coalesce into one huge creature. It was approaching rapidly.

"Oh, no," I mumbled, staring.

The massive creature was plowing through the ground as if it were ice covering a river.

I looked down and saw I was now standing on a frozen lake, a dusting of snow covering the ice. I brushed against it with my boot and slid, falling on my side.

"OOMPH."

I scrambled to my feet.

The creature was nearing me, rapidly pumping its head up and down in its haste.

I could not move; all I could do was stare at its rapid approach.

It was a slimy grey, with horns protruding from its head and back, like the fluctuating horns of a snail. Mucous dripped from its head as it came.

The thing's body was a mottled grey and blue, and it undulated as it swam, breaking the ice as it came, plowing through it like a barge through a frozen lake.

It was almost upon me. It was going to hit me any second with its massive neck.

It opened its mouth and lunged for me, and I could smell the rotten stink of decayed fish and seaweed coming from its maw ...

I screamed. "AAHHHH!"

"Babe, Babe wake up," Tam's hand was on my arm, rubbing.

"Wha? Huh?" I opened my eyes.

It had seemed so real.

I sat up in bed.

"You were calling out in your sleep," Tam said softly.

I blinked my eyes.

It was still early.

I shivered. I could still smell the stink of the monster's breath as it reached for me ...

The next morning, Arya and Tilde were there early as we ate a light breakfast.

"Our science advisers tell us that they have gathered data that would seem to indicate that there is some unnatural spell over our land," Anya said.

"Yes, it is some kind of magic, and it is unnaturally warming all of Swerighe," Tilde said.

"We have noticed an unusual amount of foul weather, as well as strangely strong inclement storms," I said.

"There are far more water spouts this season than there were last year, I've noticed," Tam said.

"And the storms are severe," said Tupu. "The sea is normally so still, and the wind so slight, that we have five giant manta rays pulling our ship. Without them it would take forever to sail anywhere."

"I am certain it is all connected," I said. "The warming of the air and land, the rising waters, all of it."

"The air temperature greatly affects the storms," Tam said.

"The question is, what is causing this unnatural warming of the land?" Khepri said.

"In my oasis, the weather can be greatly affected by magic," Kym blushed. "I know this personally."

I smiled at her, remembering the Aoudaghost oasis the young chimera had lived in.

"Weather and magic: invariably intertwined," said Khepri. "It's a delicate balance."

"Indeed," Anya said.

"Charlotte," said Tilde, glancing at her partner. "We would like to suggest you take along three more on your journey to the northern villages. Do you remember your cousin Håkan?"

"Oh my God, how is he doing? I haven't seen him in years," I said.

"He is fine. He had moved to the eastern coast many years back," Anya said.

"I remember," I said.

"His wife is visiting family in the capital here, and he is here with his nephew, and the boy's best friend," said Tilde. "They have expressed a strong interest in helping to fight the creature that is ravaging the northern villages."

"They do, do they?" I said.

"Is he a farmer?" Tam asked.

"Yes, actually," Anya answered.

"Wellllllll, I don't see why not," I said. "Do they have their own weapons? Can they fight?"

"Yes, and yes," laughed Tilde. "Wait till you meet them. You'll understand."

We were ready to go, and it was still quite early, which made me happy. I loved to get a jump on the new day when adventure was afoot.

We gathered in the meeting room, our weapons and packs ready, for one last consultation with Anya and Tilde.

"Charlotte!" a huge, booming voice filled the room as a huge man entered. He was nearly as tall as Jim, with heavy muscles and a bald head. Silver beads were woven into a reddish-brown beard that was groomed to perfection. He wore bright, new leather armor, and a long sword was strapped to his side.

Two teenage boys followed him in, and I was surprised to recognize the final boy I had helped out of the sea yesterday.

"Håkan!" I walked to embrace him, slapping him on the back heartily. "It's been forever!" I laughed.

I turned to my troupe, "Håkan, this is Tam. We are handfasted just last month,"

Håkan grasped Tam's arm and shook it, "My new cousin, then, wonderful to meet you!"

"Then here, this is Caroline, Khepri, Christianne, Tupu, Jim, and Akim," I said, pointing to each of them in turn. "We are a force to be reckoned with!" I smiled.

"I remember you when you were younger. You were a force to be reckoned with back then, too!" He laughed.

"Well, yes," I ducked my head to hide my smile.

"And here are my fighting troupe, ha ha!" Håkan turned and gestured to the boys next to him. "This is my nephew, Inge, and his best friend, Olof. They are both thirteen and

growing up too fast. They need to be tempered in battle."
He threw his head back in a belly laugh.

I grinned and shook each boy's hand. "Pleased to meet you, Inge. Olof."

"Have we met before, your Highness?" Olof said, a curious look on his face.

"Just recently. I fished you out of the sea, with the help of a friendly beluga whale," I smiled.

"Oh! Oh, That was you! I knew it. I never got the chance to thank you! Oh, Your Highness." Olof pumped my hand again, then fumbled and put his hand on his midsection, and bowed deeply.

"We were glad to be able to help," I said.

"Well," said Tam, "Is everyone ready to head out to the stables?"

"More than ready!" Håkan said heartily.

I turned to my cousin, the duchess of Västergötland. "Anya," I embraced her and touched foreheads with her. "You have done well in the absence of the queen."

Anya blushed and shook her head. "We have barely held things together."

"But nobody could have held the kingdom together better than you," I said, then turned to the duchess of Ångermanland. "With Tilde's help, you have done as well as could be expected." I turned back to Anya.

"I must ask you now, to please hold things together while I go retrieve the queen and prince."

Anya nodded slowly, her eyes filling with tears.

"Be careful, Your Highness," she said. "It is a dangerous situation."

"I know, I am well aware," I said.

"Take care, Princess. May the Gods protect and guide you," said Tilde, turning to encompass everyone in the room. "All of you."

I embraced Any and Tilde, and we left.

We made our way outside through the kitchens, and it was a short walk to the stables.

"Shêtân," I murmured, petting the great black horse and running my hand down his sleek neck. The stable workers had brushed him to a shine, and his coat gleamed with health. I checked the saddle cinches and the two packs, while the others did the same.

We each had a mount, and there was a donkey loaded down with supplies.

Hmmm.

"A donkey," Tam said dubiously.

"Oh, sir, this donkey will not ever fail you, he is steadfast and strong, and he is accustomed to harsh terrain," said the stable worker who held the donkey's lead.

"His packs are loaded with food and supplies, and grain for the horses."

"I really don't think ..." Tam began.

I gave him a look that said, *We may need it, you never know.*

Tam changed midsentence, "... and thank you for this noble steed, he looks perfect for the job of aiding us in our quest." He smiled at the beast, which swished its tail at an errant fly.

A half hour later, we were on our way.

We followed a path along the sea, across high moors overlooking the slate-blue sea below us. Today it seemed calm, but I could see grey clouds to the south, so I knew the weather could change at any hour.

Especially with the unnatural warming.

The moors were stark, and the brush that grew alongside the cliff was thin and brown. Wild grasses grew short and stubby alongside the path, and it looked sparse and dark from what I could see.

The trip to the northern village was uneventful, with the exception of Christianne and Kym challenging the two new boys to race on the first evening.

"Oh, no, ha ha ha!" Caroline laughed. She was bent over the fire, tending a large pot of stew, and watching the four younglings talk a ways off.

"Do you think they'll fall for it?" I asked Jim as we stood together.

"Ahhh, yes. I do," Jim laughed.

Inge and Olof had tried very hard to impress Christianne, who, being sixteen and taller than either, had become their instant goal. Kym had seen this and had challenged the two boys to a footrace.

They'd moved to the valley next to us, to have room to run. It was a few dozen feet away, still close to camp.

"I think they might have a chance at beating her," said Håkan. "They have grown quite good in the last year."

"Yes, but, well ..." Tam said.

"Håkan, Christianne has an added advantage. You'll see," I said.

"An added advantage?" Håkan said.

I gestured to the four, who were gearing up to start the footrace.

They lined up, and bent to a half-crouch. I could hear their voices say, "Go!"

And they began to run.

The boys were pulling ahead.

Then Christianne's wings emerged from her coat and began whirring, propelling her forward like a whirlwind.

She shot forward and was across the valley in a few seconds.

The boys ran after her, calling in astonishment, and Kym followed them, trying to run while laughing.

"What is this? The girl has wings on her back? How can this be?" Håkan exclaimed.

"Well, you see," said Tam, and explained the whole thing to the large man, whose eyebrows rose higher and higher on his forehead, until Tam finished his story.

"That is amazing," Håkan said, staring at Christianne as she walked back to camp, the two boys clamoring around her and talking all at once.

Chapter Nine
Storsjöodjuret

That evening was storytelling time. The campfire crackled merrily as we all sat, eating and talking.

"Oh, Christianne's wings are just one of the surprises we have to offer," Jim was saying.

Håkan listened, completely engrossed.

"Look at Kym," Jim pointed.

Håkan turned to look at what appeared to be a six-year-old girl.

"Do it," Jim said, smiling.

With a sheepish grin, Kym set down her now-empty bowl of stew and rose, walking a half dozen feet away from the fire.

She closed her eyes and concentrated, transforming into the chimera.

"Oj, o, å!" Håkan exclaimed. "Åh, hur otroligt!"

"I know, right?! HA HA HA!" I laughed, holding my belly.

"It's not that funny," the chimera said.

"Hon kan prata!" Håkan asked.

"Yes," I said, "the chimera can talk. She's still the same person, still Kym."

The chimera shimmered and was the small six-year-old girl again.

"That was amazing, cousin," Håkan said.

"Incredible," Olof said. Inge just nodded, his jaw dropped open in astonishment.

"Kym is invaluable when it comes to not only adventuring, but combat, as well," Tam said, patting Kym's hand as she took her seat again.

Khepri handed Kym a piece torn off the crunchy loaf of Swerighe bread she'd brought from the castle.

"Thanks." Kym smiled at her.

"Rest. Do you want another bowl of stew? Khepri asked.

Kym picked up her bowl and handed it to Khepri. "Yes, please."

Khepri handed it back, and Kym was soon wolfing down a second helping of the fragrant dinner.

"It takes energy to transform, you see," I said to Håkan.

"Ahh," he said. He turned to Jim. "I noticed you look a bit odd. Are you human? You appear to be, except for the hint of odd coloring you have."

In answer, Jim began to transform into the djinn. At ten feet tall, even sitting, he was an imposing figure.

Håkan's jaw dropped open.

Olof and Inge's eyes widened in surprise.

The djinn completed his transformation, winked at Håkan, then nodded at me, and transformed back into his human form.

"No, I am not human," Jim said, grinning.

"By the gods, you are impressive, my new friend," Håkan said.

"Yes," said Tam. "And also incredibly useful in many different situations."

"Hey, you ...," sputtered Olof. "You were helping people in the flood on Gåsö! I saw you and I thought I was dreaming!"

"It was not a dream," Jim chuckled.

"Oh, my goodness," Inge said.

"I will tell you something, my new friends," said Håkan. "I would not want to come up against you in battle." He raised his cup of mead. "Skål! May we be victorious tomorrow!" he drank deeply, and grinned.

"Skål!"

"Skål!"

"Oh, yes, indeed! Skål!"

"Skål!"

"Skål! Skål!"

The merriment lasted well into the night.

The next morning, the sun rose slowly into the sky, and we got a late start.

The horses meandered through the sparse forest, and out the other side.

By midafternoon, we were approaching the village. We made the descent from a low hill, and stopped just as the rise allowed us a clear view.

The fishing village looked deserted.

"The village was attacked three times in the last fortnight," said Håkan. "After the first time, the people evacuated into the inland town, and a skeleton crew was left to maintain things. Well, that crew was attacked, and they fled, joining the villagers in the other town. The queen then had guards posted back a ways, just there." He pointed behind the village to a low building far back from the seashore.

"And what happened the third time?" I asked.

"The monster came and sank all the boats. It seemed especially unhappy it was robbed of its prey. We think it wants blood," Håkan said.

I scanned the sea.

"What happens when the beast comes? Is there any warning?" Tam asked.

"It storms. Lightning and thunder," said Håkan. "Either the storm is brought by the monster, or the monster is brought by the storm. Either way, that is how it comes."

"Hmmm," I said.

"Well, since the skies are not showing stormy weather today, why don't we go down and look around?" said Tam. "Maybe even stay down there."

"Are the guards still there?" I asked Håkan.

"No. After the last attack, it was clear they could not defend the village, so the queen withdrew them," said Håkan. "It's been almost a month. The village has been deserted all that time." He looked down at the building.

"Let's check it out," Tam said.

I urged Shêtân forward, and we slowly approached the village.

We camped in the lee building the guards had taken, where it seemed safest.

There were beds and shelter, and we lit a fire in the center, beneath the smoke hole.

"We'll stay here for a few days, and hope it shows itself," I said.

"If there is a storm, it will come," Håkan said.

"Let's hope so," Tupu said.

While the others settled in, Tam, Tupu and I decided to go exploring.

We looked inside the houses along one of the two main roads.

I kicked at an abandoned doll in the corner of one room in a small house we'd entered. "It's so sad."

"Hopefully, they can return," Tam kissed my hand. "All is not lost."

"Hey, look over here," Tupu called from outside the small house.

Tam and I hurried out.

Tupu was pointing to something in the dirt.

It was a drawing in the dark soil.

"That looks like some kind of monster in the sea," Tam said, crouching down to touch the indentations. "It looks big."

"We should have Håkan look at this," Tupu said.

"No need," I said, studying the figure. "I recognize the drawing. It is called Storsjöodjuret. It is a monster from Swerighe folklore. A six-meter-long serpentine sea monster. But it was only a folktale."

"Perhaps it was more than that," Tam said.

"Maybe the warming has something to do with its sudden appearance," said Tupu. "That can't be a coincidence."

"Indeed," I said grimly, looking out at the beach.

That night, we rested only a few hours. Jim took first watch and stayed by the fire.

It was a quiet night, and I had a hard time falling asleep, unlike Tam, who snored softly beside me.

I nudged him, and he moved to his side, and the snoring stopped.

"Does he always make that noise when he sleeps?" Jim whispered from across the dwindling fire.

I smiled. "Sometimes."

Jim rose and retrieved two more logs of wood, placing them atop the glowing coals. He poked the dying fire with a long stick until it flared to life again.

I watched Jim, and my eyelids grew heavy. I glanced outside the window of the low longhouse, and saw a few stars twinkling in the night. My eyelids grew heavy, and I dropped off to sleep.

A few hours later, I was awakened by low talking.

"Do you think we should rouse the others?"

"No, let them sleep. It's nothing, really."

"It's not nothing. It's storm clouds."

"Which have done nothing more than block out the stars. It's not even raining."

"Yet."

A low moan of wind reached my ears.

I opened my eyes.

"What's going on, you two?" I yawned, sitting up.

"Now look what you did," Olof said.

"Your Highness, there's a storm rolling into the area," said Inge. "Uncle Håkan went outside to investigate the shoreline. He's been gone a while."

What?

I pulled my boots on. Dawn was just pinking the village, making the windows something less that black outside.

I strapped on my scimitar. "You two stay here," I ordered.

"Wait," Tupu said from her sleeping roll. "I'll come with you."

I waited while she pulled her boots on and strapped on her sword.

As we walked outside, I turned and pointed at the two boys.

"STAY. HERE."

They nodded, their eyes big in the firelight.

I shut the door, which wedged into the doorway.

Thunder rolled overhead.

"That's promising," Tupu said.

"I wonder where Håkan went," I said. "Let's go check by the seashore."

It was a short walk down through the houses along the path.

"I think this used to be a cobblestone street," I said, brushing the toe of my boot against the mud that had flooded over the stones.

"This weather could be trouble, especially with all the flooding," murmured Tupu.

We walked along the shoreline.

We passed an older fishing boat that was half sunk in a few feet of water. I splashed into the surf and grabbed hold of its tall edge.

"Seems a sturdy build." I looked around. "The houses, too. All built well of strong wood."

"I wonder where he went," Tupu said.

I looked around, swinging my head around several times. There was no sign of Håkan.

"Håkan!" I called out. Lightning danced across the water about a half mile off shore.

"Håkan! Håkan!" called Tupu.

"Here, lass," Håkan's voice answered.

We turned and saw him emerging from a small wooded area, carrying more firewood.

We walked to meet him.

"Have you seen anything?" I asked as we approached, glancing back out to the sea.

"No, not yet," Håkan looked out at the water. Rain was beginning to fall in fat drops, making wet cups that flooped on the surface of the water.

"I'd better get this wood in by the fire before it gets wet," Håkan said.

We turned and trotted back to the longhouse. Just as we passed through the door, the clouds opened, unleashing a deluge.

"Just in time," Inge said, smiling and taking the wood from his uncle.

"This should hold us for a while," Olof said.

Behind us, there was a loud roar coming from the shoreline. "RAAWRRR!"

"I'm up! I'm awake." Tam sat up, rubbing his eyes.

"Whazzat?" Christianne said, opening her eyes.

"Okay, okay!" said Kym.

"Ughhh," Khepri said.

"REAARRRRRYEEEA!" came another roar.

"I think the Storsjöodjuret has arrived," I said grimly.

Chapter Ten
A Tough Beast to Battle

The troupe hurriedly pulled boots on and buckled sword sheaths on while Tupu, Håkan and I watched from the window. We couldn't see much, but we could hear a crashing sound down by the water's edge.

"There goes the last fishing boat," Håkan said grimly.

I laughed despite the gravity of the situation, then ducked my head to stifle it.

Oh, dear lord, Charlotte. Be serious. This is an important battle.

I grinned as everyone walked up to the door, and we opened it and stepped out.

Storsjöodjuret was a childhood legend, told to keep children from sneaking out at night for mischief. I couldn't help but grin and feel in high spirits as we walked down the path to the shoreline.

"Well, there it is," Tam said.

We stopped behind the last house, and watched as the monster attacked the half-sunken boat I had examined earlier that morning.

It was indeed nearly twenty feet long, from tip of nose to end of tail. It looked like an aquatic dinosaur, except it had nostrils instead of gill slits. Its hide was a dull brown, mottled with grey, and its belly was a paler shade of grey. There were blotchy looking spots along its back, which sported several fin-like appendages. Its head look very seal-like, but much larger. It held itself up on four legs, each of which ended in a strong-looking flipper.

It paused in its wanton destruction, raised its head, and screamed in apparent displeasure.

"ARRARRARRTTTT!"

Its voice was high-pitched, almost an ultrasonic screech. It hurt my ears.

It hadn't seen us, thank goodness. We had time to form a strategy.

We ducked back behind the house and sat down.

"Okay, ideas?" I asked.

"Well, we could rush it," Kym said.

"Are you insane?"

"No. Maybe." Kym laughed.

"Actually, that's not a bad idea," Håkan said. "It's on the beach and out of its element. And we have the element of surprise on our side."

"I agree. Let's stop talking and do this!" Tupu said.

I grinned.

Tam stood and nocked an arrow in his bow. He nodded to me and stepped out from behind the wall of the house.

TWANG!

A howl of rage emanated from the beast. We ran.

"YAAAAAAAH!" I yelled as I sprinted toward the sea monster, my scimitar raised high.

The others follow me, calling out war cries as well.

I reached the beast and swung at it, slamming my blade full-force against its neck.

It bounced off.

Uh oh.

The others sliced at the Storsjöodjuret as well, at different parts of its body. Tail, neck, flipper, back; wherever we could reach, we tried to slice and dice this monster.

It had no effect. It didn't even draw blood.

Wait.

I saw a trickle of blood running down the side of its neck and saw it was coming from the arrow embedded in the thing.

Tam's arrow.

"FALL BACK! FALL BACK!" I screamed.

The thing screamed in rage and swung its head at us, catching Håkan on the side and sending him flying.

"FALL BACK NOW!" I grabbed Håkan's arm and pulled. Jim grabbed the man's other arm, and we pulled him back a dozen feet.

"I'm fine, I'm fine," Håkan yelled, flailing his legs.

We dropped his arms, and he got up and ran with us, limping slightly.

The others were running, finally.

The Storsjöodjuret roared again and again, as it tried to come up out of the water on its flippers. But on land, it was slow moving.

We were able to run from it and get away.

Live to fight another day.

"Okay, well, that went poorly," Tam said.

"Its hide is tough, I think it's tougher than a shark's," Håkan said.

"Tam's arrow got it. We may have to shoot arrows at it to kill it," I said.

"How many arrows have you got, Tam?" Caroline asked.

"About three or four dozen," Tam patted his pack. "Should be plenty."

"If the arrows can be placed deep enough to really harm it," I said. "I only saw a small trickle of blood from the arrow you got into it just now."

"We'll have to distract it so he has the time to shoot it full of arrows," Khepri said.

I glanced at Håkan. "How are you doing, cousin?"

"Eh, I'll have a bruise tomorrow, but I'll live." He winked at me.

"You're tough, old man," I smiled.

" 'Old man' is it?" Håkan exclaimed in mock rage.

I laughed.

"Okay, okay. So, I think we should go back and shoot it full of arrows," said Tam. Thunder sounded again, and he looked up. "Before it leaves again."

"Agreed."

"Yes."

"Let's go."

"I agree."

"I'm in."

"I'll distract it."

"You will not," I said. "Inge, please do not go close to that thing. You saw what it did to your uncle."

"Yes, Your Highness."

"Okay," I said, looking around. "Everyone ready?"

"Let's roll."

We ran out around the buildings again, down the path, and out onto the beach.

It was farther out to sea, I saw to my chagrin.

"Tam, quick, shoot it a few times," I said. "Try to get its eyes if you can. That ought to hurt it."

Tam nocked an arrow and crept forward, his boots nearly in the water.

TWANG!

TWANG!

TWANG! TWING! TWANG! TWANG!

Six arrows appeared in succession on the beast.

One hit the creature's eye.

It screamed in pain and began swimming back to shore.

"Okay, be ready!" I called out. "Keep the monster off of Tam! Keep out of the arrows' way!"

The thing was getting closer...

Thirty yards.

Twenty.

Ten.

TWANG! TWANG! TWANG! TWANG! TWANG!

Arrow after arrow hit the Storsjöodjuret as it approached.

We stood ready, swords out, in case it came up on the beach after Tam.

Blood flowed down its body in a dozen rivulets. The sea water began to run with blood where it swam.

"I need to hit its other eye," Tam said.

"You have my blessing," I said.

He smirked at me and nodded his head to the side in a sardonic gesture, then stepped a foot into the water, took careful aim, then let an arrow fly.

"TWINGGGGGTHUMP"

The arrow landed in the beast's other eye, and sunk in farther than any other arrow had so far.

It screamed.

Blood ran down its neck heavier than before.

The beast collapsed in water about two feet deep.

It floundered there, tossing its head back and forth.

"It can't see," Khepri said.

"We've got to finish it off," Håkan said.

"No need," I said. "It's dying."

One of the arrows must have pierced the beast's brain, because its movements slowly ceased, and it lowered its head farther into the water.

"It's done for," Olof said, creeping forward.

The Storsjöodjuret was barely moving now. Its sides heaved as it struggled to breathe. The eyes were completely gone, punctured and embedded with arrows. A clear fluid ran down its face into the water.

Olof stepped up to it and stuck his sword into the monster's neck where an arrow had pierced it. The blade slid in a few inches and stuck.

Inge came up then and stuck his sword into an eye and it fell in easily. He quickly withdrew it, and more clear fluid ran out of the wound.

"It's dead," said Inge. "I think." He stuck his sword back into the eye and pushed it in a foot, until it stuck.

The beast shuddered and then lay still.

We pulled the monster onto the sand, and examined it. After all, it wasn't every day one got the chance to see a sea monster up close.

It had a tough hide, we had seen that, but now we could poke and prod it and find out how tough it really was.

"Oh, that's definitely thicker than a shark's hide," Håkan said."

"Very tough hide," said Khepri, examining the corpse closely. She poked an arrow into the eye, and was rewarded with more cerebral spinal fluid coursing out. The eyes were each easily the size of my hand, fingers spread.

Strangely large.

Khepri was looking at the other side of the thing.

It lay on its side in the sand.

"Hmmm," she said from the other side.

"What is it, Khepri?" Jim asked.

"Well, and I can't be completely sure. ..." She paused, then continued. "I think," she spoke slowly, "I think this specimen is a juvenile."

"What?" Håkan said. "It's a what?"

Khepri stood upright again. "A juvenile," she said. "A child. Not a full-grown adult."

"You mean to tell me this is not an adult Storsjöodjuret?" Håkan asked.

"That's what I said," Khepri said.

"So, the full-grown adult would be larger?" I said slowly.

"Oh, most assuredly," said Khepri. "In fact, if I'm right, it would be much, much larger."

"So, where did this young sea monster come from?" Caroline asked.

"In the legends," said Håkan, straightening himself and stretching his back, "the Storsjöodjuret is said to live in the ice. It is said to come from the ice itself."

"If there is truth to that legend," said Jim, "And there almost always is some truth in legends, that could mean the creature was frozen in the ice. Entombed in the ice. Possibly hibernating."

"Until it was set free by the warmer climate," Tam said, "The ice is melting all over this land. Remember the glacier?"

"Yep. So, the legends might all be true." I looked down at the creature.

"I wonder why it targeted the fishing village," Caroline mused.

"Maybe it was upset at having been melted out of the ice," Kym speculated. "You never know. And it's too late to ask the Storsjöodjuret."

"Okay, Khepri are you nearly done? I want to go wash up," I said.

"Nearly, I just want to take some samples," Khepri said from the other side of the corpse.

I smiled and met Tam's eyes. Khepri was our healer, but also the troupe's resident scientist. She always kept empty ampules in her bag for collecting samples. And her medicinal bag was nearly always hanging from her shoulder.

Someday, Khepri's going to make some huge, important discovery, and it'll be fantastic.

I walked back to the ocean and began washing my sword off.

Tam brought the arrows he'd dug out of the creature's body, to wash off and examine.

"Are most of those undamaged?" I asked.

"I think so," he said, turning them over in his hands. "Too valuable to go to waste. They take a ridiculous amount of time to make."

"I've seen you crafting them. They are intricate," I smiled.

"Not only must the wood be carved perfectly straight, which is a much harder thing to do than it sounds," said Tam, "but the arrowheads must be mounted into the wood just right, so the arrow is correctly balanced."

"Hey, Charlotte, look at this," Khepri called.

I trudged back through the sand.

"What's up?" I asked.

"I found something strange, look here," Khepri lifted a flap of hide she'd been able to cut through, and pointed at something embedded inside the Storsjöodjuret's body.

I leaned closer, then decided to just kneel in the sand, to get a better look.

"Tam, can you turn it over a bit more?" I called.

"Sure," answered Tam. The massive corpse turned over a few feet.

"More, please," I called.

The body turned a bit more.

"See," said Khepri. She pointed an arrow she was using to push through the organs, indicating a glowing blue sliver deep inside the cadaver.

"What the heck is that?" I asked slowly. I reached a finger out to touch the thing, despite the gore surrounding it.

"OWW!" I pulled my finger back, resisting the urge to suck on the aching tip.

"Are you bleeding?" Khepri asked sharply.

"No, it was more like a ... a stinging cold. Like, really, really cold," I said.

"Hmmmm." She reached into the cavity and pushed the organs aside more, then looked up.

"Tam," she called. "Do you have a bit of leather I can use to grab something?"

"Sure," Tam handed her his hood.

"Perfect," Khepri said. She wrapped her hand around the leather hat and reached in again. "If I can just ..."

I waited, holding my breath.

"There! Got it." She slowly pulled out the blue sliver. It was longer than I first realized, measuring about ten inches.

It was like a long splinter, glowing blue with an unearthly light.

She held it up for us to see.

"The cold is burning my fingers through the leather. Ouch!" she grasped the thing with her other hand, careful to keep the leather between her flesh and the sliver.

We all leaned in.

"What," asked Kym, "is that?"

"Well, if I were to make an educated guess," said Khepri, "I'd say it's what brought the Storsjöodjuret out of its icy hibernation. I think it's part of the unnatural magic that's harming this land. And," she said grimly, "I've read a bit about this kind of magic, in *The Book of Mysteries*. And it's not good. Not good at all. It's incredibly destructive."

"What kind of magic is it, Khepri?" asked Christianne.

"It's Ice Magic."

Chapter Eleven
A Story of Abduction

"Charlotte, we need to gather information," Jim whispered in my ear as we walked back to the longhouse to retrieve our bags. "If we are going up against ice magic, well, it's not just hard to defend against. It's nearly impossible."

"I was thinking the same thing, actually," I said. I glanced around the deserted village as we walked. There was an air of desolation about it that unnerved me.

"Okay, I think we should go back to the castle," I said.

A few days later, we trotted our horses back into the stables and met the duchesses inside the castle kitchen.

"Anya, Tilde, hello again," I said.

"Oh! You surprised me, Princess!" Anya turned suddenly to face me, and I saw she had a bowl of cold chicken in her arms.

"Oh, Anya, don't stress eat," I said. "Take a ride in the countryside instead."

"That's a great idea," said Tilde. I looked over at her and saw crumbs at the corner of her mouth.

Sigh.

"We need to talk to any eyewitnesses who saw the intruder that kidnapped the queen and prince," I said.

"Ah. Hmmm. I think ..." Anya glanced at Tilde. "Tilde? Can you think of anyone who ...?"

"Only Elias," Tilde said. "You can find him in the stables," she added helpfully.

A half hour later I walked back out to the stables while the others cleaned up and washed for dinner. It had been decided we'd gather information and head out as soon as we could.

Hopefully tomorrow morning.

"Come with me, Jim," I asked. "But stay out of sight." I put my finger to my lips and we left.

Walking into the stables, I grabbed a bucket of oats and walked to visit Shêtân. I arrived at his stall and saw an old man shoveling manure into an ancient wheelbarrow.

I poured the oats into the trough and patted Shêtân's neck as he bent to eat it.

Looking around, I saw several stable hands nearby. I decided to ask them where I could find this witness.

"Oh, Elias?" said a smartly dressed young man about to exercise a dressage mare. "He's mucking out stalls, I think he's near the big black stallion," he waved vaguely back in the direction from which I'd come.

It couldn't be.

I walked back to Shêtân's stall and peered in.

The old man was still hard at work, his back bent nearly double with his task. I watched him for a few minutes, not wanting to interrupt. Finally, he took a break and stood, stretching his back with a groan. He reached into his pocket and pulled out a tan rag, using it to mop the sweat from his brow.

I ducked low so he wouldn't see me.

"There, there, big fella," the old man said, petting Shêtân's neck. "You're such a beauty."

He set the pitchfork into the barrel and wheeled it out of the double stall.

"Oh, hello," he said as he saw me.

"Hello. Are you Elias?" I asked.

He looked me up and down. I hadn't changed clothes from the journey back from the village, and I was covered in road dust and grime.

"Well, now. It depends who's asking," he smiled.

I smiled back. "I'd like to talk to you about the kidnapping," I said, sitting on a nearby bale of hay. I reached into my bag and withdrew a bottle of mead. "Care to join me?"

"I always have time for a new friend," he chuckled, settling himself on the next hay bale.

I uncorked the bottle and took a small swig, then passed it over to him.

He took a long drink and smacked his lips in relish, passing the bottle back to me.

"Are you new in town?" he asked. "I don't recognize you."

"I've been away for a few years. But I grew up in town." I pointed down the hill. "I used to steal apples from the orchard down by the creek."

"Oh, ho ho ho, now," he tilted his cap back on his head and scratched his forehead with a grimy hand. "I used to steal a few apples from that very orchard myself, when I was nobbut a lad. 'Course, that was a long, long time ago," he smiled, remembering.

"I heard about the kidnapping. Can you tell me about it?" I asked.

"Yes, sure. Well, it was about three weeks ago, if I remember correctly. Little thing, no bigger than yay high," he put a gnarled hand out about two and a half feet above the ground. "Snatched right out of her bed, in her parents' cottage down by the kitchens," he said slowly.

Another kidnapping? Hmmm.

"The cottage down by the kitchens? Is that the green one? Under the big tree?"

"No, no, lass. It was the small one farther down. It's brown and grey."

"Ah. And she was snatched out of her bed?"

"Aye, aye. Right out of her bed, as she slept. Left her mama dead and took the little mite, cold."

"My god. Her mama was killed?"

"Aye, aye. Killed dead. Her head bruised and bleeding. Old George found his daughter t'next morning when he come to visit. Märta worked as a maid in the castle until last year, when she was accused of stealing. They'd dismissed her and threatened to throw her in jail, until Old George intervened. He knew his Märta would never steal from the queen." He leaned in close. "We suspected it was the new cook – only worked there for a month before things started goin' missin'. She accused Märta, but we all knew better. We could all see what kinda person the new cook was. And Märta workin' there for twenty years herself. 'Tis such a pity. Old George had been supportin' both Märta and his granddaughter ever since she'd gotten the ax." He sat back up. "Old George was beside hisself, findin' his daughter laid out like that, and no sign of poor Tuva. He's not been the same since."

I leaned forward. "Did you see what happened?"

"Welllll, see I was comin' back late from t'tavern that night. Not somethin' I normally do, you understand. But my friend Nil had 'is birthday that evening, and I couldn't very well leave early, could I?"

I waited.

The old man took a deep breath, remembering.

"It was long about one in t'mornin' and I was takin' a shortcut," he paused, lost in thought.

I passed the mead back to him, and he took another healthy swig.

"Ah, that's fine drink, yessir, fine drink."

"So, it was one in the morning?"

"Aye, aye. T'was late. An' there was no moon that night. Black as coal it was. Luckily, I know that path by heart, walked it every day o' my life." He closed his eyes. "Now let me think. Ah, yes." His eyes opened, and his finger came up. "The night was dark, but it was warm, warmer than normal. And I was walkin' behind the green cottage and betwixt the brown one and the creek. And I remember, I says to myself, I says, 'Elias, what's that cold you feel?' "

"Cold?"

"Yessir, all of a sudden t'warm night got cold, like a blanket settlin' down on the land. Cold and quiet. T'crickets and owls quieted, and everything was still. It was like a shock. Stopped me in my tracks." He gazed out into the middle of the stable, lost in thought again.

I passed the mead to him again, and he gratefully took another few gulps.

"Aye, cold it was, and quiet, like death had come to the castle. I saw a pale grey shadow detach itself from t'dark wall o' Märta's cottage. It was right next to Tuva's room. Like a large woodsprite, but made of grey mist, it was. It went into Tuva's window. Slipped in like a shadow. I stared and hid behind a tree; it was such an unreal sight."

I waited.

"Then I heard Tuva scream Then I heard bumping around and Märta's voice. Then another scream, and t'shadow came out of t'window, pulling Tuva with it. And the darnedest thing happened."

"What happened?" I whispered.

"The shadow carried Tuva off, through the air. Like she was a feather. She went screaming all t'way. Her scream went through the sky, as the thing spirited her away, through the sky like the wind. Toward the far mountains." His eyes had a faraway look.

I spied the djinn high in the rafters, his eyes wide. He gave me one nod, then disappeared.

I rose from my seat.

"Elias, my friend, here, take this." I tucked the half-empty bottle of mead in his arms, and the old man cradled it like a baby.

Unshed tears sat in his eyes as he remembered the kidnapping.

I patted his shoulder and quietly left him there. Then, I went in search of the stable master.

I found him in an outbuilding. He was tall and strong back; a bushy blond beard and rolled-up sleeves were his most prominent features.

"Hello, Hans is it?" I said.

He straightened from his task of planing a door, which lay on two sawhorses.

"Aye. Oh, yes, sorry." He snapped his heels. "Your Highness. Sorry, I didn't recognize you at first."

I nodded. "Hans, you're in charge of everything out here on the stable's grounds?"

"Yes, Your Highness."

I pointed toward the main stable building. "And Elias works under you?"

"Yes, Your highness. Is there a problem with the old man?"

"No, there's no problem. In fact, whatever you're paying him, I want you to increase it by twenty percent. And assign him easier tasks. Old men should not be doing back-breaking work." I nodded toward a stable boy who was standing nearby.

"Have the stall mucking done by the young, understand? Set Elias to grooming and tending the royal horses."

"Yes, Your Highness," Hans said.

"Make sure this happens immediately. Do you understand?" I asked.

"Yes, Your Highness."

"And I want him treated well. Gently. With deference to his age."

"Yes, Your Highness."

"And I just gave him a bottle of mead. see that he gets to keep it."

"Yes, Your Highness."

I nodded and walked away.

I started back toward the castle, and Jim, back in human form, trotted up to me.

"We need to talk," he muttered out of the corner of his mouth.

"Talk to me, Jim," I whispered as I walked.

Jim spent the next few minutes whispering into my ear as we walked. He'd heard other stories similar to Elias'. This was far worse than I'd been led to believe.

When he was finished, I stopped, feeling rather upset, and looked into his eyes.

"Come with me," I said.

I strode around the side and into the kitchens. "Anya? Tilde?" I called.

"Your Highness, they returned to the dining room," said the cook. "We set out a meal for you and your troupe. They're in there now."

I looked at her, and her dozen assistants. "Where is the head housemaid?" I asked in a clipped tone.

"Right here, Your Highness," said an older matron coming through the door to the hallway. Her uniform was starched and her hair tidied.

I pointed to the cook. "Have her fired." I looked at the astonished cook. "I know you've been stealing from this household. I want you to gather your things and leave immediately. You're lucky I don't have you arrested."

The cook's face went white. She bent to gather her skirts and bag, mumbling, "Yes, Your Highness."

I turned back to the head housemaid. "You will take far greater care in hiring castle staff from now on. You will hire according to merit, nothing else. Yes, I know the cook was your niece. She's also a thief and is responsible for the maid Märta's firing."

The head housemaid's face went white.

"If I hear of any more trouble, I shall replace you, as well. Do I make myself clear?" I said.

"Yes, Your Highness," the head housemaid whispered, bowing her head.

I stood there, looking at each person in the room steely-eyed. Then, after a minute, I strode out into the hallway and made my way to the dining hall.

Jim walked behind me, not saying a word.

Chapter Twelve
Strategies

"Troupe," I said as I strode into the hall and sat down. "We have a problem."

"Charlotte, good to see you."

"What's the problem?"

"We are dealing with ice dryads," I said in a steely voice as I stared at them.

"Oh, no," whispered Caroline.

"What are ice dryads?" asked Christianne. "I've heard of dryads, but not ice dryads."

"Ice dryads are dryads born from the glacier. They are usually in service to an ice wizard, who stays hidden and sends out the ice dryads to perform tasks," Jim said.

"The night the queen and prince were kidnapped, a number of other people were also kidnapped. At least one was a child on the castle grounds." I looked at Anya and Tilde at the far end of the room. "Cousins, when you rule a kingdom, it is important to take note of everything that happens, not just mischief occurring to the royal family."

"I have been gathering information. Seventeen different people have been abducted in the last month, including fifteen children. This is besides the queen and prince," Jim said.

Both duchesses went white with shock.

"We had no idea," Anya murmured.

"You need to do better. Learn to make friends among the commoners. You'll get a lot of information that way." I got up and paced. "Royal Counsel and the Master of Whisperers do not give you every bit of information you need to keep the kingdom, and the people, safe. That is all I will say on this for now." I looked at the two duchesses until they left the room.

"Now, troupe, we are dealing with multiple ice dryads and quite probably an ice wizard. This situation is more dangerous than I thought." I glanced at Khepri.

"Find out if there's anything on ice wizards in *The Book of Mysteries*," I said.

Khepri nodded.

I turned to Tam and Tupu. "We will need new weapons against these creatures. They have been known to shatter steel with their power of the cold."

"Miss," Caroline began.

I held up my hand.

"One more thing," I said. "And this is of paramount importance."

They all stared at me.

"It is true ice dryads can control the cold, and transform into mist and shadow, and fly, among other things. But if we are dealing with an ice wizard, and it looks like we are, you must know that ice wizards are very rare, which is a good thing, because they are misnamed: they can control both the cold and the heat. They can control the temperature of the air, of the land, and of the seas. They can turn things cold," I looked at them significantly, "or warm."

Khepri consulted with me later that evening.

"Charlotte," she said quietly, coming into the room I was resting and talking with Tam and Jim in.

"Yes," I sat up. "You're back. Good. What did you find out?"

I looked at her and her bag. I did not see any huge, heavy books on her person.

Khepri saw me looking and said, "I left it on board, locked away."

"Good," I said. "What did you find out?"

"Well, the book does mention ice wizards. Apparently, they are normally encased inside the glaciers, where they live. They are able to enter other dimensions through the glaciers, and the other dimensions are their normal habitats. They are natural creatures in these other dimensions. But if they emerge into our world, they are incredibly destructive and malicious."

I waited while Khepri took a sip of water.

"The book does not speak of them extensively, and something tells me they haven't made an appearance in eons."

This explained why Jim knew about them. He'd been trapped in his bottle for centuries, but I'd never asked how long he'd been around before that. It wasn't polite to ask people their ages.

Khepri continued: "But the book does mention one very rare potion that can be used to drain them of their power and send them back into a glacier," said Khepri. "Oh, and the glaciers are actually created by encasing the ice wizards and sending them back to their own dimensions. That is how glaciers are formed."

I shook my head in disbelief.

"So, if that is how glaciers are formed, does this mean ice wizards are a normal part of this world, too?" asked Caroline. "Since glaciers are a normal part of this planet? At least on the ice caps?"

"Yes and no. Our two worlds coexist," said Khepri. "So they complement and sustain each other. We have no idea what the other dimension gets from our world, but this world derives its glaciers from that dimension."

I blinked.

"I am not entirely sure exactly how it works, but I am studying this every chance I get," Khepri said.

"You could spend many lifetimes studying it and still not learn all there is to know about the essence of all the universe," said Jim. "I have gleaned a small portion of it, but I consider myself still an infant in terms of the learning."

Khepri nodded.

"Okay. Now." I thought for a minute. "This potion, Khepri, are there instructions on how to brew it?"

"Oh, yes. Fortunately, the book goes into great detail on that," said the healer. "It is called a potion of black feather flames. It will drain the ice wizard's power, and may encase the wizard in a glacier. In fact, the book cautions that whoever gives the potion to the ice wizard may be trapped inside the glacier when it's created: Its effects are instantaneous."

Oh, dear.

"You mean to tell me," Caroline stood up and walked around the table, "that whoever is able to get the potion into the ice wizard might be encased inside the glacier too? And be *killed*?"

Khepri looked thoughtful. "That's what the book says. It says the effect of the potion on the ice wizard is nearly instant."

"Wait," I said. "Does the book say it's instant or *nearly* instant?"

Khepri looked troubled. "I think it said 'nearly'. Nearly instant."

I took a deep breath.

"I would very much like to know exactly what 'nearly instant' means." I looked at Khepri.

She looked troubled, but had no other information to offer.

I took a deep breath and closed my eyes.

Breathe, Charlotte.

I looked around. I noticed Jim in a corner, looking troubled.

"Jim? Buddy? You okay?" I asked.

Jim shook his head, then stepped forward.

"*The Book of Mysteries* may have little on ice wizards, but I remember something I learned eons ago. Tens of thousands of years ago." He took a deep breath. "I remember learning about an ice wizard who had set in motion a spell, a spell so devious and so intricate, that no one could undo it. Mostly because the wizard had cast it on himself, and he had just been entombed inside a glacier."

Uh oh.

We waited.

"I didn't understand then, but I think I do now," Jim continued. "Ice wizards can sometimes cast a spell upon themselves, if they know they are about to be entombed, that will age and mature, like a cask of mead, and eventually allow the ice wizard to escape from their imprisonment. A spell designed to be so slow moving, that it takes thousands of years to complete."

"I fear this is the spell we are dealing with," he said. "It may not be the same ice wizard I heard about, but this is a spell they are all taught to perform if they fear entombment."

"Tell me more about this spell," I said.

"The spell itself is so gradual that men don't notice it. It is called The Warming," Jim said quietly. "It is said to thaw the ice wizard." Jim gulped.

I have never seen him afraid. Until now.

"It is said that if The Warming is not halted, if the spell is continued to progress, it will gradually warm the entire land. It will warm the entire globe."

I studied his face. "Jim, can you explain what you mean?"

"The Warming would take decades, perhaps longer, but it would gradually warm the entire earth. Well, I say gradually because it would not be fast before our eyes. But the world has cycles, and it should normally take forty to fifty thousand years for the planet to cycle from cold to warm, and then back to cold. So, the world would naturally move from cold to warm over a span of twenty thousand years. Not less than a hundred years."

Khepri stood up. "Oh, no," she said. "Ohhhhh no. If the temperature warms that fast, it won't just change the weather patterns and force strong storms and flooding. Animals, magical or otherwise, won't be able to adapt, and most of them will die out. Quite rapidly." She looked stricken.

The bears, the phoenixes, the giant manta rays, the water dragons, all of them ... gone.

Tears sprang to my eyes. I stood up.

"I want to find this ice wizard and force an end to The Warming, immediately."

"Me, too!"

"Yeah!"

"They can't hurt so many animals! We're going to stop this!"

"We have to."

"We must."

"Let's go!"

"Let's kick some ice wizard butt!"

"Hold on," said Khepri.

"What?" Kym asked.

"We need to make the potion, so we can trap the ice wizard again," Khepri said.

Khepri, always the voice of reason.

"Yes, of course. Let me eat a little something and then I'll help you with that. Jim, you need to eat, too," I said, sitting back down.

Later that night, Khepri and I studied the parchment where she'd transcribed the list of ingredients and recipe for the potion. It was incredibly complicated.

I sighed, for the third time in ten minutes.

"Troublesome, isn't it?" Khepri grinned.

"Incredibly," I replied.

"Maybe Jim can fetch this one," Khepri pointed. It was an herb that was normally found at the bottom of the shallows in a cold bay. "It should be around here."

"And this one, I think we have this one," I said.

"Hmm, nope. Well, what I mean is, we'll need fresh, just recently picked. I can go hunting for it tomorrow, if I can borrow Christianne," Khepri said.

"Of course," I murmured, looking over the list. "Is it my imagination, or are most of these found in colder climates."

"Makes sense, since the potion is to entrap an ice wizard inside a glacier," Khepri mused.

"I guess."

"Okay, so the only one I'm clueless about is this one," Khepri said.

"What is it?" I leaned close to read the words on the parchment she held.

"It's a rare form of the wormwood herb, it's called Nepenthes, and it's very rare. The book says it's nearly gone from this planet, and, oh! there's a note here, I remember, I copied it from the book's index ..."

"There's an index in *The Book of Mysteries*? That's actually awesome," I said with a smile.

"And useful!" Khepri agreed.

"Now, what did it say, what did it say ...? Hmmm ..." said Khepri, bending down to read her own cramped writing. "Oh, okay, it does say it's very rare, but it says it was last seen in the northern mountains, so I will try to find it. Hmmm..."

"What?"

"Well, I remember reading in the book that there are a lot of herbs that were going extinct at the time they wrote the book, which, as you know, was thousands of years ago. So, they wrote that they had taken some of the herbs back to their world to grow, in hopes of repopulating the species back here on our world." Khepri looked up. "You know? I wonder if that's how the plants on that world evolved to be aggressive and carnivorous."

"I don't know," I said, my mind whirling with the possibilities. "It actually sounds like a nightmare if that were true."

"Just imagine, you're trying to grow a rare plant from another world, and a specimen gets out of your laboratory and into the general population of flora, and the indigenous plants react very badly to it, and start evolving to become aggressive," she shuddered.

"But surely not," I said slowly. "I mean, travelers have brought back plant specimens from across the globe and replanted them in new lands here, and it's never resulted in …. um …" I stopped, remembering the huge carnivorous plant on Iq Ameq'el. "Hmmm."

I looked at Khepri, my eyebrows raised.

"I guess anything can happen," she said quietly. She bent her head to the potion recipe again.

"Let's hope we can find the Nepenthes in the forests," I said.

I felt skeptical.

Chapter Thirteen
A Bad Feeling

We decided go in search of the ice wizard, and collect the remaining herbs we needed for the potion along the way. I was chomping at the bit to get started: My parents could be in danger every day. This could not wait.

"Okay, everyone check your packs and supplies, make sure you're ready to go," I said for the fourth time that morning.

"I think we're ready, Babe," Tam said with a grin.

"Aye, Your Highness, let's go get the queen and prince," said Håkan. "I'm eager to meet this ice wizard." He hefted his ax in heavily muscled arms.

I almost felt sorry for the ice wizard. I looked over the troupe, all of them eager to get going. We were formidable and deadly.

"Okay, let's go!" I led the march out of the castle and to the stables.

Twenty minutes later, we were galloping out of the castle grounds and northeast across the moor, heading to the dark forest.

It was slow going the first few days. Three of the horses threw a shoe and had to be reshod. Luckily, Håkan was an accomplished blacksmith. Inge had been apprenticed to Håkan's cousin, a blacksmith herself, and had learned the basics of the trade, so he was able to help. Olof spent much of his time soothing the horses being shod, feeding them wild carrots he'd found.

We made camp for a day, and the horses were ready to go in the morning.

"Remind me to have a word with the castle blacksmith and stable head. They should have checked the shoes of each horse to make sure they were perfect," I murmured to Caroline, who nodded.

Caroline was my confidant. Someone I could share information with and bounce ideas off. She was indispensable to me, and irreplaceable.

On the third day out, we entered the dark forest. Patches of snow lay in the cool shadows, and took days to melt after a snowfall, if they were out of the sunlight.

The trees were new to most of the troupe. Caroline and I, as well as Håkan and the boys, of course, were used to the northland's trees, but Khepri spent much of the downtime collecting new herbs and bark samples.

We found numerous signs of The Warming: rotting trees at the base of the mountains, ruined meadows on the moor, flooded with mud and muck.

But we continued onward.

On the fifth day, we came close to a mountain, icy and looming high. Its cliffs were utterly insurmountable. And yet there was a multitude of life on the mountain.

Some of it unfriendly.

"HRRRRR!!!" The roar reverberated across the trees as we passed through one late morning.

I stopped my horse. Shêtân snorted nervously.

"The horse knows," said Håkan, staring out at the mountain.

I glanced at him and mentally shrugged, then clucked to Shêtân to move forward again.

We rode out from the trees, following a path beside the mountains to our left.

"AHHRRRRR!" came the scream again.

"Where is that coming from?" Christianne asked, staring up at the mountain. The shriek reverberated off the mountains and trees. It was impossible to know where it had originated.

It made me nervous.

"Let's pick up the pace," I said, squeezing my knees and urging Shêtân into a lope.

We covered several miles before slowing again to a trot.

Everything stayed quiet for nearly an hour.

The path through the area continued, and it had been well maintained by the crown. We were able to make good time, the great icy mountain on our left, the dark forest on our right.

"Charlotte," Tupu rode alongside me. "I've been meaning to ask: How did this forest get so thick and wild?"

"Ah, that. Yes. Actually, it was by order of the crown," I said. "My great-great-great grandmother, who was queen back over a hundred and fifty years ago, decreed that the forest should be allowed to run wild, with permanent settlement forbidden, so that wild game might flourish and provide meat for the land, and hunting for the crown. Two centuries ago, Swerighe endured a period of famine, and the memory of it lasted a good long time. We now have more food than we need for our people, enough to send much of it overseas."

"Wow, that's crazy," said Tupu, looking over at the ominous woodland. "How many square miles does the dark forest span?"

"Oh, it's over twenty-eight hundred square miles. Nearly three-quarters of a million hectares."

"Holy moly," Tupu murmured.

"Yeah."

That evening we built a campfire out in the open, on the side of the trail, next to the forest. Sitting on my bedroll, chewing on the leg of a rabbit Tam had shot and Caroline had roasted on a spit, I felt uneasy.

This is weird.

I'd picked our campsite. Everything had seemed good with the spot. Even Håkan had been enthusiastic about the area.

"I see a river up ahead, let's go fishing, lads!" He took Inge and Olof with him. They'd brought Kym and Christianne as well. Håkan had lopped off a few saplings and they'd fashioned fishing poles and were having a grand old time.

Why do I feel uneasy?

"Here, Babe," Tam handed me a small branch. "Let's roast some marshmallows."

"Okay, where on earth did you get marshmallows?" I asked, surprised.

"While you and Jim were investigating the witnesses, Caroline and I went down into the marketplace. She showed me the best stalls." He grinned.

"I had to, Miss. He forced me to," Caroline laughed.

"Anyway, I brought a small bag of sweet treats. Most of them are marshmallows," Tam handed me a long, white spongy orb, then pushed one on to the end of his own stick.

"I haven't done this since I was a child," I smiled, licking my lips in anticipation. I held my stick, marshmallow on the end, high over the fire.

We munched on the sweet, toasted treats for an hour. My face and fingers got all sticky, and I decided to walk down to the creek to wash. I was on my way down when I saw Håkan, Inge and Olof running back.

"Don't go down there!" Håkan said. "I'm getting my sword." He grabbed my arm and tried to turn me around.

"Why, what's wrong?" I craned my neck and couldn't see any danger.

"We couldn't see it, either," said Olof, "but we could feel it."

"Something bad, very bad," Inge said.

We hurried back to camp.

"What's wrong?" Tupu said, looking up from sharpening her scimitar with a whetstone.

"No idea, but they're freaked out," I said.

"We felt there was bad things, dangerous things, coming near us," Håkan said.

"It was a bad feeling," Olof said.

Inge nodded.

Jim stood up. "Describe the feelings. Was it a feeling of imminent danger? Or hostility? Or just unnamed fear?"

"The fear," said Håkan. "It just felt like fear, all of a sudden, in our minds."

"Fear," Inge said, shuddering.

Jim looked grim. He bent and retrieved his sword, strapping it on.

We all followed his lead.

"What do you think it is, Jim?" I murmured next to him while I scanned the area.

"Harpies," he said, quietly. "They can project waves of fear, to force people away from their nests."

"I felt something earlier, too."

He looked at me sharply. "Here? At the campsite?"

"Yes."

He scanned the area, trying to find ... something. His gaze narrowed as he focused on a dark thicket high up in a tree halfway between our camp and the creek, and about a hundred fifty feet up.

"There," Jim whispered. He moved to stand next to the tall tree. Then he pointed to the sky. "See that clear blue sky? Just a few clouds off to the side?"

I nodded.

"If it becomes stormy, that's when we have to worry. And the creatures nesting at the top of this tree can create that storm, just as easily as they can become active if a storm approaches on its own."

"So," I said, looking up into the tree. I couldn't see much. Just a dark mass of branches. "That's a nest of some sort?"

Jim nodded.

"What's up there?" asked Tupu.

"Harpies," answered Jim.

Oh, lordie.

"Okay, well, this was a crap place to make camp," I said.

"It was rather unfortunate," Jim acknowledged.

"Well, hmmm." I thought for a minute. Staying in this location was dangerous. "Do you think we can break camp and move?" I whispered to Jim.

"I think it might be too late for that," he stared into the sky, and I glanced up to see what had caught his eye.

A lone figure, looking like a huge bird with black and grey wings and huge, taloned feet, had launched itself from the top of the tree and begun a low glide around the gorge.

"Uh oh," said Jim. "Charlotte, we need to take cover." He glanced down at me. "And staying quiet no longer matters; they've noticed us."

I wheeled around. "People! Take cover!" I grabbed my bag and sword and rushed about, shooing the troupe into the trees.

146

Khepri, Tupu, and Caroline grabbed weapons and ran for cover, followed by Kym, Christianne, and Tam.

Håkan had been talking with Inge and Olof while they unhooked the few fish they'd caught and laid them next to the fire. They were the farthest from the trees.

I ran toward them, glancing up at the sky. The harpy had been joined by three of its companions, so there were now four large forms gliding through the sky, wheeling in circles.

Watching us.

I grabbed Håkan's arm. "Come on!"

He grabbed the boys, and we all raced for the cover of the forest, where the rest of the troupe had already taken cover.

I glanced up again. The harpies were descending. Fast.

"RUN!" I screamed.

Håkan and the boys ran fast, but Inge stumbled and went down on the uneven ground.

One of the harpies was nearing, in a dive faster than the wind.

Storm clouds were gathering above.

"That's not good, Charlotte!" called Jim. "They get their strength from the storms!"

I ran back to grab Inge, and stumbled, falling to one knee before scrambling to my feet again.

The harpy was almost upon us. I could hear its scream.

I heard a whirring sound, and suddenly, Christianne was there, her wings fluttering so rapidly they were a blur.

"Come on!" She grabbed my arm, and Inge's arm, turned, and fled into the trees lightning fast. Inge was dragged, his exclamation of surprise a yelp in the air.

We entered the trees and turned.

The harpy hit the ground with its talons, a second after we'd left the spot. Its scream of outrage was deafening as it rose back into the air.

Christianne was folding her wings back into her coat.

Inge picked himself up off the ground and brushed out the dirt and forest flotsam that had accumulated in his clothes as he was dragged.

"Take cover! They're coming back!" Jim shouted. "And these trees won't stop them, they'll just slow them down."

Two of the harpies flew into the trees and lit on some nearby trees, gripping the bark of the trunks with their long, sharp talons.

"LOOK OUT!" called Tupu.

Tam was taking aim with an arrow, his eye steely, his gaze unwavering.

"SKREEEEYA!"

"SKREEEEYA!"

"Swords out!" I called unnecessarily.

"Won't matter," muttered Jim beside me.

"Why not?" I asked.

"They throw things," he answered.

"Huh?"

A flying object, hurled by the closer harpy, whizzed past my ear and hit the tree behind me with a splat!

What's that smell?

"Ohhhh no. No no no no," Khepri said.

"Be careful!" called out Jim. "It's acidic."

"It's what?" Christianne said.

"It will sting. It will burn. It will HURT," Jim clarified.

Another projectile barely missed, hitting the tree so hard it splattered against my arm. I looked down to find brown dots on the leather armor of my sleeve.

They were smoking.

"What the hell?!" I said, brushing the stuff off.

What is this?

"OH MY GOD IT'S THEIR POO!" called out Caroline, who'd apparently been hit. She brushed the stuff off her leg. "HOLY HELL!"

Three more harpies joined the first two, their sharp talons hooked onto the side of the trees about forty or fifty feet up and off to one side. They held on sideways like this, and screamed at us as they threw ... stuff.

"Take cover!" I called, ducking behind a large tree.

"Behind you!" Tam cried.

I swung around and saw two more harpies had latched themselves onto tree trunks on my other side.

They're surrounding us.

"Tam, can you reach them?" I called out.

"Nearly. I need cover!" he answered.

I crawled toward him, and held up my bag to cover him. He peered out from behind a tree and launched a succession of three arrows.

One of them hit its mark.

"CRIIEEEJKJKJK!" one of the harpies screamed before falling out of the tree and hitting the ground hard.

"SKREEEEYA!"

"SKREEEEYA!"

"SKREEEEYA!"

Thump! thumpthump! *thumpthumpthumpthump!*

Crap hit the trees above us and slowly slid down, leaving a trail of smoke from burning bark.

"SGHAAFVVVV!!!" came an angry cry from the harpy closest to me.

"Remind me to craft my own bow soon," I said.

"Will do," Tam said, then shot off another rapid succession of arrows, hitting a second harpy. It screamed and fell to the ground in an unmoving heap.

Christianne was suddenly moving, her wings out, whirring faster than the eye could see. She ran forward and jumped, hitting a tree, then pivoting and jumping again, her wings propelling her forward so fast that her momentum kept her aloft.

She slammed into a harpy, grabbing it and stabbing her dagger into its side.

"Got you!" she cried in triumph.

The nearest harpy dove at her.

"Christianne! Behind you!" Tupu called.

"I've had enough of this," said Kym, and she began to grow. In a few seconds, the massive chimera was there where a little six-year-old gild had stood a moment before. It growled in rage and jumped, landing on the side of a tree.

But she was too low and too heavy, and she fell short of her prey, who taunted her from a dozen feet above.

The chimera screamed in pain as the harpies flung their shit at her, easily hitting the large beast on her back in several places.

The chimera began to slide down the tree she was gripping. The fur on her back began to smoke as the acidic substance burned into it.

Christianne was jumping over to attack the harpies above the chimera.

She was joined by the djinn, who flew fast, knocking the first harpy out of the tree.

"SKREEEEYA!"

"SKREEEEYA!"

The chimera gripped the tree trunk and bunched her hind legs, leaping up again. Razor-sharp claws extended from her huge paw and caught one of the harpies. The thing screamed as the chimera's claws penetrated its midsection.

Blood flew.

The chimera snarled with rage and let go of the tree, grabbing the harpy with her other front paw.

The two plummeted to the forest floor, the harpy screaming all the way. The chimera bounced, but quickly gained her footing, her rear goat legs coming up and kicking at the harpy. Giant, sharp hooves at the end of those legs were eviscerating the harpy.

The chimera kicked until the harpy was dead, its intestines pulled out and tangled in the chimera's goat legs.

Christianne took down a third harpy, her trusty dagger finding its mark even as she slowed to stab a second harpy, before she descended to the ground, having lost the momentum that had kept her aloft.

The djinn grabbed another harpy and sliced it in half with his sword.

When did he start carrying a sword?

I shrugged. New weapons, new surprises.

There was only one harpy left.

Tam took aim.

The harpy drew its arm back.

It brought it forward just as Tam let his arrow fly, then another and another, in quick succession.

The last act of the harpy, to fling its acidic bomb toward the man who was about to kill it, landed on Tam's head, even as he tried to duck.

It splattered in his hair.

"Oh OH OH!" he screamed, the brown substance sliding down his neck.

I hurried tried to wipe it off, and the acidic poo began to sting and burn the palms of my hands.

"Here," Khepri splashed Tam's head with water from her water skin, quickly wiping the stuff away. I caught some of the falling water and hurriedly slapped my hands together in it, trying to get the stuff off.

"Got them all!" cried the djinn.

"Good, now come help me!" I called, unable to get all the acid off my hands.

"Run to the stream!" Khepri called.

I picked up my bag, grabbed Tam's arm, and raced to the stream. On my third step, I hit a tree. My eye burned like the devil.

"Ahhh!" I screamed.

"Come on," said the djinn.

I felt my body being hoisted up and flown through the air.

Less than a minute later, I was dropped gently into the stream, landing in a few feet of water.

I ducked my head, washing my face where a drop of stinging poo had touched my eye when I'd bumped into the tree.

I plunged completely into the moving water, the coolness feeling like a heavenly balm on my skin.

I could not get enough of the water. It felt so good, so healing.

I finally stuck my head up, and my feet found the sandy bottom.

I looked around.

I was a dozen feet downstream from the others, who were all washing and looking much happier.

I love water.

We all reconvened at the campfire. The sun was dropping below the horizon, and I felt slightly chilled.

"Here" Jim placed a few more logs of firewood onto the flames, poking at them with a branch until they caught fire.

I shook with chills and inched closer, my feet nearly in the coals.

"Charlotte, look at me," Khepri said.

I turned to stare at the healer.

"Hmmm. You look like you've got a sunburn where the acid fell." She reached her fingers into a jar in her other hand, and dabbed a liberal amount onto my face. "Close your eye. There you go." She spread the unguent across my skin, and I felt a cool, healing sensation. "Try not to touch it or rub it off. You should feel better by tomorrow."

I looked over at Tam. Most of his hair and part of his face was wet with Khepri's balm, and he was conversing with Kym, a smile on his face.

Khepri saw me staring. "He'll be fine. We got it washed off quick enough." She closed the jar of salve and placed it into her bag. "Luckily the acid was weak, or we'd have been in much worse shape.

"Hey," said Jim, sitting down next to me. "How do you feel?"

I smiled at him. "Pretty good Khepri's salve is like magic. Oh, Jim! Thank you for warning us. I think things would've gone much worse had you not sounded the alarm."

"My pleasure. Harpies are nasty creatures, on the best of days."

"Are there any more left in that nest?" I glanced up at the trees.

"Nope. They all came to join the attack. Between Tam, Kym and Christianne, all were bested. Tupu dragged them off and tossed them into a gully."

"Don't kid yourself: you helped a lot too," I said.

Jim blushed. "I wish I'd seen them sooner. I should've known, I felt the uneasiness too. It'd just been so long that I'd forgotten what kind of creature threw off that kind of psychic scream."

"Hmmm, 'psychic scream' that's an interesting phrase."

"Jim smiled. "Believe it or not, all creatures are at least a little bit able to throw off a psychic vibration. Most of them are very low key, not like those nasty harpies, screaming their feeling everywhere."

"All creatures?" I asked.

Jim's right eyebrow rose in amusement. "Yes, everyone. Even you," he chuckled.

"Jim is correct," said Khepri from where she was setting up a spit over the fire. "I learned this when I was an apprentice healer."

"Now this I gotta hear," Tam said, moving closer to us.

"Me, too," said Christianne. "This sounds interesting."

Kym smiled from across the fire. "I already know this."

"Kym!" I grinned. "You already know this?!"

"Sure do," she smiled wider.

Jim shifted on his blanket and handed Khepri a cleaned fish steak, which she skewered onto a stripped stick and leaned against the spit she'd erected, to join the dozen others in a fragrant, sizzling cookup.

"Well," said Jim. "I think the reason Kym knows is that this is part of most magical creature's defense mechanism. It's part of yours, too." He winked at me and Tam. "Some people call it a psychic smell."

"All right, let's hear it. How do I have a psychic smell? It sounds impolite," I laughed.

"Well, the thing is," said Jim, "Everyone gives off a certain psychic 'vibe', if you will. The harpies' vibe screams 'Uneasiness. Danger.' Do you understand?"

I nodded.

"Now, humans have a much softer psychic cry, or smell, as it were. You, for instance. Charlotte, give off a smell of adventure and courage." He turned to Tam. "You, Tam, smell of bravery and levity. Almost humor." Jim winked at Tam.

"What about me?" asked Christianne.

"You, hmmm." Jim regarded the sixteen-year-old thoughtfully. "I sense your psychic smell is in flux. It used to be innocence and joviality. But it's slowly changing and becoming more adventuresome and courageous."

"Like Charlotte?" asked Christianne.

"Sort of. Like Charlotte but with wings," Jim smiled at her.

"Ha ha ha!" I laughed in delight.

"I'm like Charlotte, but with wings!" Christianne jumped up, and flexed her arms. Her wings came out and fluttered in the air.

I looked closer.

"Chrissy are they turning purple?"

Christianne stopped and tried to look behind her. Her wings slowed until they barely move, flexing slowly in the firelight. "Are they?" she asked.

Kym jumped up. "Oh! They're more purple than green now!" She clapped her hands in delight.

"Cool," Christianne posed, her hands on her hips.

Chapter Fourteen

Celebrations and a Yeti

We celebrated long into the night. Jim transformed and floated up to look inside the harpy nest. He found an egg, which he destroyed, and something else.

"A barrel of mead?!" I exclaimed when the djinn floated back to the ground with it.

It was a small barrel, maybe a few gallons. It bore the seal of the queen.

Mother's seal.

I brushed my fingers across the blue and golden colors painted onto the sides of the wooden cask, still visible on the surface that had been scratched up by the harpies talons.

"Oh, my goodness," said Caroline. "This is from a theft that happened a decade ago, I remember it! She pointed at the number on the cask. "Look here, it's the batch number."

"Wait, wait, wait." I put my hand up. "Carrie, are you saying ... that this is ... aged AGED MEAD?!"

"Yes."

"Let's get it opened. Is the seal still intact?" Tupu said.

I bent down to examine the wax plug, then straightened. "Yes."

"I'll get it open," Tam said, prying at the stopper with his dagger.

We had the small barrel open in no time, and spent the next four hours in revelry.

"Ohh boy!"

"This is ..."

"No, none for you Christianne!"

"Why not?"

"I um ... I don't know."

"Well pass it over then."

"Charlotte, you shouldn't have more than a few cups."

"Okay."

"Kym, hand me your cup."

"Got it."

"Ohhhh man, this is good."

"Isn't it?"

"The finest mead in the world comes from Swerighe's breweries."

"Yum!"

It was a long night.

And we slept well into the morning.

This will never do. We need to find the queen and prince.

These thoughts greeted my wakening brain before I had even opened my eyes.

I groaned, feeling my stomach roil.

I turned over and tried to get to my feet.

How many cups of mead did I drink?

I was a softy when it came to booze, it didn't take much to get me sloshed. I stood up and slowly walked down to the stream.

Håkan was already there with Inge and Olof.

"Fishing, huh?" I asked, then held my head until the spinning sensation stopped.

"Aye, lass." Håkan smiled.

Inge lifted three large trout.

I splashed into the stream, mumbling an apology for startling the fish.

"Och, it's all right. After last night, I'm surprised you aren't sicker."

"Oh, I am. I am," I held my stomach. "I'm not used to drinking that much."

Håkan grinned.

I walked back to the fire, which was dying out, and tossed a few more logs on.

Caroline groaned from her sleeping blanket.

The coffeepot was settled into the coals, and mostly full. I poured myself a steaming cup and held it with both hands, trying to warm up. The fragrant steam drifted up and enveloped my face, and I closed my eyes, inhaled, then took a sip.

Oh, that's good.

I slowly sipped my coffee as everyone woke up, groaned, and then went to wash in the creek.

Håkan returned with another rainbow trout, making a cache of four, which he proceeded to scrape clean by the fire.

Olof brought a bucket of water, and they soon had the fish filleted and on the spit.

Tam returned from tending the horses. "Is that coffee?" he asked.

"Sure is," Caroline smiled, handing him a cup.

"Ohh, good, good." Tam drank deeply from the cup, then turned to me. "Charlotte, it was a smart idea to tack the horses up the trail. They were completely out of sight of the harpies. They may have heard some commotion, but they seem none the worse for wear, and still secured on their lines."

"Good."

"I think we'll make good time today, barring any more encounters with anything aggressive," said Jim. "That tends to take up a lot of time."

"You're not kidding," Tupu said.

Jim smiled at her and gave her a kiss.

"Smoochy woochy woo!" Kym said, laughing.

Jim blushed a rosy shade of purple.

"Oh! Ha Ha! Oh, my darling!" Tupu covered his face in kisses.

I smiled, and began to pack up in preparation to move out.

A half hour later, we were riding on.

"Now, we want to reach our destination by nightfall: the mountain the ice wizard was seen entering," I said as I walked. "Then we'll camp just a ways away ..."

"A ways away? How far is that?" asked Tam.

"Over yonder, a ways." I laughed.

"She means about a half mile back from being seen, sir." Caroline said.

"Yeah. Yes. That's what I mean," I said, grinning.

Tupu looked at the icy mountain and the snow on the ground next to it. "It's getting colder."

"Yes, and it will get colder still, the farther north we go," Håkan said from behind.

We were soon trudging on rugged ground through the snowy ravine, our boots crunching on the icy path.

Everything was snow covered.

We pulled our coats tighter, grateful we'd added more fur before we departed.

My nose was red, and I was glad of the fluffy fur surrounding my neck. I loved the new collar. It was thick and white and made of bear pelt. Everyone had one, and they tied around the tops of our coats and helped us not to freeze.

Shêtân snorted in the cold air, his breath visible in front of him. He pranced about, eager to run.

"Easy, boy," I said.

It was very quiet, as it always is in the snow.

I swear I can hear my heart beating.

"Hold up," Håkan whispered. He gestured for Olof to ride ahead on the path, while we waited.

"I heard a grunting sound," said Håkan softly. "Sounded like a Yeti, although they've not been sighted in generations."

"Could it have been thawed by The Warming?" Caroline asked.

"Aye, that's what I'm afraid of," replied Håkan. "Legend has it they're quite grumpy when they awake from hibernation."

Inge rode on ahead to check on his friend before Håkan could stop him. Håkan raised his eyes to the sky in a gesture of futility.

We waited.

Ten minutes later, both boys appeared, trotting their horses swiftly.

"Ya, Ya, that's a yeti all right. It looks just like the pictures in the books I've seen. It's foraging. I think it's hungry," Olof said.

"Damn," Håkan swore. "That's not good, Your Highness, not good at all."

"Håkan, you may just call me 'Charlotte' on this quest," I said.

"Oh, I could never do that, Your Highness," Håkan blushed.

Good lord.

"Okay, well, ... the yeti." I turned to Olof. "Did you see it up close, or from a distance? Was it growling? Did it have blood on its mouth? Was it calm or angry or frightened? I need details."

"Oh, um, let's see. I spotted the yeti from maybe a hundred yards away. It was not growling that I could see. I couldn't tell if it had blood on its mouth, but it looked like it. That or dirt. It seemed calm yet desperate. It was foraging and seemed frustrated."

Olof looked at me, his eyebrows raised.

"That's better. Thank you." I turned to the troupe. "We need to go down this gorge, it would be a delay of a hundred miles if we went around. Any ideas?"

"Hmmm."

"We could fly over?"

"No, I think we all remember what happened last year, when I was too weak from flying you all up the ice cliffs to help with the cyclops," Jim said firmly.

"I agree," I said.

"Okay, well, maybe we can sneak past it?"

"On horseback??"

"We could lead the horses."

"Do you think we could?"

"Yetis are not stupid. And they're wild creatures. It'll hear us."

"It'll hear us, all right."

"Well, it's sneak past or get into a fight with it."

"I vote we fight it."

"I'm getting tired of killing wild creatures."

"Now, you know we only fight if we're attacked."

"Håkan, do yetis fight interlopers?"

"I'm not exactly sure. But I would put money on it, yes."

"Yes, they do. We were just learning about it last month in our lessons."

"Yes, I remember. Inge is right."

"Okay, well, we may have to fight, then."

"At least there's only one."

"At least."

We headed back out onto the trail, riding together, trying to move quickly yet quietly.

I feel like we're riding into a fight.

I rode with my scimitar in my hand, glad I'd sharpened it yesterday. I hefted it in my hand. It was a comforting weight.

"It's just up here, around this far turn," said Olof.

"Be ready, everyone," I said softly.

We hurried along, eager to get this over with.

I rode at the front, Tupu beside me.

I grinned at her.

"It's awesome to have you back by my side. It was weird without you."

She grinned back at me. "I am glad to be back. I was bored in my village."

"I'll bet."

"Boredom is a killer."

"It is."

"Shhhh, there it is," said Khepri, pointing.

We looked.

Just coming into sight, maybe a hundred and twenty-five yards away, was a large, white, hairy beast that walked upright and looked for all the world like a gorilla, only taller.

Ohhh dear.

I stopped and backed Shêtân up, until I was out of sight of the yeti.

"Okay, Olof was right, it's foraging. We need to hurry and try to get past it. We can't give it any excuse to view us as a threat."

"I'm ready."

"Let's do this."

"I hate waiting."

"I hate talking."

"Let's go, Charlotte!"

"Okay, fine," I said. Gripping my scimitar, I turned, and raced Shêtân around the corner and ran him down the gorge's path.

It led straight to the yeti.

I kept my head down, trying not to look aggressive, but running Shêtân as fast as I could.

I heard the troupe behind me.

We got maybe sixty yards from the yeti before it noticed us.

"Keep going," I said out of the corner of my mouth, as I galloped Shêtân down the path.

All of a sudden, Christianne was riding alongside me, her wings whirring behind her.

"Hi," she whispered.

I glanced at her and put my finger to my lips as I rode. She nodded.

She must be able to push her steed faster, using her wings.

I made a mental note to ask her how she did that.

We raced toward the yeti, who had straightened and turned to watch us, a look of surprise on its furry face.

It turned to face us.

Does it think we're charging it?

Apparently, it did.

As we got within fifty feet of the yeti, it let out a roar and raised its snout, sniffing us.

"Faster!" I urged Shêtân forward faster, speeding up.

The yeti dropped to all fours and lumbered toward us, looking like a massive ape-bear.

But much bigger than any bear.

It came closer.

And closer.

We galloped.

At some point, the yeti had to realize we weren't attacking, that we were just running past, and I hoped that would persuade the creature to leave us alone. After all, we numbered eleven, were brandishing weapons, and compromised a visually impressive fighting force.

The yeti stopped about a dozen yards away from us, and waited to see what we would do.

We galloped on, nearing it, our trajectory taking us in a diagonal toward it.

The yeti watched us.

We galloped our horses.

I almost thought we were going to make it past it. I really did. I had it all in my head: We would gallop past, and the yeti would be surprised. Too surprised to react, and by the time it knew what had happened, we'd be on the other side of it, running away. And he'd just stand there watching in astonishment.

It was not to be.

As we got within twenty feet of the yeti, he roared a challenge.

The massive snarl echoed in the canyon, reverberating between the two sides, making the sound louder and longer than any sound had any right to be.

"RAWWWRRRRRRRR!"

RAWWWWRRRRR

RAWWWRRR

RAWWRR

RAWRR

RAWR

Oh, lord.

The yeti charged us, a scream of rage issuing forth from deep within his throat.

"ARRAOARRRR!"

The beast lumbered toward us, its face a snarl of rage and challenge.

We stopped and dismounted.

I lifted my scimitar and prepared to fight.

A whirling blur passed in front of me, between the troupe and the raging yeti.

It flew across my field of vision once more, in the opposite direction, then back again.

It was Christianne, trying to distract the beast.

"Run," she called, as she made another pass.

The yeti kept coming.

"I don't think we can outrun ..." I was cut off by the yeti.

"ROAARRRRR!"

It swung its huge paw and swatted at the blur that was Christianne.

I heard a noise, and the chimera appear. She jumped on the yeti, knocking it to the ground.

The djinn was there, as well. He flew in fast, punching at the yeti's back as it tumbled with the chimera.

Blood flew.

"Well, I'm not going to let them have all the fun," Tupu cried as she charged in, her sword held high.

I jumped into the fray as well, but by now the jumble of people was so thick I couldn't be sure if my scimitar would hit friend or foe.

Christianne ran in fast, swiped at the yeti's face, hit its nose, then ran back out again.

Caroline, Khepri, and Tam jumped in. as well as Håkan, Inge and Olof.

The yeti was overwhelmed, at the bottom of a dog pile. I think even Shêtân wanted to jump on top of it. He pranced and whirled and turned and stomped his foreleg in frustration.

We pummeled that yeti so hard that after a while, we were just hitting dead meat.

Khepri raised her hand. We stopped waling on the yeti and stood up.

The chimera stood still, one leonine foreleg still on top of the white, furry beast.

It was quite dead.

One leg lay off to the side, nearly hacked away from its body.

The yeti's chest was nearly flat from the weight of the chimera's paw on it.

Blood ran from dozens of wounds.

It lay still.

Blood dribbled out of his mouth.

Its eyes stared ahead, unseeing.

Awwww.

I knew it couldn't be helped: The thing had attacked us. But I felt remorse. Despite my efforts to move past it, maybe the beast had thought we were attacking it.

I would never know.

We left the yeti there in the middle of the gorge, and proceeded on horseback through to the end of the icy canyon, staying silent the whole way.

Killing something was a serious thing, and it hit us harder the more human our foes looked. I felt bad for slaying the ogre on our previous quest, and now this yeti, more than for the manticore, the vicious unicorns and some of the others.

I wonder why?

I slouched more and more as we rode, feeling worse and worse.

"Hey, Babe," Tam rode up alongside Shêtân, his huge brown mare prancing in her eagerness. He cooed to her and patted her neck, and she slowed down. "Charlotte, you okay?"

"Yeah, I'm okay."

Tam remained silent.

"I'll be fine. Just moody," I said.

"Hey, Charlotte," Khepri rode up on my other side.

I glanced at her, and she pointed up ahead.

My eyes went wide.

Off to the side of the trail was another yeti.

Oh, no.

I looked closer. This beast had obviously seen us, but it made no move to thwart our approach. It sat in a cave a few dozen feet up the icy slope of the mountain, regarding us as we passed.

"It's not charging," I said, stating the obvious.

"It's not," Tam repeated.

"I wonder why not," I said.

Khepri just watched it as we went by. The yeti did not even seem that interested in us. It was concerned with something beside it in the cave.

I clucked and Shêtân trotted faster, then changed to a gallop.

I could hear my troupe behind me, following close.

Just as I moved out of range, I glanced back and took one last look at the yeti in the cave. It was still there, not leaving, not moving down toward us, not interested in us at all.

Chapter Fifteen
Folktales

We had ridden the horses for most of the day, after leaving the yeti gorge behind us. An overcast greyness now blanketed the landscape. A fine mist descended on us at midday, making everything cold, moist, and dreary.

It would be dark soon. The mists parted a bit as the day drew to a close. The sun was low in the sky, already looking lopsided as its light refracted against the horizon.

Twilight was upon us.

Our horses plodded along, their heads hung lower than usual, as Tam rode ahead, scouting for a suitable place to camp.

The moor was flat and covered in marsh and patches of purple-grey heath. The entire effect was a greeny-grey, swampy dismal place. It took a while to find a high spot that wasn't damp.

"Here's a good a spot as any, I guess," said Tam, sounding tired.

We camped on the moor that night. The ice mountains had receded and melted into a shallow valley, though more of them loomed in the distance. That was our destination.

We made an uneasy camp that evening, tying the horses on a long line, which spanned the side of our campsite, off about twenty feet.

The fire was weak and harder to keep going. Most of the firewood we found was damp, and sputtered like crazy when we tried to light it.

"I'm going to cut some peat; I'll keep the camp in sight," Jim said, walking off toward the east.

"I think I'll join him; we may be able to carry more together," said Håkan. "You young men stay here; help guard the camp."

Inge and Olof nodded and took turns walking the perimeter.

"I think I'll make a stew," said Caroline. "It will settle well in our stomachs on this damp night."

"A stew sounds wonderful," I smiled at her.

Tam hefted his bow and walked to the edge of camp. We'd noticed rabbits jumping out of the heath as we'd made our way onto the moor. It was obvious they were abundant here.

I made my blanket-bed and sat there, sharpening my blade with a whetstone and thinking of rabbit stew.

My stomach rumbled.

A half hour later Tam returned, a clutch of four large hares in his hand.

Caroline hurried to skin and gut the creatures, and Tam walked over to join me.

He took out his own sword and whetstone and sat next to me, and drew the whetstone slowly along the edge of his sword's blade, making a rasping sound to match mine.

We watched the moor swallow the sun together.

As the deep orange globe slowly disappeared beyond the grey, wet landscape, the sky turned from pink to purple.

A night mist began to roll in, slowly but surely.

"I hope Jim and Håkan get back soon. They could get lost out here," I murmured.

Tam kissed my forehead. "How have you been feeling, my love?"

"Okay, I guess. A lot of emotions, but nothing physical." I looked down at my hands. "The redness is nearly gone."

"That's good."

"I am eager to rescue my parents. I felt bad about the first yeti, until I saw the second yeti. Then I felt better."

"Why?"

"I guess I felt desolate when we saw the first one die, as if it was the last yeti in the land, and they were gone forever. It was an empty feeling. Partly from the yeti's death, but partly from the worry we had killed a rare creature."

"Ah."

"When we saw the second yeti, my spirits lifted. Especially when it didn't emerge from the recess of its cave. It stayed up there, safe and sound. Safe from us."

"You know, we would not have attacked the first yeti. It came at us. We were just meeting its attack on the battlefield."

"I know."

"Did you see why the second yeti did not leave the cave?"

"No, do you know why?"

"Yes, Jim transformed and flew up, to look. I guess he was curious."

"Well, tell me. Why did it stay in the cave?"

"The second yeti had cubs."

"Ohhhh." I thought on that for a while. I looked down at my belly. It was still flat, wasn't it? I thought I saw a slight swelling in the dim light from the dying sunset.

I put my hand against my belly. I wondered how I would feel after my baby was born. I glanced at Tupu, who was deep in conversation with Khepri and Caroline. She threw back her head and laughed at something Khepri had said.

How would I feel after the baby was born? Would I be able to leave it with a wet nurse, safe on board the ship, while I went out adventuring? Or would I feel compelled to stay with my child? To nurture it and cuddle it and nurse it myself?

I had no idea.

"I think they're heading back," Tam said, pointing.

A dim light bobbed up and down on the horizon. After a few minutes, the light broke into two, and they both bobbed up and down as they approached.

Jim and Håkan on horseback, torches in hand.

I stood up, and stretched, arching my back.

"Ah, good, they brought peat," Tam said.

A half hour later, Håkan had tossed the first of ten rectangles of peat onto the fire. It was a strange substance, and burned brightly, despite being damp.

"We cut it out of a high bog," Jim was saying. "I was glad to have Håkan there. We were able to carry twice as much back."

Håkan nodded and smiled.

"Okay, stew is ready," Caroline called. We reached for the bowls as she filled them and handed them out.

I took a spoonful into my mouth. It was hot and delicious, a thick broth filled with chunks of fresh rabbit, wild carrot and wild garlic.

"Mmmm, this is delicious, Carrie. Thank you," I said.

"You're very welcome, Miss." She smiled.

"How do you make such a delicious meal with so little?" Håkan asked.

"I cheat," smiled Caroline. "I brought a small sack of wheat flour with me, to thicken the broth. And I gather wild vegetables and herbs as we travel, just as much as Khepri does with her medicinal herbs. And lastly, fresh game will make any stew taste like a feast."

"Well, you are to be commended. I've not eaten so well in my life," Håkan said.

"Ohhh, I'm telling Aunt Ebba," Inge said with a chuckle.

"You'd better not. I'll be sleeping cold for a month!" Håkan said.

"Oh, she wouldn't do that ..."

"Wanna bet?"

"No," Inge laughed. "I don't want to lose out on her meals, either." Inge turned to Caroline. "Besides, everyone in Swerighe knows Caroline cooks the best stew in the land. Everyone was sad to see her leave for those years."

I chuckled. I could see Caroline smile.

"Enough. You are going to make me blush," Caroline said.

"May I have seconds, Caroline?" Tam held out his bowl.

"Mmm, me, too, please!" Kym held out her bowl as well.

Everyone ended up having a second portion of Caroline's stew.

Afterward, we built up the fire until it flamed several feet into the sky.

"To keep the mist at bay," Håkan said, glancing over the moor.

"Are you nervous, Håkan?" I asked.

"A bit," he said. "I have heard stories of these northern moors, stories of bad things happening, and bad creatures. Creatures I wouldn't want to meet on a sunny day down by the castle's gardens, let alone out on a misty moor at night."

I felt a cold trickle on the back of my neck and blinked. I was not one to be weirded out by stories. I looked out across the dark night. The wet mist that had covered the moor made them appear brighter than they normally would have, yet the mist was so opaque my gaze could not penetrate it, no matter how long or how hard I stared.

"Håkan, I'm not from this land," said Christianne. "Tell me these stories?"

"Ah, lass, you don't want to hear about the moor and the bewitching creatures said to roam it at night," Håkan said.

"Yes, I do," Christianne said.

"Me, too," said Kym.

Inge and Olof were trying to look brave, but they had likely heard the same stories Håkan had, and I couldn't help but notice how close they sat to the fire, and the other warriors.

"I'm curious now, too," Tam said.

Uh oh.

I said nothing. My eyebrows rose, and my eyes looked down, though, when Håkan spoke.

"Well, if you're insisting ..."

Håkan settled in his blankets more, and pulled his coat tighter around himself, then began to speak.

"The worst tale from these northern moors is of the Witte Wieven. They are found near graveyards, mostly. Mostly. But on rare occasions, they can be found anywhere out on the moor. They walk and moan and search for their lost life. Their lost children. Their lost loves. These wights are the spirits of the dead women, and they roam the countryside and moors at night." He paused, and took a sip out of his waterskin, then continued in a sing-song voice.

"Woe to the traveler who wanders the northern moor at night. Stay away from graves and burial mounds after sunset, when the fog pours from them. This fog is not a natural mist, but the Witte Wieven themselves. They descend from these burial sepulchers and wander, looking for someone, anyone, as long as they're alive. They are drawn to the life force itself." Håkan looked out at us. "If you ever hear a ghostly moan out on these northern moors after the sun has set, hide your face. Do not look up. Do not even open your eyes." He fell silent and stared at us, unblinking.

We all stared back at him. I shivered again.

I had heard the legends, of course. Growing up in Swerighe, you couldn't help but hear them. Stories told around campfires at night, stories told by candlelight to children, to keep them abed and keep them from wandering out alone at night. But I hadn't heard the stories told quite like this.

Håkan was a genius. Or a madman. The youngest in our party were Inge and Olof, and they were huddling next to Håkan.

Those boys won't be wandering off tonight, I'll bet.

"Do you know any other stories of these northern moors?" Kym asked, her eyes alight with curiosity.

Oh, no no no Kym, why would you ask that?

"Well now, lass, if you want to know..." said Håkan, stroking his beard.

Here we go.

"There're stories of the Nuckelavee, a wicked devil of a man who comes to steal away the breath of the folk who live on the edge of the moor, over that-away," Håkan pointed to the northwest. "There are a few tiny towns, right up against the sea, on the edge of the moorland, and they say they've been terrorized by a specter of a rotting, living cadaver that's sewn with thick thread onto the corpse of a horse, and they move as one. The creature's breath is said to be so foul that it can wither whole crops that are near harvest, it can sicken entire paddocks of livestock, and it can kill a man before he can set eyes on the creature."

Håkan looked at Kym.

"Now, the thing to beware of is this. If you smell the sweet, cloying scent of this creature, it smells of death. Say you shot a deer, bled it dry from a tree, gutted and skinned it, then filleted it into roasts, then put these roasts in the smoker, or in the cold freeze. And say that, while you were packing them all away, you forgot one. And left it on the table overnight for a few days, then came in to find it, the whole room would smell of death, the sweet smell of rotting meat. And of flies buzzing nearby, taking the rotted juices as their sustenance. That smell. That is what the Nuckelavee smells like. If you ever smell that scent, run. Run for your life."

Kym leaned forward so far I thought she was going to fall on her face. Her eyes were wider than I'd ever seen them.

The fire crackled, and the peat popped and burned, and we all jumped in surprise.

Khepri laughed nervously, then fell silent.

Kym was straightening.

Oh, no.

"Mister Håkan, sir. Please, just one more tale?" Kym said.

"Och, lass, you are a brave one, I see. Now let me think," Håkan tapped on his cheek thoughtfully.

"Uncle, there's the Nøkken," Inge said helpfully.

Håkan stared down at his nephew, a dazed look in his eye, almost as if he had forgotten where he was.

"Ah, yes, Inge. The Nøkken. The Nøkken," Håkan's voice drifted off, then he jerked to alertness again. "The Nøkken is a dangerous creature." He looked out at all of us, then settled his eyes on Kym and Christianne. "Do you know why we had to find some high ground to make camp?" He did not wait for an answer. "It was because of the Nøkken. This creature lives in the wet spots of the moor. The puddles, the rivulets, and especially the hidden marshy grounds that you don't know are there, until you ride across it and your horse's foot sinks down - down - down into the water. Sometimes down into an early grave. The Nøkken lives in such places, the darkest places of the moor. It is said to play its lute in a ghostly tune, so softly you aren't sure if you're hearing it, or if it's the song out of your memory from the time you lost your mother ..."

Håkan paused and took another sip from his waterskin, then continued.

"The Nøkken plays this tune to trick your mind and lure you into the dark, deep spots of water out on the moor. And if it is winter, and the water on the moor is frozen, the song from the Nøkken will lure you out onto thin ice, make it appear to be firm and steady. And when you step onto it, the music will become irresistible. You will not be able to refuse the lure. And you will walk onto that thin ice, and fall through, to the bottom of the deep water ... to your death." He finished, his eyebrows riding high on his forehead, his eyes wide with the telling of his story.

"But sir," said Kym. "You are telling us tales, is it not so?"

Håkan nodded and said quietly, "But who's to say these tales are not true?"

"But," said Kym, "at the beginning, when Charlotte asked you if you were nervous, because you were building up the fire, you said, to *'keep the mist at bay.'* You said you'd heard stories of the northern moors, stories of bad things happening, and bad creatures. Creatures you wouldn't want to meet on a sunny day down by the castle's gardens, let alone out on a misty moor at night."

Håkan laughed heartily, then winked at me.

"Och, this one, she has a memory for details, does she not?"

He regarded Kym then with a serious gaze. "It's getting late, lass. Don't you think we should be getting some sleep?"

"No. Not until I find out what you meant in the beginning," Kym said.

Håkan looked solemnly into the fire.

"Aye, okay lass, I'll tell you. But you have to promise to go to sleep then, after the telling."

"I promise."

Håkan took a deep breath and began to speak.

"I was not much older than Inge here," he touched his nephew's head fondly, "when my father's father brought me out to a small town not far from the eastern edge of this vast northern moorland expanse. His own grandfather was ill, you see, and he wanted to visit him to see if there was anything he could do to help. He brought his wife, my grandmother, who was a Wise Woman, a healer and a midwife, and she brought an extensive number of wild herbs from the capital, to see if something hadn't yet been tried. Something that could help him. But my father had told me before I came, that great-great grandfather was nearing a hundred years old, and that no herb could treat him. He was just worn out. But my grandfather had to try, so we came."

"It was summer back then, a bright cheerful sunny time when the sun hardly ever sets and the flowers were in constant bloom. We came to the town, which has since fallen empty, and my grandmother set to work on great-great grandfather. She boiled and stewed and rubbed and oiled and made all manner of salves and ointments and unguents and teas, and applied it all to the old man's body. And old he was, for I remember his face. It was brown from working on the moor all his life, and so wrinkled that when he slept, you could not tell fully which wrinkles were his eyes and mouth, and which wrinkles were just there for always. He had been a farmer, you see, and had led his cows into the moor to graze during the day, and back home at night, for nearly a hundred years."

"Well, on the seventh night that we were there, my grandmother told my grandfather that she could do no more. His grandfather was dying, and to let him die, because he had earned his rest. And the afternoon of the next day, she spooned her good broth into the elder's lips, he burped and smiled his wrinkled face at her, and then fell asleep for his midday nap. And he did not waken."

"The whole village mourned for him, because he had been the eldest one living, and had been the child of the family who had founded the village. That night, he lay on the table in his house, as neighbor upon neighbor, more than fifty of them, came to pay their respects. They brought food and drink, and stayed the whole night, waiting, to make sure great-great-grandfather was indeed gone."

"The next morning, they put two coins on his eyes and placed him in a coffin my own grandfather had built of the strongest oak wood he could find. And they dug his grave in the village's burial site, on the edge of the moor. And that afternoon, they buried him with a cord they attached to a bell above the grave. They loved him that much, to give him one more chance, so if he woke up in the coffin under the ground, he could pull the cord and ring the bell, and they would come get him."

"That night, as I slept in great-great-grandfather's house, I heard the bell ring. So faint I couldn't be sure of my own ears, but strong enough so that I went and roused my grandfather, who sat up in bed, his eyes wide. He could hear it, too. He grabbed his scythe and handed me both a knife and a shovel, in case either was needed. And we took our dog and went out to great-great-grandfather's grave."

"The moon was full that night, and everything was bright with the moonlight. We could see everything. As we approached the grave, we could still hear the bell ringing, and as we moved closer, we could see it ringing, too. The cord was slowly being pulled, then let loose, then pulled again, and the small bell was swaying back and forth, and tinkling softly in the night air."

"My grandfather stood there, and watched the bell move slowly back and forth, for many minutes. Then it stopped. The bell stopped moving, and the tinkling stopped, and all was still as death. And we stood there, watching and holding our breath." Håkan paused and took a deep shuddering breath.

"Then the mist came. It had been a clear summer night, not a cloud in the sky that day, and in summer, the darkness tarried for but a few hours. As we watched great-great-grandfather's grave, a mist came pouring out from every inch of that burial mound, where the village had buried its dead for near on eighty years. And the dog began to growl. A low growl, his head down. He stared at the grave, growling, his hackles rising at the mist rolling off the ground." Håkan took a sip of water.

"It was the Witte Wieven. She came from the mist, formed out of the mist. She was just one, and she was beautiful. She rose from the mist and came walking toward us, toward my grandfather and me. The dog began to whimper and lay down on the ground as if he couldn't move. We couldn't move, either. We just stood there, spellbound, as the Witte Wieven slowly glided toward us. When she was about ten feet away, she reached her hands out, moaning. My grandfather couldn't help himself: He reached out to her. Their fingers almost touched. The Witte Wieven's face changed then, from that of a beautiful young woman, to the face of a rotted corpse. Her mouth opened wide, and she began to scream."

"I pulled on my grandfather's hand, tried to pull him back, cried out to him to come away, but he was mesmerized. Their fingers touched, and the Witte Wieven's face changed back to that of beauty, but my grandfather began to scream, and I saw that his face was turning dead. I pulled on his hand one last time, and he turned and looked at me and his face was rotting away. That's when I let go of his hand and ran, and the dog jumped up and ran with me, yelping all the way. I ran faster than I'd ever run before, screaming all the way, back to the house my grandmother was sleeping in, hysterical."

"They found him at dawn, lying across great-great grandfather's grave, dead and rotted as if he'd been dead for a year."

Håkan looked up at us, a haunted look in his eyes.

"So you see, my fear was real. I have seen a Witte Wieven's face with my own eyes. And we are out here again, on the northern moors, and I will sleep restless

190

tonight, and be grateful when we can cross through them and be out the other side."

Chapter Sixteen

The Witte Wieven

We were all quiet as we readied for sleep. The mist circling around us was thicker than ever, and the moors looked haunted.

I volunteered to take first watch, because I did not think I would be able to sleep, not after that story.

"You okay?" Tam came and put his arms around me.

"Sure," I said lightly, smiling.

I glanced over at Kym lying next to Christianne. Her face looked troubled.

"Hey, watch over Kym. I think she's regretting asking Håkan about things, okay?" I looked into Tam's eyes and kissed him on the nose.

"I think everyone's regretting she asked Håkan about things, to be honest, but yes, I'll keep an eye out." He winked at me, gave me one last squeeze, and walked back to his blanket.

I looked over at the horses: They stood in a line, their halter ropes all tied to the long staked-out rope we always set them on. They chewed a few mouthfuls of heath, and seemed unconcerned. We'd given them their share of oats earlier, and they were well fed animals.

I looked at Shêtân on the end. He was pushing his head fondly against Kym's pony, Taimim, who whickered back in reply.

The animals are unconcerned. I should be as well.

I settled in for the watch, and threw another block of peat onto the fire, stoking it with a branch.

The troupe was soon asleep, and I was alone.

I was used to moors. Growing up in Swerighe, heck, anywhere in the northlands, you got used to the huge expanses of bleak wetlands, the scrubby heath bushes growing stubbornly here and there. The dark, wet patches of bog, sometimes invisible under a thin layer of bracken and thicket and gorse bush. You could put your foot down and meet with solid ground, then with the next footstep, plunge ankle-deep into the sop – ankle-deep, or farther.

I remembered once, I'd been out riding my favorite pony, I must have been around twelve, and had rode too close to the moorland. It sometimes crept up on you. I'd been riding on a meadow trail, the flowers growing wild and distracting me, my pony sweet but a bit stupid. Wild roses and honeysuckle were in bloom, and their scent filled the air with so much heady perfume it was almost intoxicating.

We rode on this path, and the pony veered off to nibble at some wild lavender he saw growing past the side of a low hill. And so, I'd let him go, riding in that sunny day, with a long stalk of wheat in my mouth and a meat pie to look forward to in my pocket. I was scouting for a place to picnic, some nice clearing with flowers nearby. Maybe hoping to come across a faerie ring of mushrooms, for good luck.

The pony had walked down a new path, toward the wild lavender, and onto the moors, and I hadn't noticed where he was stepping. It was an oversight I'd soon learn to regret.

The pony stepped a dozen feet onto the moor, trying to reach the lavender a dozen yards away, and had fallen into the peat. He went down, his right foreleg folding unnaturally under him, and screamed in pain.

I'd fallen to the side, a wet plop onto the moist, spongy ground, and rolled away a few feet.

When I could stop my roll, I hurried back to the pony, but his leg was broken. My father and lady-maid had come running, being not far away, and he'd scooped me up and put me on the back of his large horse.

The pony had to be killed. He screamed in his suffering, and it was the only thing they could do to ease his pain. The foreman had come, I'm sure, and stuck a sharp dagger into his heart. Then his corpse would have been dragged out of the bog and disposed of.

I didn't know. My father had galloped away with me, back to the castle to have me looked over by the court healer. I hadn't seen what happened, but that was almost worse. My imagination had taken over, and I'd cried that night, so sorry for my dear pony.

I'd had nightmares for many nights after that, until my mother relented and found another pony for me. This new steed had been fat and hard, not sweet at all, not like the pony I had killed by being so feather-headed I hadn't seen where he'd been walking.

My father had taken me aside and given me a stern talk about how we must always take care of our horses, and watch over them, and feed them good food, and above all else, take careful watch of where they walk or run while we're astride them. How we, as their owners, are responsible for where they place each step, and responsible if they came to injury.

I sighed, remembering.

I rose to my feet, grabbed a wild carrot out of the bag Khepri had used to collect them, and walked over to Shêtân.

"Ooh, ooh, coo, there my sweet boy, coo, coo," I crooned as I fed him the carrot. The wild carrots were so sweet that Shêtân nodded his head as he munched it.

I salvaged a small bite and fed it to Taimim beside Shêtân.

I ran my fingers through Shêtân's mane, untangling a small snarl and laying the black, shiny hair flat on his neck. I had pampered his coat and mane, encouraging it to grow long, brushing him out every day, until his mane dropped several feet in a gorgeous cascade of black. His tail was even longer, and reached almost to the ground.

Shêtân's ears turned to prick up at a new sound.

The hair rose on my neck.

I turned my head, but all I could see was the thick mist rolling across the moor.

I glanced down at the campsite, at my friends, both old and new, slumbering soundly.

The fire crackled and a peat block fell, bringing a shower of spark up into the air.

I took a deep breath, smiling.

Shêtân snorted, his ears swiveling again, and my senses were instantly alert once more.

I turned to gaze out on the moorland, eyes searching.

An owl hooted.

Those stories really got to you, Charlotte. You're starting to hear things.

I decided to take a walk around the camp perimeter, which was a normal watch duty.

Normal. Yeah. Keep thinking that.

Shêtân snorted and stomped his foot impatiently.

"What is bothering you, my sweet? Hmmm?" I murmured to him.

I loved this horse. Really loved him.

"I'm just going to walk around the camp. You'll be able to see me the entire time, okay?"

Shêtân looked into my eyes, his long lashes brushing against my cheek.

"I'll be right back," I patted his neck and kissed his long nose, then turned to survey the camp once again.

The fire was bright and high, the peat block I'd tossed on earlier burning well. The mist, though thick outside the camp, seemed held back by the campfire. I took a few steps away from Shêtân, my eyes scanning my sleeping troupe.

Everything seemed quiet and normal. Everything was still.

Then why am I feeling such an intense foreboding?

I wondered if the harpies were nearby, projecting their feelings of fear and ill-will out to the camp. It seemed doubtful. Jim had said harpies lived in elevated places. Mostly trees, sometimes hills, or cliffs.

This moor was flat. Flat and marshy and spooky.

Spooky. Now where had that come from?

I snorted as I started walking again. I knew where the word had come from. It had come from my imagination, and the moors and my freaked-out condition.

"Maybe I just need to talk to myself as I walk, huh?" I said. "Yeah, that's better."

I walked the outside of the camp and whistled a sprightly tune, a lullaby from my childhood.

♫♫♫

"Gumman ville vagga

Och inga barn hade hon;

Då tog hon in

Fölungen sin,

Och lade den i vaggan sin.

Vyssa, vyssa, långskånken min,

Långa ben har du;

Lefver du till sommaren,

Blir du lik far din."

♫♫♫

I stepped around the camp and whistled my lullaby, about an old woman who had no children, but who wanted to cradle a baby, so she took inside her foal and put it in a cradle and ...

I stopped. I had never realized how creepy that lullaby was. I turned and looked out on the moor.

The mist rolled just outside the camp.

But there was no breeze at all. The air was still. As still as a graveyard.

I stepped closer to the mist just outside the camp, watching as it turned and tumbled in on itself.

Behind me, Shêtân shorted and stomped his foot again. I glanced back and was greeted by the sight of my horse, head down, nibbling at the heath at his feet. I turned back to stare at the mist. I heard Shêtân short again, several times. Whirling around, I looked and saw him placidly standing there, his eyes half closed.

That's odd.

I took another step toward the camp perimeter.

The mist swirled and tumbled.

I took another step.

And another.

And several more.

My foot was now outside the perimeter of camp, and the firelight was very dim.

How did I get this far from the fire?

I looked back and saw the camp was a dozen paces behind me. The mist swirled between the camp light and the place where I stood, threatening to cut me off entirely.

I heard a sound, and turned back to the mist.

A form was coalescing out of the fog.

The form of a ghostly woman.

I heard a whisper in my mind.

"This night will be bad ... the next day will be beyond imagining ..."

"What?" I said, in a strong, loud voice.

The sound of my voice brought my head back to the moment.

I looked closer.

The ghostly form of the woman took a more solid form. She was beautiful. She reached out her arms for me ...

"Not today, I'm afraid," I said, cutting the air with a strong slash from my scimitar. The sword made a

WHOOSH! sound as it cut through the fog and the woman, a familiar and reassuring sound.

The ghostly woman dissipated into mist as soon as my scimitar sliced through her. I heard a faint scream.

A shiver went through me, and I grimaced.

"That's enough of that crap," I said aloud. "I deal in reality, not in mists and ghosts. DO YOU HEAR ME?"

I stomped my feet and swung my sword in great arcs, making it whistle through the air. I turned and could see the campfire clearly. I turned and walked back, slashing my scimitar through the air in practice swings, lunging and stabbing into the mist for good measure.

As I walked back into camp, I checked every one of my companions.

Tam, Khepri, Kym, Christianne, mhmm. They're all here. Caroline, Tupu, Jim, Olof, Håkan, mhmm. All here. All where they should be.

Wait.

Where was Inge?

I swung around, scanning the camp, then swung my eyes back when I detected a slight movement.

There, by the horses.

Inge was peeking out from behind the brown mares we had brought.

"Hey."

I walked forward.

The boy had peeked out and then ducked back behind the large animals.

"What are you playing at, Inge?"

I trotted around the horses, to the back of camp, expecting to come upon the lad urinating or something.

Why else would he leave his bedroll?

As I came behind the horses, I saw there was nothing there. I ran the length of the staked-out equines, trotting the distance behind them, and out the other side, next to Shêtân.

There was nothing there.

Was the mist playing a trick on my eyes?

I stared back at Inge's sleeping blanket.

Was he back? Had he rushed and taken his place next to his uncle and Olof? Was he playing a trick on me?

I walked decisively back to the troupe, stepping between each pair of sleeping figures, counting them again.

Caroline, Khepri, Christianne, Kym, Tupu, Jim, and Tam, then Håkan, Olof and Inge.

I stared down at the sleeping form of Inge. His head was turned sideways, and he was curled up, one hand under his cheek, one hand gripping the blanket, pulling it tight over his shoulder and across the lower half of his face.

What was that?

I thought I saw Inge's eye flutter.

I poked him with my sword, nudging his leg a bit.

He did not move.

I leaned in, to get a better look at his face.

Inge's eyes slowly opened.

What the heck?

The boy's eyes looked black.

It's a trick of the campfire light. It has to be.

I leaned in closer, and Inge turned his head, bit by bit, outward to face me.

He stared at me with those coal-black eyes. I could see no irises at all; it was as if Inge's eyes were the color of black ink.

But the boy has blue eyes.

Inge slowly opened his mouth to grin at me, revealing a mouthful of huge, sharp teeth.

I stared, my eyes wide and unblinking, unable to look away.

Inge's teeth began to grow, until they were enormous, until he could not possibly be able to close his mouth around them.

A cold shiver crept slowly down my back.

I gripped my sword, raising it.

Shêtân snorted then, louder than I'd ever heard him snort, and I looked over at the big, black horse. He was stomping his foot repeatedly, looking at me.

I turned back to Inge, and he looked normal again. On his side, fast asleep.

I crouched down and put my hand on the boy's shoulder.

His slow, deep breathing told me he was fast asleep.

I pushed my finger into his mouth, trying to see if he still had the nightmare teeth, and encountered a normal mouth, full of normal young-boy teeth.

I pushed my finger in farther, and Inge opened his mouth in his sleep, and then groaned and turned over.

But he stayed asleep, and I withdrew my finger.

I shook my head, and sheathed my scimitar, patting it a few times, before rising to my feet.

That was a close one.

I took a deep breath and returned to my watch seat by the fire.

That was so weird.

Had I imagined all that? The wight in the mist? The boy hiding behind the horses? The black irises and enormous, growing teeth?

I knew I hadn't been asleep.

"You know what I think, Shêtân?" I said out loud. "I think this mist is haunting and the stories Håkan told did not help matters."

Shêtân blew bubbles and nodded his head, and I smiled.

The rest of the night's first watch passed without incident.

About 1 a.m. Tupu woke and came to relieve me.

"Be careful," I looked around. "The mist has ways of playing tricks on your eyes," I cautioned her.

Tupu looked at me and nodded. "I don't hold with such mischief, and I don't have patience for apparitions. If anything appears out of the mist, it'll have to deal with the business end of my sword."

I remembered the incident with Inge, and looked at my friend solemnly. "Tupu, be careful. And be sure of what you are dealing with."

She nodded, and I went to curl up in my blanket; sleep overtook me quickly.

I had been asleep for perhaps an hour, when I heard a shriek that woke me up.

I opened my eyes and lifted my head, looking around.

The camp was still fast asleep, and the mist was beginning to hold just a hint that it would soon become daylight.

I looked around, sitting up, and rubbed my eyes.

Everyone is there, everyone, but ... wait.

Where was Tupu?

I knew I had left her to take the second watch, before I had ... I looked around.

Shêtân was gone as well.

What the heck?

Everyone knew not to touch my horse. Everyone.

I pulled on my boots, buckled on my sword in its sheath, and walked over to the line of horses.

Every horse was there except Shêtân.

I swung my head around and looked back over the camp, then stared out into the mist.

I thought I saw Shêtân's receding form, the huge horse's back, his haunches, his long tail, swinging side to side.

"Shêtân?"

I trotted over to where I had just seen him, and the mist swirled around me, closing behind me.

"Shêtân!" I called out, cupping my hands around my mouth.

I heard whispering voices coming from the mist, multiple whispering voices, coming from multiple directions.

I ran forward a dozen more steps.

"Shêtân! Shêtân!" I called.

Suddenly, he appeared out of the mist, saddled and bridled.

I had left him with just his halter on, the saddle and bridle still back in camp, but here they were, on the horse.

I put my hand out, cooing, "There, there, pretty boy, coo, coo, coo, Shêtân," I put my arms around him and felt his strong warm neck against my cheek.

This was no apparition. This was my horse.

I gathered up his reins, and halter rope, and swung into the saddle.

I turned him around several times, trying to see through the thick mist.

It was now growing slightly more white that black, and the promise of the sun's return should have cheered me, but there was still the question of Tupu.

Where was Tupu?

I decided to check back at camp, to see if she was there, and I turned Shêtân to walk back, but he turned his head the other way stubbornly, and refused to walk the way I wanted him to.

Shêtân stared out into the far mist, and his ears pricked up, swiveling to point toward something only he could hear.

"You want to go that way, boy? Do you hear something?" I patted his neck soothingly.

Shêtân's ears swiveled back to listen to my voice, then immediately forward again. His attention was focused, and he wouldn't even blink.

"All right, boy, let's go where you want to go," I squeezed my legs and clucked to him, and he began to walk forward.

"This way, eh? Good boy, Shêtân, good horsey." I tried to see through the mist, but it was too thick for my eyes to penetrate. My gaze couldn't make out anything in the white expanse. I had to trust the horse.

Shêtân walked forward, resolute.

At one point, he turned slightly, sniffing the air, then continued.

After ten minutes of walking away from camp and into the mist, Shêtân's ears began swiveling like crazy, as if he could hear ...

Voices. Coming from all around us.

"I hear them, too, boy," I said, patting his neck.

Although Shêtân's ears were moving to take in multiple voices all around us, his steps kept going forward in the same direction. He was resolute.

Another few minutes and he stopped, putting his head down to the form of a crumpled Tupu curled up on the ground.

As soon as Shêtân's wet muzzle began nibbling at Tupu's neck and shoulders, she raised her head.

"Tupu!" I exclaimed.

"Oh, OH! Thank goodness you found me!" She stood up, wiping her eyes. "I ...I heard something and went to investigate, then got lost in the mist. I took Shêtân, hoping he would help. I did everything wrong, forgot everything you taught me about taking a watch over camp."

"It's okay, it's okay," I said soothingly. "It was Shêtân who found you."

I put my arm out, and Tupu took hold of it, and, swinging onto Shêtân's back behind me, settled herself there. Her arms gripped me tightly around my waist.

"Thank you," Tupu whispered. "Also, please don't tell anyone what happened."

"I wouldn't think of it," I said.

I urged Shêtân forward again, and he turned and trotted back the way we'd come, eager for camp.

I resolved to give him even more treats from then on. I had never known such an intelligent and resourceful horse.

Tupu sniffed behind me. "Your horse is amazing, by the way."

"Yes, he is," I agreed.

Chapter Seventeen
The Mountain Gnome

The day was spent traveling out of the moor, which I think everyone had gotten tired of, especially after all of Håkan's bedtime stories.

"Yeah, Håkan?" He looked at me. "Next time, let's keep the scary stories to a minimum, okay?"

Håkan threw his head back and laughed. Inge and Olof grinned broadly beside him.

It was a sunny day, and our horses were just stepping off the moor, leaving the bracken and heath behind us.

Ahead, another thick forest loomed, and an icy path through the snow-covered hills.

Even the horses trotted a little faster than normal, eager to leave the mist and bog behind them.

"Tam, do you think we'll get to the ice wizard soon?" Kym asked. Tam had been in charge of the crude map the duchesses had supplied us with, and pored over its markings often.

He put his head up, distracted. "I hope so, my friend," he said with a grin.

Kym's pony trotted out in front, and she was teaching it tricks.

"Taimim, prance!" said Kym, and the pony's front legs began to arch and prance.

Kym laughed in delight.

"It is good to be back in the sun, isn't it?" I said to Tupu, who rode next to me, Jim on her other side.

She looked at me, a smile on her face. "It sure is. It sure is."

The landscape had turned freezing cold. That night, it began to snow, and the next morning, everything was covered in a white blanket.

The cold, crisp air turned everyone's cheeks red, and we all lifted the fur collars on the hoods Anya had supplied us with, up over our heads. The fur surrounded our faces, warming us.

By midmorning, we were approaching the massive cliffs Tam said were our destination.

"The ice wizard has been tracked to these cliffs. It is thought he is holed up someplace nearby, possibly in a cave or crevice or large area," Tam said, folding the map again and placing it in his bag.

"Okay, we should approach the him cautiously," I said. "But first, we've got to pinpoint his location."

We rode alongside the thick forest and, at one point, stopped to gather some clean snow.

"Snow, see?" Caroline showed Christianne and Kym. "For snow candy."

Khepri dribbled some honey and molasses from her jars, dripping it back and forth onto the fluffy cold snow.

Kym tasted it.

"YUM!"

"Let me try it?" Christianne said. She took a bite. "Delicious!"

Kym took another bite.

"Careful, it can give you a headache," Caroline cautioned.

"A what?" asked Kym.

"A headache. A special kind of headache produced from the cold in your mouth," Caroline explained.

"But I've had cold things in my mouth before," Kym protested, taking another bite of the snow candy.

Christianne spooned another mouthful in as well. They both spent several minutes wolfing down the snow candy.

Inge and Olof helped themselves, but only ate a few spoonfuls.

Then ...

"OWW!" Christianne held her hand to her forehead. "OHHHH!" Her eyes closed in agony.

"I guess only humans get the headach ... oh oh OHH!" Kym dropped her spoon and put both hands to her head, groaning.

"Nope, not just humans," Khepri said, looking interested.

"Nope," I laughed.

"OHHHH, help!" cried Christianne.

"It will ease soon," reassured Caroline.

Inge and Olof nodded knowingly. They had felt the snow headache before, as well.

Håkan shook his head, smiling.

It was while we were trying the snow candy that the creature creeped up on us.

"Hello? Hello?!" I heard the high, squeaky voice a few feet into the trees and turned.

"Hello?" I said loudly, searched for the owner of the voice.

"Hello," the squeaky voice repeated, and out of the forest came the saddest looking creature I had ever set my eyes on.

I blinked in surprise.

"Oh! OH! It is a mountain gnome!" Inge said in delight.

We all slid off our horses and walked forward to meet this sad creature.

He was about two and a half feet tall, and very skinny. His nut-brown face was pinched and bony, and his nose came to a sharp point.

He wore patched clothing, his pants were of old tweed, and a nondescript color I'd call "forest floor." His coat was the color of mud. On his feet were wooden shoes and striped stockings, which he kept smoothing over, as if he were afraid they would fall to his ankles any moment. Straggly hair was topped by a cap that looked like it had been fashioned from the top of a giant acorn. I looked closer and saw it was made of felt.

How clever!

He held his hands together, and moved them constantly in a nervous gesture.

"Hello," he said again, walking forward. "I need help."

"Well my goodness, we are here to help," I said, bending down to meet his eyes. "Are you in trouble, little friend?"

"Yes, yes I am," the mountain gnome looked behind him nervously.

"Do you want something to eat?" Khepri asked, crouching alongside me and extending her hand with a morsel of fish steak.

"Oh, oh, oh." The little man came forward and gently took the snack from Khepri, then sat down right there and began to nibble daintily on it, holding it with both hands.

Håkan dropped his pack and smiled, and Inge and Olof followed suit.

"I guess we're stopping here to camp," said Tupu. She shielded her eyes and looked at the sky. "Although we have many hours of daylight left."

"He may have useful news for us," I said over my shoulder. "Besides, I want to help him."

"You want to help him because he is so cute," said Håkan. "If he were covered with warts and shit, you would not stop."

"Oh, I would, I would," I said. "Especially on this particular adventure. We need to gather information."

I sat down next to the mountain gnome and rifled through my bag for my water skin.

But the little man wrinkled his nose at the water, and shook his head.

Tam came forward. "How about this?" He held out a small cup, which the little gnome took, and then brought forth a bottle of mead.

The small creature nodded enthusiastically, smiling. Tam chuckled as he poured a bit of the golden liquid into the cup.

The mountain gnome took a sip of the mead, and wiggled his eyebrows, then drank the whole cup down.

"I guess you like it?" Tam said.

In answer, the little man held the cup out, indicating to Tam he wanted a refill. Tam obliged.

After the second cup of mead was gone, the small man sat back. I handed him a cracker, which he took and began to nibble on.

"Well, you're a mountain gnome, then?" I asked.

He nodded his head vigorously.

"And you say you need help?" I asked.

"Yes, yes I need help," the little gnome said around bites of cracker.

"What is your name?" Tam asked.

"Farryn," said the gnome. "I work in the snow."

"What do you mean you 'work in the snow'?" I asked.

"I mean, I work in the snow. Every day I go out in the cold snow and I work it," Farryn said.

"What do you do with it?" Christianne asked.

"I make bombs," Farryn said.

I blinked.

What on earth?

"Farryn?" I said. The little gnome turned to me. I handed him another cracker, which he eagerly took. "What do you need help with? Are you being chased or something?"

Farryn nodded, stuffed the rest of his cracker into his mouth, chewed two times, and then dropped his head and promptly fell asleep.

"Miss," Caroline said softly. "Come away from him."

"What happened?" asked Tam. He prodded the mountain gnome. "Farryn?"

The gnome opened his eyes sleepily.

"Don't fall asleep, buddy," Tam said. "We want to ask you a few questions."

Farryn nodded and then closed his eyes again. He seemed so sleepy, watching him was making me drowsy.

"Take care," Håkan's quiet voice came from behind us.

I took a deep breath, and vigorously shook my head back and forth, trying to invigorate myself.

"Move away from him and you'll wake, Your Highness," Håkan whispered behind me.

I rose and stepped back, stumbling a bit.

What's happening?

I walked back a dozen steps to where Håkan was waiting.

"Well?" I asked.

"Remember your nursery rhymes?" Håkan said quietly. "Gnomes will project their states to others in the area, especially sleep."

I paused and thought about gnomes. So much had happened in the last fifteen years, I barely remembered anything of my early childhood.

Wait.

Oh my gods, Håkan was right.

There were several nursery rhymes in the northlands about how gnomes can make whole villages fall into slumber, and how eating food made them very sleepy.

My jaw dropped open, and I looked at Håkan, then at Caroline, who gave me an "I knew it" look.

"Those of us with children remember, because we've repeated the old nursery rhymes to our own littles," Håkan said softly.

I glanced over at Farryn. The gnome had curled up on the ground, his hands folded under his head, and was snoring softly.

"I wanted to ask him questions," I said regretfully.

"He'll be awake in the morning, Miss," Caroline said.

"But what if he runs away before we wake?" Christianne asked.

"Let's camp here and watch him. Maybe even tie a rope around his waist and have the watch hold it," Jim said.

I sighed.

"I guess it can't be helped," I said. "Okay, troupe, make camp here."

We got to work and made a fire and set our bedrolls out in a circle.

We always preferred to arrange them in a starburst pattern, heads toward the fire, feet pointed outward. It had become our custom ever since we'd started adventuring together.

I pulled some rope out of my pack and gently tied it around Farryn's waist. The little gnome snored through the whole thing. He was so soundly asleep that nothing could rouse him. I felt myself getting groggy just from bending over to tie the rope, and I hurried to finish, then backed away, settling down ten feet from the mountain gnome.

"According to our legends, he will not wake until night has passed," said Håkan. "Not even if he is trampled."

"Whoa, that's ... that's drugged," said Tupu.

I nodded, giving her a knowing look.

"Well, it can't be helped, I guess," Caroline said. "Tam, go get some rabbits?"

"With pleasure!" Tam unloaded his pack and grabbed his bow, and hiked off to find dinner.

An hour later, there was rabbit meat, skinned and cleaned and sizzling over the fire.

My stomach rumbled.

Caroline chuckled. "Hungry, Miss?"

"I guess I didn't realize how much, Carrie." I smiled at her.

"Here, chew on some blackroot," Khepri handed me a twig.

"Oh, thanks. I ran out a while back," I said.

"Most of us did. I will have to ration the remaining sticks," said Khepri. "And get more when we're in Alkebulan."

"Blackroot? We grow it here in Swerighe, too," said Håkan. "Down in the southern shores. We'll get some to you before you set sail."

"Thanks, cousin!" I smiled at him.

"You're quite welcome, Your Highness." Håkan grinned back.

Christianne walked up with Kym, her hands full of wild carrots and onions. "Okay, who wants roasted carrots with their rabbit meat?"

I raised my hand, still hungry.

"Feed the princess first, I think she's actually ravenous," Caroline said, chuckling.

Ten minutes later, I settled onto my blanket, a bowl heaped high with crispy rabbit meat and roasted wild carrots in my hands.

Delicious!

Chapter Eighteen
A Wet Journey

"I know, I know!" Farryn's high voice came to me at dawn.

He's awake!

"But I'm hungry!" Farryn said.

"I don't care if you're half starved," said a voice, "You're not getting a crumb until we're done asking you questions."

I opened my eyes.

Håkan sat by the fire, the mountain gnome's rope held tightly in his hands.

I sat up.

There were marks on the forest floor, scrabbling and scratching marks, right next to were Farryn sat.

I rubbed my eyes.

"Did he try to get away?" I asked

"You bet he did," Håkan grumbled. "But I knew he would. I fell asleep with his rope tied to my arm." The big man glowered at the small mountain gnome, who pouted.

I looked over at Jim, who'd taken second watch. "You know anything about this, Jim?"

Jim shrugged. "I knew Håkan had things in hand. No little gnome was going to get away from him." He grinned at Håkan, who smiled.

"That's right," Håkan said.

Farryn crossed his arms and looked sad.

A half hour later, everyone was awake and alert. The sun rays reached through the trees and lit up camp, and we sat eating breakfast.

Farryn moaned the whole time.

"Pleaseeeeeee!?" "I'm hunnnnnnngry!"

"You are pitiful, is what you are," said Tupu, grimacing. "Seriously pitiful."

We were careful to keep all manner of edibles away from the mountain gnome. He had tried desperately to reach the food we were preparing.

Tam had finally tied him to a tree.

"Don't you dare untie that knot!" He'd warned the gnome.

Farryn had immediately tried to untie it.

"Stop it!" I ran up to the little man. "Just stop it!" I untied the rope from the tree and wrapped it around Farryn's arms. He struggled, but I pounded him on his head until he sat still.

"My parents have been kidnapped, and you are going to help us find them, do you understand?" I had unshed tears in my eyes.

Farryn looked at me solemnly. "Okay."

I set him down next to me. His arms were pinned, so there wasn't much he could do to grab food.

All he could do was complain.

"Give me food give me food give me food give me food give me food ..." the gnome chanted.

I reached over and brought my fist down on his head again, and he fell silent.

We finally ate our fill, and I turned to him.

"Okay, you're going to answer our questions. Do you understand?"

He nodded.

"Afterward we'll give you a bit to eat. Do you understand?"

He nodded and smiled.

I rolled my eyes.

"Such a skinny little creature, and he wants to eat all the time," I said to Caroline.

"It is odd, Miss."

"Okay, what should we ask him?" I said to the troupe at large.

"Ask him if he knows of the ice wizard," Tam suggested.

I looked at Farryn. "Well?"

The gnome nodded.

"Speak," I demanded.

""I know where he is," said Farryn. "He makes me work for him. He makes everyone work for him. I just got away yesterday, and came through the forest, and that's when I ran into you."

"What do you mean, the ice wizard 'makes you work for him'?" Tupu asked.

"We make bombs for him all day long. All day, every day. And he gives us food at night, but only a tiny bit to each of us." Farryn began to cry.

"Stop that," I said. "Now, tell us: Have you seen two humans that the ice wizard took? They would be held somewhere, maybe away from everybody."

"Yes, but he keeps them in a cage right out in the open. We can see them while we work," Farryn said.

"While you work?" asked Håkan.

"Making the bombs," Farryn answered.

"What are these bombs?" Kym asked.

"They're bombs. He's planning to store them away with a cold spell, while The Warming heats the world up. Then he will attack," Farryn said.

"And the ice wizard, he started The Warming, didn't he?" Caroline asked.

"Of course, he did. That how he came out of the ice!" Farryn said.

"What?" asked Jim. "How?"

Farryn sighed. "I forget you don't know anything."

"Hey, we know plenty," I said.

"Farryn, tell us more," Tam prodded.

"Okay, okay," said Farryn, taking a deep breath. "The ice wizard is one of the last of his race. The others died out a long, long time ago. But he found a spell to save himself from what killed the others. A spell called The Warming. He cast it before he went into hibernation. I heard him say it was meant to take effect after a certain amount of time. I think he said twenty-five thousand years. So he would be safe, he said. The spell releases gas. It's pouring bazillions of gas clouds into the sky. But you can't see them. This is what is causing The Warming."

Farryn stopped to catch his breath.

"Farryn, this spell that is pouring out gas, when is it supposed to stop?" Khepri asked, speaking slowly.

"I looked over at her, and saw her eyes looked shocked.

"It's not," Farryn said.

Khepri's face went white.

I turned to Farryn. "Tell me when it started."

"The ice wizard said the spell started back about eighty or ninety years ago, he said. He was upset because it took such a long time to finally thaw him out, Farryn said."

I looked at the gnome and blinked.

Imagine setting a spell in motion that took twenty-five thousand years to begin.

"Did the ice wizard know it would take twenty-five thousand years to start? That seems like a long time," I asked.

"No, he is angry at that. He is also angry because the spell was supposed to save his family, and they all died before they could get to him," said Farryn. "He set it in motion after the landslides and explosions, he said. He couldn't stop it. He was very mad."

"So he messed up, and lost his family, and now he's mad," Tupu said.

"Yes. He's so mad he wants to hurt people," Farryn said. "He wants to hurts the people he stole."

"My parents!" I exclaimed.

"Your parents," repeated Farryn.

I balled my fists, wanting to pummel this ice wizard.

"Charlotte," said Khepri in a quiet voice. "This is bad."

I looked at her.

"This gnome says the ice wizard's spell is a gas that's been pouring into the sky for eight or nine decades?" Khepri asked.

I nodded.

"And it's warming everything up too fast?" Khepri asked.

I thought about what she was saying.

"And it's not going to stop?" Khepri added.

A cold feeling began to flood me from head to toe.

"Ohhh," said Christianne. "Oh, no."

We broke camp and readied for the day's journey.

"Okay, Farryn. Tell us how to find the ice wizard." I demanded.

"Why should I? He'll kill me if I tell," Farryn said, sounding scared.

I held out a strip of rabbit meat.

The mountain gnome's tongue waggled, and he reached for the tidbit.

I pulled it back.

"How do we find the ice wizard?" I asked again.

Farryn hesitated.

Håkan stepped forward. "Listen, laddie," he pointed his finger in Farryn's face. "I promise we'll take ye with us, back to Swerighe, where you can be safe from this baddie, if ya tell the princess where he's holed up with the queen and prince." He brought his finger right up to Farryn's nose and prodded it.

Farryn sneezed. "Okay, okay, I'll tell you."

Håkan nodded. "Then speak."

"I don't know how to describe it, but I can lead you there," Farryn said.

"Fine, lead us then," I said, mounting Shêtân and wheeling him around.

Tupu reached down. "Come on, Farryn, you can ride with me."

The gnome smiled and hopped up to Tupu astride her big white and brown horse. She pulled him up and set him in front of her, where he immediately began braiding the horse's mane.

"Okay, let's head out. Tupu, ride in front with me?"

Tupu trotted up next to me, and we were off.

We followed Farryn's pointing finger through the trees and out into a valley. Gorse bushes grew in abundance, their leaves poking up through the snow.

The sky was a cloudy grey.

After an hour, Farryn's pointing finger led us east.

"Is it my imagination, or does the air feel warmer?" Christianne asked.

"It's definitely less cold, if that's what you mean," Tupu said.

"Oh, look! It's beginning to snow!" Kym lifted her face and stuck her tongue out, trying to catch a snowflake.

"I think we should go a little faster," said Tam. "We don't know how far it is."

"Farryn," I asked. "For how long did you run before you saw us?"

"I am not sure," Farryn said.

"Well, how many times did you see the sky get dark and then light?" Tupu asked, bending down to her riding companion.

"Oh, it was just one day. But I escaped in the beginning, and found you later," Farryn said.

"You found us in the afternoon," I said. "Tam is right, this is going to take many hours. Let's trot the horses for a while, then rest them at a walking pace." I clucked to Shêtân, urging him forward, and he began to trot.

The meadow soon gave way to a larger valley, and a thicket separated the two. We wound our way through thick bushes growing wild, and were soon through it.

It was a long day.

After a few hours, the air became warm enough that the snowfall turned into a grey drizzle.

"Wonderful," I said grimly. I was getting soaked.

"Here, Miss," Caroline rode up to me and handed me a leather hood. "I've been working on this in the evenings. It's waxed so it's waterproof."

"Oh, Carrie! Thank you!" I smiled at her. "But don't you want to share it?"

"I've made one for everyone. Christianne and Khepri helped me."

I pulled the hood over my coat and head. It worked very well, and I rode on, the rainwater running off the hood in rivulets, down the side of the hood and off my legs.

Luckily, my leather armor already offered resistance to the rain, and the water rolled right off my legs.

It was dismal riding in the rain. The grey clouds did not part for hours. But finally, the rain stopped.

I was downright warm in my new waterproof hood. Here in the middle of Swerighe, smack dab in the center of the northlands, I was warm.

This will never do.

We had to stop the spell, and it felt more urgent than ever now. The Warming was going to be bad, very bad. According to Khepri, it would be the end of life as we knew it.

But first, I must rescue my parents.

And hopefully, beat that ice wizard across the face with a wet herring.

We rode on.

It was getting late in the day when Farryn's pointing hand finally moved.

"He's up there," the gnome said in a quiet voice. I could see the fear on his small face. "Do I have to come up there with you?" he asked.

Tupu patted his shoulder. "Farryn, you stay close to me, I'm the fiercest warrior in this troupe. Nothing will happen to you if you're with me."

I rolled my eyes.

"HEY!" Kym protested.

Christianne just smiled.

Tam winked at me.

"Okay," Farryn said in a small voice.

"There you go, that's my little man," Tupu said.

The trail the gnome had indicated climbed up through the rocks, between melting snow and gorse bush, and even scattered heath.

We were able to ride all the way up on the horses.

"It's a good trail. We've been using it for a long time," Farryn confessed.

"It's a great trail," Tupu hugged him. "Thank you for showing us the way.

We climbed higher and higher, and the horses strained and jumped to get up the mountain. Finally, the path leveled off and proceeded straight, and led around the earthen side of the large mountain.

"He's in there," Farryn pointed across a canyon toward the opening of a huge cavern.

We saw a broken-down rope bridge suspended across the canyon.

"Is that safe?" I asked, looking at it dubiously.

"I ran across it and I didn't fall," said Farryn. "I would not take your horses over it, though."

"Uhhh, no. Definitely not," Tam said.

I was still worried: Farryn was a lot smaller, and lighter, than we were. But there seemed to be no other way to go.

"Let's leave the horses here and walk across." I looked out over the gorge. A wind whistled through it, making a haunted sound.

"Let's hurry so we can scout it and be back by nightfall," Håkan said.

"Agreed," Caroline said.

A ten minutes later, we were stepping across the rope bridge. I tried to keep my footing, and balance on the small slats of wood that spanned the bottom. Some of them were missing.

"It's not too bad," Tam said from behind me.

I concentrated on gripping the rope, and watching my feet. The wood that was still there was firm and steady, and not crumbling away, as I had worried it would be.

"Come on, Farryn," said Tupu. "Stick next to me. Remember what I said."

"I will, Miss Tupu. I love you, Miss Tupu," Farryn said.

I heard Jim grumble next to Tupu, and I laughed.

We need to get those two handfasted.

We made it across the rope bridge without incurring any casualties.

There are casualties. My wits.

I was grinning when I reached the other side.

I took a deep breath and turned to face the others, holding a finger to my lips. It was important to be quiet. We needed to remain undetected if we were to maintain the element of surprise.

We hiked up the path on the other side of the snowy canyon, up some steep steps, and out onto the rock ledge that preceded the entrance to the cavern.

Farryn did not speak any more; he just pointed his finger in a curve, indicating the ice wizard was around the corner.

I nodded and turned to peek.

I grasped the rock wall, and carefully stepped forward, turning my head to look into the cavern.

It was not a cavern at all. It was a deep, forest-filled gorge.

I blinked.

The gorge must have spanned several miles across. The trees growing there began near where we stood, and grew nearly sideways down the gorge slope, down into a miniature rain forest. I stared, trying to take it all in.

A rugged path stretched forward from where we stood, down the side of the gorge, and deep into the forest. I could see the whole thing from where I stood.

There was no sign of the ice wizard.

I turned back to the troupe and explained.

"Well where did he go?" Caroline asked. She turned to the gnome. "Farryn, where did he go?"

Farryn peeked around the corner, then returned.

"He was there two days ago. On the far side."

" 'On the far side'? Of what?" Håkan asked.

"Of that forest," Farryn answered.

"Of the …" Håkan looked exasperated. "Ye made it seem like he was right there around the corner. Not another day's journey through a new gorge and forest."

"Sorry." Farryn looked down at his shoes.

I took a deep breath. "Okay, okay, let's just go."

"What about the horses?" asked Christianne. "We can't just leave them there."

"I can take care of them," said Inge, standing up taller. "You can count on me."

I stared at him, then looked at Håkan, who shrugged. "I know Inge can do it. He takes care of the sheep for weeks at a time, way up in the hills."

"I guess that would be okay, Inge," I said. I glanced at Tupu and Caroline and Khepri, who nodded and shrugged.

I looked back at Inge and nodded.

He turned and began his trek back across the rope bridge.

Chapter Nineteen

Alpine Forest

"Okay, I think we'll hike down to the forest floor and then wait until daylight to approach the ice wizard," I said softly, still thinking of Inge and Shêtân.

"Let's get moving, then," Tam said, leading the way down the path.

The walls of the gorge were massive and rose hundreds of feet into the air, maybe thousands.

"How high do you think that is," I whispered, motioning to the rock sides.

"Oh, at least a thousand feet." said Khepri. "Maybe two thousand."

It was almost an optical illusion. The hike down the path to the forest floor was so beguiling it was almost making me dizzy.

"Look forward, down to the ground that's ahead," Tupu said. "Do not look up. You'll lose your balance."

I took her advice and felt instantly better climbing down the jagged path. It turned out to be a few hundred feet down, and we passed a waterfall on our way.

"Farryn, is that new?" I whispered as we approached the roaring water.

He nodded.

So much is changing in my land, so much is thawing.

I worried it would get much worse before it could get any better.

Tam rubbed my shoulder from behind, and I instantly felt better. I glanced behind me at his smiling face, and felt reassured.

It took several hours to get to the forest below, but we finally stepped onto pine needles from the dirt-and-rock path.

I took a deep breath, inhaling the heady scent of the conifer forest.

Delicious.

The forest was so thick we had to turn sideways to get through some of the trees. This was a vast, untamed wood that had been undisturbed for a very long time. Birds and squirrels and rabbits flourished here, and seemed unafraid of us.

Farryn now rode on Tupu's back, his hands gripping her shoulders and his weight balanced on her pack. His eyes searched keenly ahead as we hiked, scanning the woodland for any sign of the ice wizard.

At one point, we came across a small, abandoned cottage.

"What the heck is this doing here?" I asked in a whisper.

Tam and Caroline and Håkan just shrugged. The others peered in the window.

I tried the door handle, and was surprised when the latch moved. I pushed the door open and looked inside.

"Ohhh! Books!" I whispered, stepping into the small room.

An old bed lay in the corner, its quilt covered with a heavy layer of dust. This dust also covered the desk and chair on the opposite wall, as well as the old, broken-down bookshelf. The fireplace in the corner looked forlorn and desolate.

"Maybe we can camp here, and continue in the morning, Charlotte?" Kym asked, looking over the objects on the desk.

"Maybe," I said quietly.

I turned to the mountain gnome, "Farryn, how much farther is the ice wizard?"

"Not far," Farryn answered.

"That could mean anything," Håkan said wryly.

"True," I responded.

We decided to camp in the old cottage for the night.

"Do you think it's okay to have a fire?" Caroline asked.

I turned to Farryn. "Well? will the smoke drifting up from the cottage's fireplace be noticed? Answer carefully, Farryn, our safety may be at stake."

"The ice wizard is still a long way away," said Farryn.

"I thought you said he was 'not far'?" said Khepri.

"Tupu explained how you measure distance, and now I understand," said the little gnome. "The ice wizard is farther away than we have already come since the rope bridge."

"Oh, my God," I said, plopping down on the dusty bed. A cloud of particles poofed up into the air, and I coughed.

Kym laughed, then began to cough herself.

"I found a broom!" called Tam, and began to sweep the cottage out.

Khepri, Caroline, Christianne, Kym and myself helped, and we had the dirt and grime out in ten minutes.

Håkan made a fire, from dry wood Olof brought in from the forest.

"This wood is so thick, I seriously question whether anyone would ever be able to even see the smoke," Olof said.

"Let's get some dinner started," said Caroline. "We still have rabbit meat."

"A stew sounds great!" Kym said, her stomach growling.

I smiled.

This was going to be okay.

That evening, we feasted on Caroline's good rabbit stew. She had added a few bulbs of garlic Christianne and Olof had found foraging in the forest, and it was delicious.

We'd spread our blankets out on the stone floor. It was not as comfortable as the dirt or forest floor, but at least we stayed dry.

I looked outside the window. It was beginning to drizzle again.

"I wonder how long this forest has been thawed out?" I mused.

"Likely fifty years, lass," said Håkan. "The trees look like they've been here longer, but they're evergreens, and grow just about everywhere in the northlands."

I turned to the bookcase on the far wall. It was tilting at an alarming angle.

"I fear if I touch it, it will collapse completely," I said.

"Probably," said Tam. "Here, look. There are books over here," he gestured to the old desk in the corner, and I walked over to it.

I bent to examine the different things strewn about the work space. "Hmmm, this is interesting." I sat down to look closer at the various books.

There were maybe a half dozen books of various sizes strewn about the top. I picked up the first one, and brushed the dust off the cover.

The book was heavy and bound in green leather. It had ornate tooling across the front, and someone had meticulously carved an oak tree onto it, each leaf outlined in detail. I opened the cover and began leafing through the pages.

It was a detailed accounting of plants. Each page noted their shape and size and applications to spells and enchantments, and even recipes. On each facing page was an intricate painting of the plant, the whole thing, as well as a few leaves depicted in greater detail.

I wondered if the book was a glossary of all the flora found in this forest. Such a book would be very valuable.

Khepri walked to stand next to me, and read over my shoulder. Her eyebrows went up in surprise after a few minutes.

I smiled, and handed her the book, which she took eagerly and began to peruse herself.

I turned back to the dusty desk and picked up another book. This one was smaller, bound in brown leather, and the tooling on the covers depicted a strange flying animal, which I did not recognize. It looked large, with wide wings that expanded outward a great distance. The animal's face was of an almost bird-like quality, even though the wings looked more bat-like than bird-like. For one thing, there were no feathers.

I opened this book and saw it was full of paintings of the same animal depicted on the cover. The paintings looked like whoever had crafted them had a great love for the animal. They showed the creature in various poses, and I could tell some of them had been inside this very cabin. I glanced up and looked at the fireplace and the window, then glanced back down and saw the same features in some of the paintings. The fireplace had a special design across the mantle, and very distinctive. I recognized it immediately.

Some of the paintings showed the flying animal sleeping, perched on some kind of rod suspended above the table. The animal had its beak-like face tucked under a wing, and looked very calm and content.

Another few pictures were of the animal outside, two paintings had it perched in a tree, on a low branch. Another three were paintings of it soaring in the sky. I got a feel of its size from these outdoor paintings, and it was big. Bigger than Farryn.

I flipped through the book of paintings and came across one of an arm and hand reaching out to stroke the creature's wings. The animal was leaning into the hand that was petting it, and I was reminded of a cat enjoying a caress.

This artist has captured his love for this creature perfectly.

I looked around the cottage again, feeling sad I could not meet them both in person. But they were probably both long since passed away.

I sighed, feeling melancholy.

Khepri had taken the flora book and settled herself on her blanket by the fire, and was poring over it, her head bent in concentration.

I would not be surprised if she brought the book with her, in her pack.

I looked back onto the desk, then rose and wandered outside. The porch was small and the overhang short, but there was just enough room for me to stand outside the door and watch the rain fall.

I saw an abundance of mushrooms growing off to the side, and profusion of ferns growing in wild abandon, dipping their fronds as the rain fell on them.

The smell coming from the forest was fantastic. It was a loamy, delicious scent that made me want to stay there forever.

My thoughts wandered to my parents. My mother, the queen, was the strong one, always a great ruler. She was firm in her rule, but kind and gentle to those less fortunate.

I thought of my conversation with the old man, Elias, in the stable back at the castle. And of the girl Märta, who had been abducted along with the others. And of her mother, Tuva, killed trying to help her daughter. I felt sad they hadn't been noticed by the duchesses as they focused their attention on the queen and prince's abduction.

Tam opened the door and step cut next to me.

"How are you doing, Charlotte?" He kissed my cheek and then my neck, and I shivered.

"Oh, I was just thinking of all those others the ice wizard had abducted." I turned to look at Tam. "Anya and Tilde hadn't even taken notice of them when they told us how my parents had been stolen." I wiped away a tear.

"I think," said Tam, "that the job of ruling a kingdom is very hard, and it fell on their shoulders very suddenly. And they are older, and probably not very closely in tune with the people. I don't think they meant to be malicious or insensitive in their blindness of what happened." He thought for a minute, then continued. "I would very definitely question the Royal Counsel and Master of Whisperers and possible discharge them both. To ignore the loss of seventeen abducted citizens is not only callous and cruel, it is grossly negligent."

I nodded. "You are wise, Tam. I will instruct my mother to address these issues. Such people on staff is a huge detriment to the castle and royal household, and the kingdom itself."

I put my hand out, palm up, to catch a few raindrops.

"This woodland is so beautiful and untouched, it is a privilege to be here," said Tam. "It feels like paradise."

"Mmmm, it does, it does," I answered. "I am especially bewitched by the scents of the forest." I inhaled deeply, closing my eyes and savoring the moment as I leaned back against Tam's strong chest.

I placed my hand onto my midsection, and thought of the baby inside.

Tam kissed my shoulder. "Have you felt the quickening yet?" He murmured.

"Not yet," I sighed. "I am not even sure I have begun to grow thicker."

Tam bent and put his hand across my belly, and leaned forward. He opened my leather armor there and parted the shirt underneath. Lowering his lips to my belly, he hummed.

"Hmmmmmmm. Hello Baby!" Tam hummed.

I giggled.

He pressed his lips down and blew a long raspberry.

"PBBLLLTTTT!"

I laughed. "Oh, Tam, you're tickling me!"

I smiled and reach my hand down to caress his rough bearded cheek.

"Let's go inside," I whispered.

Tam stood up. "It *is* getting colder." He looked out at the forest. "I can even imagine it snowing here. Maybe it does, in the winter."

He pushed the door open and gestured with his hand. "After you, M'lady."

I grinned and walked back into the cottage.

Khepri was still bent over the book she was studying.

Håkan was deep in conversation with Jim, over by the leaning bookcase.

Christianne and Kym were playing a game together, their hands bouncing in time to a rhyme they were reciting.

Caroline and Tupu were at the bed, examining the old tattered quilt that covered it. Caroline was pointing to the sewing and Tupu was saying how she wanted to get better at making clothes, so she could make a new outfit for Aaaqil, because he was growing so fast.

Olof was tending the fire and putting a new log on. He straightened and saw Tam and me, and nodded to us seriously, then wandered over to where Kym and Christianne sat, and watched them.

"I'm going to sharpen my sword, Babe," Tam said, giving my cheek a kiss.

I nodded and wandered back over to the dusty desk.

I was curious to see what else lay there, waiting to be discovered.

I sat down and looked at the remaining books. There were four others scattered on the desk, and I reached for the nearest one and opened its cover.

A spider fell out.

"Oh!" I cried softly, involuntarily, and brushed the dead arachnid away. It fell to the ground. I turned back to the book it had fallen out of.

"Ohhh," I murmured. The book was a museum of different insect specimens, all flattened and pressed, and quite deflated of all life. Most of them had been affixed in some fashion.

It looks like sap.

I leaned closer to examine one particularly beautiful iridescent blue butterfly that had been pressed into the book. A yellowing substance had been used, at several points of the outer wings, to fix it in place.

I studied the intricate cells of the wings.

Even though this butterfly was last alive many years ago, its wings were still brilliantly colored. I wondered what substance in its wings gave it such a color. It almost glowed.

I turned the page, but the rest of the book was empty.

Perhaps the owner started the project late in life, and could not finish it.

I closed the book and set it aside, and picked up the next one.

This book was a dark red, and I opened it to find a plethora of stew and meal recipes. There was a partition in the middle of the book, and then a new title page with the script, *"Meals for Tara"*. I wondered who Tara was, that she had had the love of the author so keenly that they had written up recipes they thought might tempt her.

I felt a twinge of envy for this Tara. To have the love of someone so strongly, was a deep treasure and a blessing.

I flipped through the pages of recipes for Tara, and felt confused. The recipes were odd, the proportions huge. I wondered how much this Tara actually ate.

"Must have been an eager eater," I murmured, closing the book.

The second to the last book was another book with flattened, preserved insects, and this one was full.

"Ah, this must be Volume One." I said to myself.

This book had a plethora of butterflies and moths, stinging insects and also ants.

So many ants.

Some of the ants stuck in the pages were quite large. One was nearly to width of my palm, and a bright red color.

I shivered, feeling an imaginary ants crawl across my shoulder.

Don't be silly, Charlotte.

I put the book aside and reached for the last tome.

This one was dark brown, and bound in leather like the others. The difference here was that this book had tooling that looked like a portrait. Unfortunately, it had been under the weight of the other books, and the figure depicted in profile was barely discernible. I brushed my hand across the face, wondering who it was a likeness of, and how their life had been.

Had they a happy life? A fulfilling life?

I hoped so.

I opened the book and saw it was a diary.

I felt embarrassed and closed it again, looking up to see if anyone had caught me about to read an old diary, then felt foolish doing so.

Then I felt guilty again.

I sighed.

Secrets are secrets, after all, Charlotte.

I wanted to respect the owner of the diary, and felt I should, being a polite person.

But then I wondered what things of importance could be revealed by a hundred-year-old diary.

I sat there, my curiosity warring with my natural dignity and esteem for another's secrets.

The fire crackled and popped.

I thought about it, then slowly opened the diary and turned it to the first page.

My shoulders fell. It was a detailed account of the writer's trip to the market.

Eggs, spices, mhmmm. Oh! A chicken! They had bought a chicken.

I closed the book, then noticed something just inside the cover as it fell into place.

I lifted the front cover again and looked closely. The writing was faded, but I could just make out the words, *Property of E.O. Spinesetter, Esq.*

Chapter Twenty

The Ice Wizard

We were up early the next day and ready to hike.

"I think we'll see the ice wizard today, for sure," Kym said, excited.

"Don't be so eager to meet him, Kym," Christianne said. "He's a very dangerous creature, and not a good person,"

"He's a damned kidnapper and murderer," I said.

"I know, I know, I'm just eager to get to him," said Kym. "He's hurt someone I love, and I want to rend him to pieces."

"Awww," I smiled and hugged the little girl. She grinned and squeezed my middle tightly.

"Okay, let's head out," I said. I had been thinking of my parents the whole night, and I couldn't wait to find them.

"Where's Farryn?" Khepri asked.

Oh, no.

"Here I am," the little mountain gnome called from the woodbin next to the fireplace. He emerged and brushed himself off. "What a wonderful feast last night! I slept so well!" he said. "Let's go get your parents, Princess Charlotte!"

I just stared at him. He grinned back at me. I finally laughed. "Okay, let's go," I said, opening the door of the old cabin and walking out into the woods.

It was a fine, fresh day. Birds sang in the trees, and early morning mist rose from the forest floor, promising a warm day ahead.

We hiked through the forest on an animal path Farryn insisted was the way he had come. He continued to ride on Tupu's back, sitting on the top of her pack, his hands on her shoulders, his head above the warrior's, watching everything, scouting the path from this vantage point.

The path Farryn guided us on led through the deep forest for several hours, and when we came out the other side, it was up against the other side of the enormous rock face of the inner side of the gorge.

We climbed up and up and up, Farryn practically jumping up and down on Tupu's back in his eagerness. He insisted we were close.

And we were, but not in the way I imagined.

I'd just emerged on a high ledge alongside Tupu and Jim, and I turned to help Tam up. The last step was hard, and a helping hand was always welcome when you were hiking.

"Look," Farryn pointed.

I stared.

He directed my eyes toward a small tunnel through the rock, barely big enough to fit us if we crouched. As I peered inside, I could see a faint light.

Was it an optical illusion?

"Farryn, is that ...?" I began.

"That's the other side. It comes out near the top of a waterfall. From there you can see the ice wizard's lair," Farryn explained.

I crouched and looked again, dubious.

"Let me go first," Kym said.

"Good idea," said Farryn. "She's the smallest."

"The smallest, and yet the largest," Tam murmured, winking at Kym, who grinned.

She ducked her head just inside the rock tunnel, then turned around. "It's not so bad, see?"

I nodded, "Go on, Kym. Be careful. I'll be right behind you."

She nodded and started down the tunnel.

I crouched and stepped in after her.

The rock tunnel was covered in moss and vines for at least a dozen feet in. The sunlight reached through the passageway and lit the way, so torches were unnecessary, at least during the day. We stepped over the small stream that trickled down the middle of the rock tunnel, and moisture ran off the walls of the tunnel to join the flow, until it grew to more than a foot across.

Halfway through, I could hear the waterfall. It was a loud, roaring sound that echoed up inside the rock, making discussion impossible to hear.

After climbing through the tunnel for more than fifteen minutes, I emerged on the other side.

Kym was standing to the side, on a wet granite ledge that looked like it would crumble at any minute.

"Careful," I said, pointing.

Kym nodded to me, and I realized she saw my mouth move, but couldn't hear me over the sound of the waterfall.

All of us gathered just outside the rock tunnel, and Farryn pointed.

I followed the direction of his arm and couldn't see anything but forest and white glinting reflections. I made a *huh?* gesture with my arms and he motioned for me to crouch down to his level, then pointed again.

I squinted.

I could just make out a dark form halfway down the side of the mountain. It was obscured by the vast forest cover and the reflective shine.

What was that?

But it was as Farryn had promised: the cavern of the ice wizard.

I turned and looked at Tam, who nodded.

He had seen it, too.

I felt a thrill. We were finally in sight of the place where my parents were being held.

I stood and took a deep breath, and smiled, and heard a massive whine as a missile whizzed past my ear and exploded on the rock face next to me.

"TAKE COVER!" Jim screamed, and grabbed my arm, pulling me back into the rock tunnel.

What is happening?

Three more missiles flew at us. One of them made it inside the tunnel and hit Jim on the side of his head.

He went down.

"OH GOD! BACK UP! BACK UP! BACK UP!" Tam yelled, trying to drag Jim's huge body farther back into the tunnel.

It was hard because the large man had fallen into the stream. The bottom of the tunnel, under the stream, was a rocky, craggy, uneven surface.

Håkan grabbed Jim's tunic and I grabbed one of his legs. Tupu had his other leg, and the four of us were able to pick him up and move him a dozen feet back.

"What happened?" I said.

"Farryn looked scared. "That's him," he said, backing up behind Tupu.

"That's the ice wizard?" Tam asked. "What was he throwing at us?"

"He's throwing the bombs," Farryn said.

"THOSE WERE BOMBS?" Caroline exclaimed.

Half a dozen more missiles came flying into the tunnel, hitting the walls and ceiling.

I looked closely at the residue one of the things made when it hit the wall beside me. I touched my fingers to it. It was snow, but hyper-cold snow. The crystals burned my fingers where they touched. I noticed bits of rock embedded in it.

Great.

"We need to back up more," Tam said.

"We need to check Jim's head, where that snowball bomb hit," I said.

Khepri was already crouched beside Jim's still form.

"All right, pick him up." I grabbed Jim's leg.

"Up," Tam said, lifting Jim's shoulder.

Håkan and Tupu grabbed Jim's other leg and arm, and we pulled him back, deep into the tunnel, at least fifty feet.

I swung on Farryn, "I thought we could sneak up on this ice wizard."

"The ice dryads spotted us. That's what I was pointing to!"

Huh?

"Those reflective lights, Charlotte," said Khepri. "I saw them, too. I just didn't recognize what they were."

"I thought those were crystals or something."

"Or water."

"Yeah, I thought they were water, too."

"I thought they were patches of snow."

"Snow? In a warm forest?"

"Well, it was snowing on us just yesterday."

"The weather has been so crazy, they *could* have been snow."

"They were not snow, though."

"They were ice dryads?"

"Farryn!"

"Farryn, you should have warned us."

"The princess said that Elias had told her of the ice dryads. I thought you knew what to look for." Farryn spread his hands in confusion.

"Oh, for gods' sake," said Håkan, sitting and holding his head.

I knelt down next to Jim and turned to Khepri. "How is he?"

"He'll live," said Khepri grimly, "but he'll have a whopper of a headache when he wakes up."

"Wake him. This is an emergency," I said in a clipped tone.

I swung on Farryn and took his arm, speaking in a quiet, steely voice. "From now on, I want a warning of anything and everything that could possibly happen. Pretend we're children and know nothing about this place. Understand me?" I stared into his face, my lips pressed together.

He nodded.

"This could have resulted in great injury. Or death," I stared at him unblinkingly. "You will not make this mistake again." I squeezed his arm for emphasis.

The mountain gnome gulped and nodded again.

I turned to the mouth of the rock tunnel and the source of the snowball bombs beyond.

"Who threw the snowballs?" I asked Farryn.

"I hope it was the ice dryads," he said.

I turned around. "Why do you hope it was the ice dryads?"

"Because if it was the wizard, he'll be coming. ... He doesn't give up easily." Farryn answered.

What?

More snowball bombs whizzed down the tunnel, falling short of us, but making a loud stinging noise as they hit the stream.

"Uh oh," Farryn said.

"Tam, ready your bow," I said quietly.

"In these close quarters, I cannot promise ..." Tam said.

"Ready. Your. Bow."

I drew my scimitar, bumping my arm on the side of the rock tunnel.

"You'd be better off fighting in the open," Farryn mumbled.

"What?" I said.

"You'd better hurry," Farryn said quietly.

WHIZZ WHIZZ WHIZZ WHIZZ WHIZZ

I looked up. The circle of light at the end of the tunnel was obscured.

"He's here," Farryn whispered.

Tam let loose an arrow. It hit the rock side with a *ping!*

This is not going to work.

Jim was coming to.

"Ahhhh," he groaned.

"We need to get out of this tunnel," I said. "NOW."

Khepri pulled Jim's arm; he got to his feet, and stumbled down the tunnel.

We began to run back, as snow bombs flew toward us in rapid succession.

One hit my pack and knocked me forward. "OW!" I could feel the freezing cold of the thing, even though it hasn't hit me directly.

I crouched and ran.

"Babe, I'm right behind you," Tam said from behind.

WHIZZ WHIZZ WHIZZ WHIZZ

"OWW!" Kym screamed, more in anger than pain. She stopped and turned her head back to the advancing ice wizard, glowering.

I grabbed her arm and pulled her forward again.

"Kym, no. There's not enough room in here," I said in a low voice.

"There would be after I was done," she grumbled.

"You can't move the whole mountain," I said.

"Wanna bet?"

"Just come on. I want to do this in the open," I said.

We ran, crouching, all the way back to the rock tunnel entrance, and poured out onto the forest.

"Spread out!" I called.

"Way ahead of you," said Håkan.

"Let's get ready," Tupu cried.

More snowball bombs were whizzing out of the tunnel. They flew harmlessly into the trees.

We waited.

The rock tunnel exploded outward with a loud roar, spraying shards of stone out into the forest.

We ducked and put our arms up to shield our faces.

The ice wizard emerged.

Oh, my god.

He was no bigger than Farryn.

A tiny man, dressed all in white and blue, his face a glacial white, his hair like blue ice, jumped out of the exploded tunnel, and landed there, fuming.

He pulled his arm back in a wind-up to throw something, and when it was behind him, a frozen snowball bomb appeared in his hand. He brought his arm forward in a swift fling and threw it out at the forest.

We had crouched behind trees and bushes.

Coming out of the darker rock tunnel, the ice wizard was momentarily blinded by the bright sun, and didn't see us.

More figures emerged out of the rock tunnel, and came to stand behind the ice wizard.

The ice dryads.

I stared.

The figures were tall and thin, and looked like they were made of ice. Dark, slitted eyes glared out at the forest. One of them bent low to whisper in the ice wizard's ear.

The small creature whirled around and slapped at the ice dryad, who backed up a step. Then the wizard turned to the forest and held out his hands.

"Oh, no," Farryn mumbled. "Duck, everyone."

The ice wizard's finger began blowing frost onto the forest, freezing the trees, the leaves, the birds, everything.

We crouched behind the trees, and I watched as the frost hit the trunks and ice crystals began moving to cover their entire length. I'd had my hand on one of them, and lifted my fingers off the tree just in time.

Tam peeked out from behind the tree next to me and let loose several arrows.

One went right through the tall ice dryad standing behind the ice wizard. One hit the rock wall behind the ice wizard. But two hit the wizard square in the chest.

He looked down at the two wood shafts sticking out from his torso.

They began to change color to icy blue. As soon as the transformation was complete, the arrows shattered and fell out of his chest.

"Great. It took me half a day to craft each of those," Tam mumbled.

The ice wizard was unleashing his snow bombs at a furious pace. The air was filled with them. They hit the frozen trees and leaves and branches, and the trunks of the trees crackled ominously at the impact.

"Exactly how many bombs did you and the other gnomes make?" I whispered to Farryn.

"Uhhh, I think ... we were making them for the last few years, with only a little time to sleep and hardly any food. So, a lot," Farryn said.

"And how many other gnomes work for the ice wizard?" I asked, ducking as a snowball bombs landed close to me.

"At least a few hundred. I never counted. Maybe a thousand. Maybe more," Farryn answered.

So millions. Millions upon millions of snowball bombs.

SIGH.

"And my parents," I whispered. "They are in that dark cavern you pointed out? When we were at the waterfall?"

Farryn nodded.

I stared at the ice wizard, thinking.

I noticed he had stopped throwing snowball bombs. He was conferring with the ice dryads in whispers.

"WIZARD!" I called out. "WE ARE NOT AFRAID OF YOU! WE ARE NOT AFRAID OF THE COLD!"

I heard Farryn groan.

I ducked back down.

"You shouldn't have said that," Farryn whispered.

"Why not? I'm tired of this creature. Tired of him, tired of his stupid bombs, tired of this whole day," I whispered back. "Tired, tired, tired." I glowered. "And I want my parents back."

"What's that?" Tam whispered.

I heard a strange crackling sound. It grew louder by the second until it was a roaring.

I felt a blast of heat on my head.

"FIRE! THAT MANIAC HAS SET THE FOREST ON FIRE!" Khepri screamed.

I looked. The ice wizard had his arms stretched out again and pointed to the mountain above us. The treetops were on fire. Great plumes of black smoke rose and hit the cavern ceiling, roiling out to the valley.

I heard a loud roaring noise.

This is new.

"AVALANCHE!" Håkan cried.

"RUN!" Tupu screamed.

I looked up the rock wall of the mountain and saw a wall of water and rock flowing down it, coming straight for us.

Chapter Twenty-One
Avalanche

We ran, forgetting all about the ice wizard. We ran for our lives, stumbling and tumbling down the slope of the forest, gaining speed as we jumped down.

"Water! The water is coming!" I heard Caroline cry.

I glanced back. The avalanche, the rocks and the water together, was barreling down the mountain. The larger boulders hit the trees, some with such force they shattered some of them, spraying shards of still-frozen wood out into the forest.

I grabbed onto a tree branch and swung down onto the ground below, then jumped and tumbled farther down, my feet carrying me fast down the mountainside.

"Charlotte!" Khepri called.

I looked back and saw she was stuck in a tree with Christianne.

"KHEPRI!" I tried to climb back up to her, but too many rocks and trees and now WATER came tumbling down.

"I'VE GOT HER," Håkan cried.

The djinn rose up in the air, and flew back to Khepri.

I clung to a heavy tree trunk and climbed up to the first branch, to watch.

Håkan had gotten to them, and was holding fast to Khepri's arm, but the water was coming down hard and he couldn't jump down. He would be swept away. The tree the three clung to started tilting dangerously.

The djinn flew up to them and grabbed Christianne and Khepri, and Håkan hung on to the djinn's huge purple arm. The large djinn then turned and flew to the side and down, and disappeared around the corner.

I looked down. The avalanche was now mostly water and forest flotsam; a few branches and small rocks tumbled down as well.

"COME ON, BABE!" Tam was there, reaching for my arm. "WE HAVE TO JUMP NOW, OR IT'LL BE TOO LATE!"

I looked down. The rushing water was coming faster and faster.

"Help!" I heard Olof cry out. He was stuck in a tree farther down, clinging desperately to the trunk. Caroline and Tupu were next to him. Farryn gripped Tupu's back and was holding on for dear life. They stared up at us, panic in their eyes.

"HERE!" Kym called from another tree, and transformed into the chimera.

She grew huge, and stood there beside a tree, her massive leonine legs planted firmly in the rushing water.

"OW!" The chimera cried as a large rock hit her leg. She turned and, bunching her hindquarters, leaped over to the tree where Olof, Caroline, and Tupu were stranded.

"GET ON!" she cried, and the three clambered up onto her back, gripping her lion hair and mane tightly as the chimera pivoted and turned to jump.

The chimera turned to look up at Tam and me.

"JUMP!"

It was about ten feet, but it was downstream and off to the side, and we had no other chance.

We jumped.

I landed on the tree branch where Olof had been, grabbing it with both hands and climbing onto it.

Tam was not so lucky. He landed at the base of the tree, half in the water.

"AH!" he cried, crumpling to the ground and holding his ankle.

The chimera reached down, grabbing Tam's pack in her teeth and lifting him out of the water.

"COME ON, MISS!" Caroline called, patting the back of the chimera behind her.

I jumped, landing on my stomach across the chimera's rump.

I pulled myself up and moved my boot over her back, and held on.

It was wet, and I immediately began to slip to the side.

I felt a strong, muscled limb wrap itself around my waist and pull me back on, and I glanced down and jumped a foot when I realized it was the large snake growing out of the chimera's hindquarters.

"AH!"

"I've got you, Charlotte," the chimera said from her lion's mouth. "And despite what you think, believe it or not, that's still me."

I stared at the snake head, its glittering eyes watching me, its forked tongue flickering in and out of its mouth. It winked at me. I grinned and nodded.

"Jumping down now," the chimera called, bunching up her hindquarters.

She leapt into the air and across the avalanche, landing on the hillside a few feet from the moving water and rocks. She pivoted and leapt again. this time landing on another small hillside.

This time, her goat hooves landed in water, and the earth gave way as her weight came down on it.

She scrambled with her hind legs but was pulled into the rushing watery avalanche.

We hung on.

The chimera was swept backward, dragging her forelegs in the flow, trying to slow her momentum.

But she couldn't.

We were pulled along the avalanche, unable to stop our momentum. The chimera flicked her head, tossing Tam onto her back, where he landed between Caroline and me. He looked very surprised, but none the worse for wear. I wrapped my arms around his waist, kissing the back of his neck.

Thank goodness the chimera was so strong. She seemed irritated but unharmed, except for bumps and bruises.

We were swept back to the forest floor. Then the flow turned the corner and we were swept sideways, and more water joined us, and we began moving faster.

"WATCH OUT!" I heard Caroline scream.

I looked and saw we were headed toward a large chasm, gaping at us like an open mouth in the earth.

OH NO!

The chimera had seen it, too. She began scrambling in earnest, shifting to the side a bit, but unable to stop her forward momentum.

We were going to fall.

Right before we got to the chasm, the chimera jumped again, purely out of desperation.

We sprang forward a couple dozen yards, but the avalanche was coming down faster than ever, and we were swept right back to where we were before.

Then we went down.

We fell into the chasm backward. The chimera held on until the last moment, and to her credit, she stayed upright the entire time, so we wouldn't fall off.

The avalanche poured down into the chasm, and we went with it, the river of water, dirt and flotsam carrying us down and through.

We hit the bottom with a huge SPLASH! and the chimera sputtered for a few seconds, scrambling to regain her footing. She tried, she really tried.

But it was not to be.

We were now partially underground, being swept along by a river of water, curving back and forth as it flowed.

The water is getting deeper.

There was still a lot of forest debris in the water, but rocks and trees no longer moved alongside us. It was just branches, dirt, leaves, and water. Lots and lots of water.

Thank goodness the chimera floated. She acted like a boat, with five very odd passengers.

It took a long time to wash out of the chasm, and our journey carried us over a mile.

The chimera's legs finally found purchase, and she wearily crawled to the edge of the avalanche river.

The flotsam flowed out of sight.

We sat on the embankment, the chasm having opened up into a huge cavern. I stared at the cathedral ceiling above me. The way we had come was open to the surface, but downstream, the water emptied into a cavern larger than any I'd ever seen. We sat on the edge, uncomfortably close to where the flood emptied into the depths of the cavern.

"Good thing you were able to get out," Tam said. "It looks like another drop over there."

The chimera lay on the embankment, her eyes half closed, her breath slow.

I got up and sat down next to her, my hand on her paw.

"Hey, you okay?" I asked.

"Yeah, I'm okay," she said softly. "Just need to rest a bit."

I patted her and lay my cheek against her chest.

"Thank you for saving our lives," I whispered.

We lay there for a few minutes.

Then I heard Farryn talking with Caroline, and I raised my head to listen.

"... prisoners ...cavern ..."

"Huh?" I sat up. "Farryn, what did you say?"

Caroline turned to me. "Miss, we are near the cavern where the queen and prince are being held."

WHAT?

I stood up, and walked to the edge, where the cavern fell away. I couldn't see much, but the space below looked vast.

"Farryn," I called over my shoulders. "Can you come here, please?"

The little man stepped next to me. and held on to my leg for support.

"Are you okay?" I asked, looking down.

"I'm just a bit wobbly is all," said the gnome. "Just a bit wobbly."

He fell against me.

"Oh, my," I said, scooping him up in my arms. "I don't think you are ready to travel anywhere."

"Perhaps not," he said weakly.

I carried him back to the embankment, and set him down next to the chimera.

Caroline, Olof, Tupu, and Tam came to sit next to us.

I rubbed the gnome's back.

"I know we've been through a lot today," I said.

Farryn closed his eyes, enjoying the back rub.

I looked at Caroline and shrugged.

Tam examined the chimera. "Can you change back to human, honey? I think you might feel better."

The chimera nodded her massive leonine head and closed her eyes, concentrating. She shimmered and shrunk down to human form.

"I'm just exhausted," Kym said weakly. "That was a heck of a thing."

"It was," Tam said.

"Farryn," I said. "Exactly how close are we to the cavern where the ice wizard is holding my parents?"

Farryn nodded, and opened his eyes. "It's just beyond that wall," he said, pointing to the far wall of the cavern.

"Do you think the others got out?" Tupu said in a quiet voice.

I glanced at her and put my hand out to cover hers.

"I'm sure Jim got them to safety. He was flying fast, and he's got a huge rescuer complex." I grinned.

"Ha ha! That's true, that's very true." Tupu shook her head. "I don't know why I worry so much."

"You worry because you love him," Caroline said softly.

Tupu nodded. "I do, I really do. Very much."

"Well, wherever he is, I'm sure Khepri, Christianne, and Håkan are safe with him," I said. "Remember how weak he felt in the ice cave last year? After carrying us all up that ice cliff? He had to rest for a couple days." I looked at Kym. "I think he may have to rest now, at least for a few hours. Overnight, maybe. And Kym needs rest, too." I patted Kym's small arm.

"Maybe we should camp here, then tackle the other cavern in the morning," Tam said.

I looked farther up the way we'd come. The earth was open to the sky a hundred feet up, so the daylight still reached us. "We'll be able to tell when the sun sets, and when it rises again."

"We're all wet through and through, too," said Caroline. "I'm going to build a fire." She looked around.

"Out of what? Everything's soaked," Tupu said.

"You can use Solace roots," said Farryn. "They burn even when wet." He pointed above us, and I looked up.

The walls and ceiling where we sat were covered in curling black roots. I looked closer. Something shimmered on the black.

What was that?

I rose and drew my dagger from my boot.

Walking over, I grabbed one of the curling black roots. It was an inch or two thick, and, looking closely at it, I saw it was flecked black and brown, with white specks.

I turned to Farryn. "What kind of tree is this?"

"Oh, it's not a tree, it's a kind of mycelium," Farryn answered.

"You're kidding," I turned back to the curling root. I tugged on it, but it held fast.

"Try your knife," said Farryn. "But be careful, it's full of ..."

Too late.

I brought my dagger up and sliced against the black curling root. It parted, and sprayed my face with spores.

I sputtered and spit, trying to get the stuff out of my mouth.

I turned to Farryn. "Is this stuff poisonous?"

"No. In fact, it's good chopped and roasted," he said.

I spent the next ten minutes hacking away at the curling black roots with my sword. Olof helped me gather the roots and bring them back to where Caroline was building a fire. She had set the roots three feet from where Kym was resting, so she wouldn't have to move.

Tam strung a rope across the side, near the fire, and draped our blankets and spare clothes on it. They were soon drying, with white wisps of steam slowly drifting off them.

I built a fire with the Solace roots. Farryn was right: They burned very well.

I dragged a large branch out of the water and brought it close to the flames to dry out, in case we needed wood on the fire.

Caroline soon had a meal bubbling in a pot, created out of leftovers, roots and veggies she carried in her bag. Thank goodness she hadn't lost it in the avalanche.

An hour or two later, our blankets and clothes were dry, and we were able to arrange the blankets and bed down for the night.

It was good to be on solid ground again. Lying back, I watched the daylight dim and vanish a hundred feet above my head.

Chapter Twenty-Two
New Magic

The next morning, Kym was sitting up and feeling much better. We let the fire die out, packed everything, and began our journey down to the cavern wall.

"I hope we meet up with the others soon," Kym said. "It feels better when we're together."

Farryn pointed to the far side, and we hiked down to the rock face. It looked impenetrable. I turned to Farryn, a questioning look in my eyes.

He smiled and motioned for us to follow.

He led us down fifty feet, and then disappeared.

I blinked, hurrying my step to where I last saw him.

Farryn poked his head back into view and waved.

"Hold up, will you?"

We all hiked to where Farryn gestured. It was a passageway between the two caverns, with room enough for us to slip through. With Farryn leading the way, we walked along the rock, following the passageway, which turned and turned again, folding back on itself before curving again the other way, then straightening out, and finally, opening out into the second cavern.

This new cavern was huge. I couldn't see the roof or the far walls.

"Where does the ice wizard stay?" I whispered to Farryn.

"Back at the other side," said the mountain gnome. "That's where he's holding all the prisoners, too."

I nodded, then gestured for the others to follow us.

We hiked along the side of the rock face, following an old trail. The cavern was full of sounds; drips and creaks and rocks tumbling.

Hiking uphill was hard work, but the far wall finally came into view.

We could see a large spray of solid ice, blue and opaque, and a dark recess in the rock, about fifty feet from where we stood.

I stared at the massive blue ice-covered wall. It was dozens of feet across.

Dark figures were barely visible through the pale, opaque blue ice. I squinted, trying to make out the faces.

"That's the prisoners," Farryn whispered beside me as we lay on our bellies on the ledge, peeking over the top.

I nodded.

We all watched the wizard's ice dryads move about. They looked solid when they were on the ground, like skinny blue-white wisps of figures. When they became airborne, they looked like smoke.

Or mist.

I wondered if the mists on the moors had been dryads. There was no way to tell. An ice dryad could hide in the thick natural mist that rose from the marshy ground, hiding inside the fog.

I shivered.

"Yeah, they're very creepy," Farryn whispered.

"Where is the ice wizard?" I asked.

"Not sure," said Farryn. "He might be checking out the other gnomes in the quarry."

"Quarry?" I asked.

"Down that way," Farryn pointed. It's a deep gorge that is frozen solid with frost. We dug into it to make the bombs."

"Okay. I just wish we knew where he was," I whispered. "It's got me worried. He could be anywhere."

As if fate had heard us, the ice wizard strode into view. A mountain gnome, taller than the wizard, followed behind him. He was close, maybe thirty-five feet away. I strained, trying to hear what he was saying.

"I need to find that human," the ice wizard said. "It is near, I can feel it."

"Yes, sire," his assistant said.

"It is the old magic. It calls to me." The ice wizard began to pace, his nose down, as if trying to scent out his prey.

I ducked my head even lower, worried he would somehow know we were up on the ledge.

A ball of fear suddenly formed in my stomach, and grew worse with every passing moment.

I looked back at the others.

They returned my gaze expectantly.

I scooted back, pressing my body against the rock wall, far out of sight, and motioned for the others to follow me. We all moved back a dozen feet.

"Okay," I whispered, ignoring the apprehension I felt. "I think the prisoners are inside that wall of ice down there. The wizard only appears to have one ice dryad with him, but," I glanced at Farryn, "I believe more are nearby."

Farryn nodded.

"And I understand there are over a thousand gnomes nearby. They could also show up at any minute," I whispered.

"I think we should move in fast, then," Tam whispered. "Catch him by surprise."

"Are you sure we can best him, though?" whispered Tupu. "I mean, he wields both ice and fire in his hands."

"I think if we rush him, and *grab his hands*," I whispered. "Restrain him, somehow, from using his magic ..."

The others fell silent, thinking, so I followed their lead and stopped whispering.

That's when I heard it.

Click ~ click ~ click ~ click ~ click

I looked over my shoulder and all around us, and saw nothing.

I looked at Farryn, and saw a look of terror on his face.

"*What is it?*" I mouthed, soundless.

Farryn buried his face in his hands, shaking.

Tam touched me on the shoulder, making a motion that we should attack now, before more dryads appeared.

I nodded, trying to ignore the sound, and my own misgivings.

I rose to a crouch with the others, and turned to jump down off the landing, looking back to the floor where the ice wizard had been.

He was gone.

I looked around wildly, but did not see him.

Click ~ click ~ click ~ click ~ click

I finally looked above us, and there he was.

The ice wizard was standing sideways, at the top of the rock wall above the ledge where we had been hiding.

I could feel the color draining from my face.

"Jump!" I cried, running and launching myself off the ledge and onto the ground. I ran as fast as I could toward the wall of ice.

Tam and Tupu got there ahead of me. Olof, Caroline, and Kym were right behind me.

Even Farryn jumped with us, wanting nothing to do with the ice wizard.

I ran up to the wall of ice and pressed my hand against it.

It burned. It burned so badly I jerked my hand away.

"AHHH!"

I stared at the palm and fingers of my hand. They were bright red.

Just like the snowball bombs.

"God, what is WITH this place?" I slammed my hand against the ice wall, then kicked at it with my boot. I stared inside. I could just make out the face of the queen, frozen in place.

"Mother ..."

Tears ran down my face.

"Uh, Charlotte?" Tupu nudged me.

I turned.

She was in a crouch, her sword held at the ready. So was Tam. And Caroline, and Kym.

Olof had a sharp knife in one hand, the other balled in a fist, ready to strike.

The ice wizard walked down the wall, defying gravity, and hopped onto the floor and slowly walked up to us.

I looked down at his shoes. That's where the clicking sound was coming from.

The look on his face was cryptic.

I took a deep breath.

"HEY, LET MY PARENTS GO ..." I began to yell.

The ice wizard waved his hand, and all of a sudden, my voice was gone and I couldn't move. I tried to call out, but my face and body were frozen.

I tried to see my friends out of the corner of my eye. From what little I could see, they were frozen, too.

I couldn't move at all. I couldn't even blink my eyes.

The ice wizard slowly walked up to us, and began walking down the length of the line we made. I heard him.

Click ~ sniff ~ click ~ sniff ~ click ~ sniff

What on earth is he doing? My eyes are starting to burn.

An ice dryad appeared next to the wizard, but following a little behind him, as the mountain gnome had just a short while earlier.

I waited. There was little else I could do.

Finally, the ice wizard came to me. He looked me up and down, then inhaled deeply.

"It is this one," he said.

The ice dryad bowed and flew away, looking like mist the second his feet left the ground.

The ice wizard was examining me up and down, up and down, then, his eyes stopped on my middle.

He turned and snapped his fingers.

The mountain gnome assistant reappeared.

"This one," the ice wizard whispered.

"Aye, sire. Yes. I will get right on it." He glanced at Tam and the others. "Sire, what would you like to do with the spares?"

The wizard waved his hand vaguely, and the gnome backed away.

The ice wizard glanced sideways at Tupu next to me.

"Ah, Farryn, there you are. Did you expect you would get away from me?"

I heard nothing, but I imagined Farryn was probably peeing his pants with fright.

The ice wizard was extremely intimidating.

He backed up a few steps and considered us all, then his eyes moved back to me.

He waved his hands, murmuring a few words I could not make out, and I felt a frozen ribbon of ice start to wind its way around my legs.

Around and around, it traveled up my leg and up to my hips, and there it stopped.

The wizard made a vague motion, and the ribbon of ice wrapped a loop around my ribs several times.

He stood back, head to the side, surveying his work.

Then he looked into my eyes.

"It is a real pity we could not have known of each other under other circumstances, Princess. When I first stole the people from the town and castle, I was just feeling my way around, trying to sense where I was, how I could now use my magic, you know, that sort of thing. But when *you* came *here*, well, I could not have envisioned a more fortuitous circumstance."

He began to pace.

"You see, every day I am awake, I grow in power." He waved his hand vaguely. "It is the spell, you see. The spell of warmth that is making everything come alive! Everything is being released! And my power grows because of it. But you! With you I sense the Ancestral Magic, the Old Ways. Inside you, especially, I sense the power." He raised his hand and pointed his finger straight at my midsection.

He stared at me, considering.

"Is that where your heart is? Is that where you brain is?" He leaned forward. "I NEED TO KNOW!"

I stared at him. Tears drained out my eyes, they were stinging so badly now. I could barely breathe.

He sighed and tilted his head sideways, then waved his hand carelessly in the air, a short flip of his fingers, and suddenly my face could move.

I immediately shut my eyes.

Ohhh, that's better.

The ice wizard was walking again.

Click - click - click - click - click

I opened my eyes a crack.

"OH!"

He was right there, a few inches from me, looking at my midsection.

I breathed hard, studying this wizard.

"Do you know why you are so special?" he said.

My mind raced.

What does he mean? What does he want?

He stepped back and looked up into my eyes.

"I don't know what is here," he pointed his finger at my midsection again, "But I want it."

He looked at me silently for a minute.

"Should I slash you in two and see what's inside?" he said.

I glowered down at him. "Keep your hands off me, wizard."

"Ah! She speaks! Finally!" he bowed with a flourish, his hands waving in front of his face. "Greetings, Princess!"

"How do you know who I am?" I asked, still glowering, but unable to help myself.

"How do I know who you are. Hmmm, let us see." he walked around the ground in front of me in a figure eight. "Well, for starters, you smell of royalty. Like those two," he waved his hand toward the people encased in the ice wall. "In fact, you stink of it!"

I blinked.

"Princess, you have an ancestral magic within you. And it is strong, so strong. Much stronger than the other two." He walked closer. "And it is strongest right here," he poked his finger into my belly, and his fingernail was long and sharp.

"OW!"

"Ha! Ha! Hahahahaha!" he laughed as he backed up.

"Keep. Your. Hands. Off. Me." I said in my steeliest voice. I bared my teeth and hissed for emphasis.

I wiggled my neck. The rest of my body was utterly immobile: The ice wizard's spell held me fast from my neck to my toes.

If he wanted to cut me open, he could do it I wouldn't be able to stop him.

I took a deep breath.

He was looking at me, a serious expression on his face again.

"Princess, you will stay with me. And I think I *will* cut you open and see what's inside."

"If you so much as lay one hand on me, I will kill you," I said in a low, hard voice. "If you so much as touch me again, you're dead. You keep your filthy, low-down, evil fingers away from my bab– ..."

I had gone too far.

"AHA!" His eyes stared at my midsection. "I remember now! Females can have a baby inside. And you have one inside right now, don't you?" He looked up at my face, his eyes dancing with delight.

I held my breath.

"Oh, this is WONDERFUL!" The ice wizard clapped his hands with joy. "Oh! I could not have asked for a better– ... but wait!" He walked closer to me. "How ... isn't ...?" he glanced up at me. "Aren't you supposed to be bigger?" he gestured around my midsection. "Around here, somewhere?" he looked back up at my face.

I rolled my eyes in spite of myself.

"Well?"

I remained silent.

"TELL ME!"

I pressed my lips together.

He regarded me with a look of deep frustration.

I rolled my eyes.

He stepped closer to me.

He leaned in. "The baby inside you has immense power, much stronger than yours, which is much stronger than theirs." He jerked his thumb toward the wall of ice. "But it will be much, MUCH stronger, stronger than I can even imagine," he whispered. "When it is in my hands and I give it a special, MAGICAL name." He wiggled his eyebrows.

I bared my teeth. "First of all, you tiny little rancid twat, you are NOT getting my baby! So just put that right out of your mind, RIGHT NOW. Second of all, go brush your teeth, because you STINK." I spat at him. My spittle landed on his cheek.

He stepped back. "Okay," he said quietly, wiping the glob of spit before it could drip far down his cheek. "We'll see about that."

Chapter Twenty-Three
Magical Baby

The ice wizard waved his hand in a huge arc, and the others – Tam, Caroline, Olof, Tupu, and Kym – were thrust into the air and off to the side, and sucked through an arch in the rock wall.

Farryn ran after them. But the wizard flicked his hand, and in an instant, the little gnome was pressed flat into the ground and lay there, still as death, his eyes wide and frightened.

The wizard turned to me.

"Princess," he said quietly, then took a deep breath and closed his eyes for a few seconds. He took several deeper breaths. "Princess." He opened his eyes and smiled at me. "I want what's best for the baby. Trust me, I do. I want it to become my apprentice! I can teach the child so many things, all manner of enchantments, and potions, and spells, and transfigurations, that your mind will be blown. BLOWN!" He laughed.

I took a deep breath. "NO."

He tried again. "You have no options, you know." He stared at me.

I remained silent.

"I could let your parents go free," he said.

My expression was unchanged.

"I could let them go, and you, and every," he pointed with emphasis, "person," point, "from," point, "the," point, "village," point, "I," point, "took."

"Now, isn't that worth something?" he asked in a wheedling tone.

I remained stubbornly silent.

He tilted his head to the side, putting his hand to his chin.

"Are you that selfish, Princess? Is it not bad enough that you live in a palace, and eat all the richest foods, and have all the most sumptuous gowns, that you have SO much more than any of the poor villagers you rule over, that you cannot take pity on them just this once?"

My face was unmoving. I knew I had to remain still.

"Trade your small, insignificant baby for all those people? Save all their lives with just one trade?"

I looked straight ahead and refused to move.

"Well. I have never in my extremely long life, seen such a spoiled and selfish princess. Never in my life." He began pacing slowly in front of me.

He paused for a few moments. He seemed to be thinking.

He glanced at me. "You know, I don't really need your permission. I don't need your cooperation. I don't even need you to be ALIVE." He screamed the last word in my face, spittle flying from his mouth.

I turned my head in disgust.

Fine, you don't need me? I am completely withdrawing from this conversation, then.

I closed my eyes and remained silent.

The ice wizard made a loud sound of disgust, and I heard him walk away.

I peeked, opening one eye just smidgen.

He had walked over to the archway he'd blown my friends through.

The ice dryad was there.

The wizard whispered to the creature, which turned to go. Then the wizard waved his hand as he turned back to me, and a large amount of snow began to tumble into the archway, fast and hard. Wet splats of partially melted snow fell heavily in, and it was soon filled to the top.

The ice wizard then waved his hand again and the snowed-in doorway froze, a shiny, translucent blue veneer spreading over the snow with a crackling sound, climbing all the way to the top.

Then the ice wizard walked to the high ledge where we had been hidden, and he walked sideways across the wall again, defying gravity. He walked out of sight, and I knew he was going to the far tunnel Farryn had brought us through.

I heard wet snow falling again in large splats, and then the icing-over sound.

He was sealing us in.

I closed my eyes again as he reappeared and returned to the ground near me.

He busied himself nearby, seemingly rearranging glass vials and packets of something.

"Don't bother with closing your eyes," he said. "I know you were watching me. I saw you."

He returned to stand in front of me, a vial in his hands. Its contents swirled with an inner light of their own.

"This," he held up the bottle, "is my own creation. I've been using it on the mountain gnomes, to create my own little workforce." He stared rapturously at the vial. "You see, if I give it to a female who has a small baby inside her, and utter my incantation, the baby grows. It grows much faster, you see. It grows until it's big enough the come out. And it usually only takes an afternoon."

My heart beat faster, and I felt the first icy touch of fear.

"Now, I've been giving this potion to the gnome females, the ones who had babies inside, and then closing them in a small cave, overnight. In the morning I return, and where there was one, there are usually two!" He put his head down, apparently considering something.

"Except that one time when there were three. But that was a special occasion." He shrugged.

"Now it's your turn to take it!" He grinned and held up the vial.

I shook my head, my lips pressed together in a thin, bloodless line.

He stepped closer.

"You are out of options, Princess."

He waved his hand and something forced my head slowly back.

It was agony.

"AHHHH!" I screamed as my head was forced back farther and farther, until I felt the back of my skull hit my shoulders.

The pain was intense.

I panted, my eyes wild. I felt the creepy little man grab my arm and shoulder, and he began climbing me, as if I were a mountain.

"YAHHHH!!!!!" I screamed.

He continued to climb. He dug his boot into my hip, using it as a foothold, and hefted himself higher.

My eyes, weeping and wide with fear, saw his face come into view.

I slammed my mouth shut so hard my teeth clicked. The muscles in my face strained as I pressed my jaw shut, and my lips pressed tightly together.

The ice wizard wrapped one arm around my shoulders, and with the other hand, stuck his thumbnail against my lips and slid it across, diagonally, slicing my lower lip open.

Blood poured down my face, and dripped onto my neck.

Tears streamed out of my eyes. I had never experienced a nightmare as awful as what was happening to me now.

He pulled the stopper out of the vial with his teeth, and carefully tipped it past my sliced-open lip. I felt the bitter liquid pour onto my teeth and slowly drip down into my throat.

"ARRGGGHHHH!" I groaned through my clenched teeth.

He continued to drip the potion through my teeth, drop by drop. I could taste the blood from the cut lip, and I could feel my mouth start to fill with blood.

"Might as well swallow, Princess, I'm going to keep you frozen like this until you do," he whispered, his face grimacing. "You'll eventually choke."

I rolled my eyes in agony, and blinked back tears that had started to pool in my upturned face.

It lasted a long time, I think. A very long time.

At one point, I heard Farryn sobbing.

He must be watching this.

My heart was in agony.

Drip - drip - drip - drip - drip - drip - drip - drip - drip - drip - drip - drip

Oh, yes. It took a very long time.

At some point, it felt like it had been an eternity, the ice wizard had emptied contents of the vial into my mouth. He tossed it aside, and I heard it smash on the floor, the sound of breaking glass loud in the cavern.

He was sweating by then, and the sweat dripped onto my face.

"Swallow it, Princess. All of it." He reached up and stroked my throat, tickling it.

I gurgled and shook my head, although I could barely move an inch.

Then he tried pinching my nose closed.

I closed my eyes as his sweaty knuckles smashed against my face.

His fingers slid because his hand was wet with sweat, but also because my face was slick with tears and blood.

I began to groan.

"ARRRRGGGGGGHHHHHHHNNNNN!"

"Swallow it," he said quietly. "We can do this all night. I've got nowhere else to be."

Oh, god. Oh, god. Oh, god. Oh, god.

My head hurt so much I thought it would explode.

"Okay, let's try something new," he said. He climbed back down and pulled my dagger out of my boot. Then climbed back up to my face.

"This dagger looks sharp. Is it sharp, Princess?" He stuck the point into my lip.

I groaned again.

He pushed, and the dagger's tip hit my teeth. He wiggled it, staring down into my mouth, and pushed the tip into a crack between my teeth.

Not the space between my jaw, but into a crack between two of the teeth on my lower jaw.

The dagger's point stuck. The ice wizard shoved the dagger hard.

The tooth broke.

It hurt like hell.

He pushed the dagger through the broken tooth and into my mouth.

It slid against my tongue, slicing it open.

Tears poured out of my eyes. I tried to blink them away.

He pushed the dagger in farther. It hit the back of my throat.

"Swallow or I'm going to push it all the way through."

I closed my eyes tightly.

"Swallow or I'm going to push it all the way through and it will slice through your neck. Probably kill you."

I kept my eyes tightly shut.

"Princess, I am not joking," the ice wizard pushed the tip of the dagger into the back of my throat. I felt the flesh part and blood pour down my throat.

I began to choke.

The potion and blood slid down my throat. I couldn't stop it.

I began to cough and choke.

"Swallow all of it? Every last bit?" The ice wizard brought his eye up to my mouth and peered in.

Nodding, he smiled. "That's a good girl." he patted my shoulder and climbed down, then waved his hand and released the magical hold he'd had on my neck.

I dropped my face forward, groaning.

"Aww, you'll be fine." He patted my arm.

"What kind of maniac are you?" I rasped icily, blood dripping from my mouth.

"Oh, just your average, every day kind of maniac who WANTS THAT BABY," he screamed.

I spat at the ground.

"Release me!" I demanded. "Release my parents! And the rest of these people!"

"No." The ice wizard grinned at me, then walked over next to the ice wall and sat down. He began muttering evil-sounding spell words, waving his fingers in and intricate manner.

I felt a cold icy feeling inside me.

"OWW!"

The coldness grew, enveloping me in its grip.

"AHHHHHHHH!" I screamed.

He continued his spell.

"AHHHHHHHHHHHHHHHHHHHHHH!"

He kept speaking the words. It went on for many minutes.

After a few more minutes, I went hoarse.

All I could do was groan. I could feel my insides twitching and stretching. It was unbearable, like my organs were freezing.

Such a deep pain. I could not withstand it.

I felt myself passing out.

I came to in a puddle of blood. Dried blood was crusted around my face, and everything hurt so much it woke me up.

I opened my eyes and blinked, looking around me.

I was in a small room, maybe ten feet square. Frozen walls of translucent blue surrounded me. I groaned and tried to sit up.

Something was wrong.

"AHHHH!!!" I screamed in pain, clutching my midsection.

Huh?

I looked down and my jaw dropped open.

My belly was full and round. The skin was so tight across it that it felt as if it might crack open with my movements.

I lay back down on the dirt floor.

Breathing harshly, the pain growing steadily worse, I clutched my bulging middle.

I felt something move inside.

WHAT?!

I looked down and unbuttoned my leather armor and lifted my shirt, then moved aside the woolen undergarment, exposing the skin of my midsection.

The skin was red and stretched very tight across my middle. Squiggly darker red lines reached across the skin as well.

I waited.

After a minute, I saw something move inside, a small bulge rolling under the skin from right to left.

I tapped the bulge, and it stopped moving for a few seconds, then pressed out farther, and then receded back in.

I stared, utterly mesmerized.

It moved again, slowly, stretching across for a few inches, before rolling back again.

I spent the next hour tapping through the skin, and the baby inside moved against my hand. It reacted to the taps, and I was amazed that I could get this reaction from a baby that had not even taken a breath.

I hummed, and the baby's movements stilled.

I lay still, and the baby moved again, as if wanting my movement.

I sat up, and the pain, excruciating, returned, and I screamed out loud.

Lying still felt the best, but it didn't remove all pain.

At least once or twice an hour, the pain returned, even as I lay still.

I stared down at my belly. I wasn't sure, but I thought it had grown larger during the time I had been awake and interacting with the little baby alive inside me.

"It's growing too fast," I said out loud, realizing that the wizard's spell had done this.

My heart seized in worry for my baby.

I lay still, hoping for it to move again, to somehow let me know it was okay in there.

I knew the rapid, forced growth of the baby had stretched me too much too fast, and I was worried it had somehow hurt the baby, too.

I decided to try to get to my feet. My back and legs hurt from lying on the dirt floor.

Everything hurts.

I groaned in pain as I got to my feet.

My balance was completely off, and I fell forward, catching myself at the last moment.

"Ohh," I groaned, holding my heavy belly with one hand, catching myself against the ice wall with the other.

I stumbled, then stood up completely.

"Hmmm, this actually feels better," I said aloud.

The baby pushed against the side of my belly. I patted the skin there and smiled.

I walked around a bit, stretching my legs.

Today has been rough.

I chuckled at my understatement.

I did a few deep knee bends while holding on to the wall for balance.

I was feeling better and better.

Then the muscles in my middle stretched again, and I looked down. I could actually see my round belly getting bigger.

I kept staring, mesmerized.

The baby kicked.

Hmmm. What was I forgetting?

It came to me like an icy bucket of water over my head.

The ice wizard is planning to steal my baby!

"OVER MY DEAD BODY!" I yelled at the walls of my icy prison. "DO YOU HEAR ME, WIZARD? I SAID, OVER MY DEAD BODY!" I slammed my fists on the ice.

A voice filled the room.

"That can be arranged, Princess."

Chapter Twenty-Four
The Birth

The pain hit me full force.

I had lain down after the wizard's voice had threatened me, lain down and tried to sleep.

I was so sleepy I felt drugged.

I wondered if it was a side effect of the potion and spellwork he had performed on me the day before.

The day before. I had no idea how I knew another day had passed, I just sensed it. I knew it in my gut.

My midsection had grown huge in the space of just a few hours. I had no idea a pregnant belly would be so massive, so, so, I don't know ... so OUT THERE.

The women in my mother's line had always carried babies "out there" – a pregnant belly that pushed out more than normal, but I never realized exactly what it meant.

Maybe this is normal?

After a few hours, my worries flew right out the proverbial window, because the pain had started.

Extreme pain.

And I was alone.

As I lay on the cold dirt floor, I allowed myself a tear or two. Ever since the ice wizard's voice had come through into the chamber, I had not uttered a word.

He was listening in, that was certain.

I would not give him the satisfaction of hearing my thoughts uttered aloud.

He would get no help from me.

The pain started in my back, then radiated around my sides and to my front. Over and over and over, every ten minutes or so.

I lay curled in a ball, my arms clutching my stomach, my face bathed in sweat.

It lasted for hours, exhausting me more than anything ever had.

After hours of lying on my side, feeling the pain, I felt something new.

Oh, god.

A cold sweat descended upon me, from my head to my toes.

My breathing was rough and jagged. My eyes open in surprise and distress.

Suddenly, I felt the distinctive signs of imminent vomit.

I scrambled to my knees, my back heaving in pain.

It was as if my entire body was beyond my control. My back undulated, my neck extended, and the contents of my stomach flew out of my mouth.

There was not much there.

My body did not get that information, because I continued to heave, uncontrollably, vomiting up clear fluid and spit, for many minutes.

It all splattered onto the dirt, rolling away in a stinking puddle.

After the heaving subsided, I felt a new exhaustion. I rolled away from the soiled dirt and sat up against one of the icy walls of my prison.

The pains were different now, they felt lower and more focused, a shrieking pain that came every few minutes.

I sat there, clutching my huge belly, trying to catch my breath between the pain surges.

I felt a wetness and looked down.

Did I pee?

A clear fluid, dotted with black, was coming out of me. I tried to stop the flow, but it just kept dribbling out.

I moved to a crouch, bracing myself against the side of the wall.

My knees were bent, and I felt another pain coming.

This one felt different.

I lifted my face to the ceiling and winced, trying to remain silent, and unable to.

"REEYAHHHHHH!" I screamed, unable to hold it in any longer.

The pain lasted a long time, many minutes. When it subsided, I looked down, and my heart skipped a beat.

Blood was dripping out of me. Bright red blood, thick and luminous, in a steady stream.

Panic bloomed in my mind. I knew enough about childbirth to know that a little bit of blood was normal, but not this. There was so much that it was gathering in a puddle at my feet.

Another pain was beginning, and the flow of blood dripping out of me was growing heavier.

"OHHHH GODDDD! I'M BLEEDING! HELP ME, WIZARD! SOMEONE HELP ME!"

"AAAHHHHHHHRRRRGGHHHHH!"

The ice wizard materialized in front of me, took one look at me, and went white, then dematerialized again.

I panted as fear filled my mind, fear and pain.

"YERRAAHHEEHHHHAAAAGGHH!" The screams were coming involuntarily now. The pain was so deep, so strong, and the blood kept dripping.

I closed my eyes tightly, holding my belly with both hands, and leaned against the wall. My knees ached and felt locked in place.

I felt as if I was dying.

I heard a pop! and opened my eyes.

The wizard was back, and he had brought help.

Khepri and Tupu blinked, looking around.

Another pain was coming, and I panted roughly, bracing myself for the agony.

"ARRGGGHHHHHHHHH!" I clenched my teeth in distress, looking down.

Another fresh squirt of red, red blood descended to the dirt floor.

"OH MY GOD!" cried Khepri, rushing to my side.

"Oh! OH! Charlotte!" Tupu crouched, grabbing hold of my arms.

Khepri ducked her head, her face nearly in the puddle of blood, assessed the situation, and got to work.

Her voice was businesslike.

"Okay, Tupu, get behind her and hold her under her arms."

Tupu moved behind me, got into a crouch, and slipped her arms behind and under mine.

"Now," Khepri glanced behind her at the ice wizard, who stood there staring. "Wizard, get us clean, dry cloths, and hot water and soap."

The ice wizard looked shocked and did not move.

"NOW!" Khepri roared.

The wizard jumped and nodded. He dematerialized and was gone.

"Where did he go?" Tupu asked.

"Hopefully off to do something useful," Khepri muttered.

"Kh–Khepri," I said weakly.

"Don't worry, Charlotte, we're here to help you." Khepri looked into my face. "I'm going to do everything humanly possible to save this baby."

"Bu–but the … the blood. S–so mu–much blood." Tears rolled down my face, then I felt the tightening start again.

"Hold her," Khepri instructed Tupu. "Hold her tightly."

The pain, THE PAIN! It was agony.

"Oh, no," muttered Khepri.

The wizard reappeared, his arms full of blankets, a pail dangling from his hand. He set them down.

"SPREAD THEM ON A CLEAN PART OF THE FLOOR, WIZARD!" Khepri screamed, furious.

The wizard hurriedly took the top blanket and spread it onto the near corner, and then spread another on top of the first.

"Tupu, move over there," said Khepri. "Be careful."

I felt myself being lifted from behind. Khepri grabbed both my ankles, and I was moved bodily to the other corner. She placed my feet down first, and Tupu gently lowered me back into a crouch.

"The baby is breech, so we have to move her to all fours," Khepri said hurriedly.

Tupu pushed me forward, and Khepri slid her arms next to Tupu's and under my armpits, and they gently lowered me face-down onto my hands and knees.

"Hold on, Charlotte," Tupu murmured.

"Get down next to her and support her shoulders and arms," Khepri said.

Tupu obliged.

"YOU, TOO, WIZARD. GET ON HER OTHER SIDE!" Khepri barked.

The ice wizard crouched down next to me.

His face was near mine.

Sweat and grime dripped off my face, and I glanced at the little man crouched next to me.

"When this is over, I am going to ..." I never got to finish, because another pain came then, and I felt a splitting feeling down between my legs. I gritted my teeth and groaned.

Khepri had positioned herself on her back, nearly upside down, her face between my legs, and a steady stream of words issued forth.

"That's it, that's it. Charlotte, try not to push. I know it's hard, but hold back if you can. Holdddd backkkkkk, that's it. That's it. Now, I am going to reach in as the contraction subsides. Don't panic. It's going to feel weird, but don't panic and don't push, whatever you do ... that's it. Okay. I'm in."

I felt a colossal pain run up my spine, and a stinging sensation from between my legs.

I trusted Khepri completely and was so relieved she was here with me.

"Okayyy, hold on, holdddd onnnn, I'm just going to ...," Khepri said.

I felt a huge pull, and the oddest sensation, as if I were about to flip over. And it hurt, ohhhh how it hurt.

"AHHH!" I cried out.

"Yes, yes, my sweet, my captain, I know it hurts. It's almost over, I promise, shhhhhh, try not to push, my darling, try not to push, you'll snap my arm ...," Khepri murmured.

I felt another pull, and a gush of fluid, and then a pressure so tight it was like I was being squeezed into nothing ...

"There, there, my sweet. Okay. Let's rest a minute. Let'sssss justtttt resttttt aaaa minuteeeee. There, there, okay." Khepri sat back.

"You're doing great, Charlotte," Tupu murmured, rubbing my back.

I looked over at the ice wizard, grimacing. "When this is over, you ..." Another pain seized my body and I was rendered speechless.

"AARRRRGGGGGHHHHHHHH!" I groaned.

"There we go, there we go, push, push, yes, that's my girl ..." Khepri murmured.

I felt a massive pressure and more stinging. "Ohhhh! It hurts, it hurts ..."

"I know, I know. You're doing great, Charlotte. Just push, push for me ..."

It hurt worse when I pushed, but I took a deep breath and pushed harder than I've ever pushed in my life ...

"There we go, anddddd the head is out," Khepri murmured, her hands working away between my legs.

Tupu rubbed my back, "You're doing great, Charlotte," she whispered.

Another pain began, and I felt a surge inside me.

"AARRRGGGHHHAAANNNNGGGGG!" I groaned, the sound coming from deep within me. It felt so primal.

"Push, sweetheart, push, push, push, push, push, pushhhhhhhh ...," Khepri murmured.

Something huge splooshed out of me.

The baby!

Tupu pulled me to the side, so I was lying against her on the blanket.

I stared at Khepri.

She held the baby in a blanket. It looked blue. Khepri set it down on the floor and bent over it, putting her mouth over the head and gently blowing into it.

"My ... my baby ...," I said in a weak, crying voice.

"Shhh, she's doing all she can, Charlotte," Tupu said.

Khepri continued to blow into the baby's mouth for many minutes. She massaged the thick, curled cord that reached from the baby to up between my legs.

She picked the baby up and turned it facing down, patting its back.

Fluid dripped out of its mouth.

The baby's face was swollen.

Khepri placed the baby back onto the floor and blew into its mouth again and again.

Finally, I heard a sputtering, and a weak cry.

"wahh wahh wahh wahh ..."

Khepri took a deep breath, then another. She wrapped the baby in the blanket, and Tupu reached and lifted my shirt, and Khepri tucked the baby against my skin, and wrapped the blanket around both of us.

I looked down.

The baby was slowly turning from blue to pink, with a smattering of dark hair, and dark red lips. It was covered in a grey smear.

I took a deep breath, inhaling the scent of this new human. It smelled like heaven.

I was smitten.

"This baby has the heart of a lion," murmured Khepri. "I was seriously worried ..."

I could not take my eyes off my little baby. My head still wasn't wrapped around that facts of its birth, or how it had been just a tiny thing the size of a bean, not two days ago.

"Hello baby," I whispered.

"It is the custom in Swerighe to give honor to the place a baby was conceived," I whispered. "You were conceived on my ship, while we were at sea ..."

"Mare ... Mer ..." Tupu murmured.

"And you're right, Charlotte, and the heart of a lion. Such courage and fortitude, such a strong lion's heart ...," Khepri said softly.

"Khepri," I looked up. "Is the baby okay?"

Khepri nodded, tears in her eyes.

"And is it a boy or a girl?"

Khepri smiled. "Charlotte, your baby is a little boy."

"Mer," I said. "Lion heart. Mer-lion. I will call him Mer-lion." There was a soft glow on the baby's face, and I smiled. The name had stuck.

"NO! NO NO NO NO NO NO!" The howl of outrage came from the other side of the tiny cell.

I jumped.

We all looked over at the ice wizard.

"Haven't you done enough?" Khepri said in disgust.

"I WAS GOING TO GIVE HIM A MAGICAL NAME! A POWERFUL NAME!" The ice wizard roared. "NOW YOU'VE STOLEN THAT AND FIXED HIM WITH A COMMON NAME! ARRGGGHHHH!" The ice mage grabbed his head and wobbled from side to side.

"That was her right, you idiot, as the baby's mother," Khepri spat in disgust.

The ice mage thrust his hands out. "I will still be able to apprentice him! He will still grow in the old magic! I will still triumph with him at my side! He still has the deep power! Give him to me!"

"NO!" we all yelled.

I squeezed my baby to me tighter, pulling him to my side and covering him with both arms.

"YOU HAVE NO SAY IN THIS!" The ice wizard waved his hand and suddenly, I was lying in a meadow, Khepri and Tupu beside me, and nearby Tam, Caroline, Christianne, Kym, Håkan, Inge, Jim, and Olof stood.

"AHHHHH! MY BABY!" I shrieked in agony. My arms were empty. The baby was gone.

Chapter Twenty-Five
The Agony and a Plan

I was hysterical.

"Charlotte, you must calm down, or I cannot do this and you could bleed to death," Khepri said.

Tupu set me down on the grass, rubbing my arm. "Shhh, sweetie, stop thrashing. She's got to stop the bleeding."

"BUT, BUT TUPU! AHHHHH!" I cried.

Tam held my head, tears streaming down his face. He was in great conflict.

"Tupu, what happened? Why is Charlotte bleeding?" he whispered.

Tupu motioned for Caroline to take her place. She stood up and motioned for Tam to draw away from me.

Tam kissed my forehead and whispered, "I'll be back, Babe. Hold tight."

I nodded, tears, grime and blood splattered on my face.

Caroline lay down on the grass next to me, and Christianne lay down on my other side.

Caroline wrapped her arm around me and nestled her face against my shoulder. "It'll be all right, Miss. Khepri will fix everything ..."

I glanced up and saw Tupu standing a bit away, whispering to Tam. A minute later he yelled.

"WHAT?! HE WHAT?!"

I closed my eyes, my heart breaking.

I wanted my baby. I wanted to hold him, to clutch him in my arms, to nuzzle his little body. I groaned with sorrow.

Suddenly, I was gripped by more extreme pain. My insides felt like they were being ripped out.

"KHEPRI, WHAT ...?!" I screamed.

"Shhh, shhh, it'll be okay, Miss," Caroline whispered.

"Okay, okay, hold on, almost got it ...," said Khepri. "Uhhhhh, okay, there." She sat up and looked at me. "The placenta is out, and clots are out, the bleeding has stopped."

"Khepri," I whimpered. "I want my baby."

Tears filled Khepri's eyes. "I know, sweetheart. I want him back with you, too. We'll get him, if it is at all humanly possible, we will get him back, I promise." She wiped her eyes, turning her head.

Tam knelt next to me, looking me over, then addressed Khepri. "Is she okay?" he asked in a quiet voice.

"Yes, she'll be okay. She's lost a ton of blood, and will be weak as a kitten for a while, but the bleeding is stopped, and the baby …," Khepri made a choking sound. "The baby was okay, last time I saw him. He was born blue and not breathing, very stressed. A breech birth. But Charlotte was a champ, and we got him breathing again." She took a deep breath.

"Tam." I touched his arm, looking up at him. "Tam, we have a son. He, he was … the wizard …"

"Tupu told me. He forced the baby to grow too fast," Tam choked out.

I nodded. "It hurt. It hurt so much. My belly expanded so fast, my muscles ripped, the skin looked like it was going to break, but it didn't, and the baby came. He came out. He's alive. I named him."

Tams face grew gentle, and he smiled. "You named him?"

"Yes, after the sea, and after his spirit …" I smiled back, tears in my eyes. "His name is Mer-lion."

"Mer-lion," said Tam, trying out the name. "A good, strong name." He leaned down and kissed me.

"Khepri," Jim said, leaning over, not wanting to intrude.

"Hmmm?" Khepri said.

"Can … can she be moved? It looks like it's going to rain."

As if in emphasis, the sky thundered ominously.

"Yes, I think so. But I don't think she can walk very fast, and she really needs to rest," Khepri said.

"Not a problem," said Jim, and transformed into the djinn. He gently scooped me up, and turned to the others. "Let's go."

It turned out the ice wizard had flung everyone back to a meadow we had camped in weeks ago, about a three-day ride from the castle. He had flung everything that smelled of us out of his realm, far, far away; even Inge and the horses.

In the blink of an eye, we had traveled hundreds of miles.

The message was clear: GET AWAY FROM ME!

I had been left weak as a kitten, unable to fight, unable to walk for very long distances, unable to do much of anything for myself.

I felt horrible about losing my baby, sore from my injuries, and extremely grateful I had the best friends in the world.

The best.

With the help of the djinn, and all the others, we made our way back to the castle.

I felt utterly defeated returning without the queen and prince, without all the snatched villagers, and without my baby.

"Charlotte," Khepri knocked on my door and stuck her head in. "Can we talk?

Caroline was spooning broth into my mouth.

"Sure," I said weakly.

"I don't think she heard you, Miss," Caroline said.

Khepri walked in. "How're you feeling this morning?"

I lifted my hand and waved it in a "so-so" gesture.

Caroline put the bowl of broth down, and dabbed at the corner of my mouth with a silken napkin.

"I think she's going to need a little more time before she's up to full strength, Caroline said.

As I lay there, listening to them discuss me, I closed my eyes.

I had lost so much blood it was a huge effort just to be awake. I had slept most of the time traveling back to the castle. Jim had carried me the whole way. He'd been incredible.

He was in an adjoining room, laid up himself, recuperating.

It was the morning after we'd returned, and I was so depressed that I struggled not to cry. It was incredibly frustrating being this weak and wanting to hurry back and retrieve my baby and my parents – and slice that wizard from head to toe – but not even be able to get out of bed.

It had been four or five days since I'd given birth to Merry, as I was now calling him. I worried the wizard wasn't feeding him correctly or taking care of him properly. A baby needs his mother!

My body had been producing milk for Merry for days now, my breasts were hard and swollen with milk, and it was agony not to hold him in my arms and nurse him.

On the way back home, Khepri had made a tincture that she had me drink, and this greatly reduced the buildup of milk in my body, but it was still heartbreaking to know my baby was somewhere off in the frozen mountains, probably crying for his mama, hungry for my milk.

Khepri and the court physicians had conferred and were handling my condition well, and I was woken at least ten times a day for poking and prodding and medicines.

I knew it would be a week or more until I was in fighting condition.

Tam hunted out in the forest, bringing fresh game that was prepared by the newly hired cook, to replenish the iron I had lost with the bleeding, and I appreciated every morsel.

Tam was so sweet. Jim told me he'd watched the man rail against what had been done to me by the wizard, punching walls and vowing to rip the head off of the evil mage.

Håkan, Inge, and Olof had offered to go back in after the wizard, but I declined their offer.

It was clear we needed a plan, and a fresh weapon that could defeat the wizard once and for all.

I could only hope that Merry, my parents, and the townspeople who were being held captive would survive long enough for us to rescue them.

"Charlotte,"

Khepri finished conferring with Caroline and came to sit close to me. "How are you feeling, for real?"

I took a deep breath. "Frustrated as hell," I said weakly. I closed my eyes in disgust at how feeble my voice sounded.

"I understand, honey." She put her hand over mine and squeezed.

I tried to sit up in bed, and Caroline moved to help me. She lifted my shoulders, and Khepri stuffed several goose-down pillows under them, propping me up. Caroline then tucked the blanket around me.

I looked down and ran my fingers along the white seam of the quilt. It was beautifully handcrafted and soft as a feather.

I looked up and cleared my voice.

"Tell me what you've discovered," I said.

"Okay, I've been studying *The Book of Mysteries* further, and found a few more things," Khepri said. "Now that I've seen what we are dealing with, what kind of spell, and exactly what kind of creature, I think we may have a real shot at defeating him. At least, I have high hopes for one."

This got my interest.

She continued: "First of all, there is no counter spell that I can find in the book, that will stop The Warming. That much is clear. But every spell has an opposite, a way to cancel it out or halt its progress. And I have found a potion that will force the ice wizard to reveal what this counter spell is."

"Remember the Nepenthes? It's the herb we needed – an herb vital to a potion that would encase him back into a glacier? I found that it's also vital to the potion that will force the truth out of him. Well, the book speaks of this herb and where it can be found." She sat back, looking satisfied.

"Well," Caroline asked, "Where is it found?"

"On the world of the centaurs," Khepri said.

"You are kidding, right?" I said.

"I am not," Khepri wiggled her eyebrows. "Apparently it originally came from their world, and was seeded here long ago, probably by the quamernats. I think they brought over quite a lot of different flora."

I nodded.

Khepri smiled. "We know where it is and how to get it. It's the last ingredient we need to defeat this lunatic." She wiggled her eyebrows up and down.

I smiled.

Ten days later, I was feeling much better.

"I swear, Caroline, I have never eaten so much red meat in my life," I said, getting into my leather armor. "And tinctures, so many tinctures."

"They sure seemed to do the job, Miss," Caroline smiled as she helped me into my coat.

"Is the troupe assembled?" I asked.

"Yes, Miss."

"And they've been briefed?"

"Several times, Miss."

I paused in my hurried actions. "And how are they doing? I know I've seen them a few times, when they came to visit me here, but I need to know the real sense of their attitudes, their feelings." I looked at her. "Carrie, tell me: What have you observed?"

"You want the truth, Miss?"

"Yes."

"They are chomping at the bit, eager to get going," Caroline said.

"Good. So am I." I pulled my boots on and stood up, surveying the room where I had spent so many days recuperating. I glanced at the maid standing by the door, gesturing her to come over.

She drew close and curtseyed, waiting for instructions.

I waved my hand all around the room. "Make sure this room doesn't smell like medicine anymore."

"Yes, Your Highness."

"And wash everything three times."

"Yes, Your Highness."

"And toss out the pot and the basin."

"Yes, Your Highness."

"That's all for now."

She curtseyed and withdrew back to her position at the wall.

I nodded at Caroline and strode out of the room.

Within an hour, I had taken care of castle business, given my cousins my blessings, taken a cursory inspection of the new cook and his helpers, and inspected supplies being loaded onto *Pride of the Sea*.

We were ready to depart.

As I walked purposefully up the gangplank onto my ship, I saw a sight I had been hoping for.

Håkan, Inge, and Olof were lined up, fully outfitted in leather armor, holding impressive weapons at their sides, and standing at attention.

Tam was nearby, looking uncomfortable. He saw me and walked over.

"They showed up a few hours ago. They want to join us, say they can 'be of noble use', whatever that means." He looked at me, his eyebrows raised.

The message was clear: *You are the captain. This is your decision.*

I smiled inwardly.

I glanced at him. "To be of noble use. in this land, means they know they can fight well by our side, and they wish to offer their swords. It's a way of strong warriors joining an army," I squinted up at the deck of the ship, surveying my small troupe already gathered there, "although we don't exactly have an army."

Tam shrugged, "Oh, I don't know, we're a pretty formidable fighting force." He grinned.

I turned to look at Håkan and the boys. No words were needed. I gestured for them to follow me on board.

All three broke into grins and fell into step behind us, and we all boarded *Pride of the Sea* together.

Greta was sitting up in the crow's nest, waving down at us. Akim was up on the fo'c'sle deck, saluting.

The main troupe were all gathered on deck, at attention. All the sailors and mates stood behind them.

The sight brought tears to my eyes.

I stopped, stood stiffly, looking them over. I kept the tears I felt forming from falling, and I spent several minutes staring at them with pride and strength. Then I nodded.

"All right! Let's get this voyage started! There are citizens of Swerighe to rescue, and the day is getting long." I looked up at the sailors at the fo'c'sle. "Let's get the mantas swimming, let's move out!"

Every one of them let out a cheer and a whoop! And just like that, our voyage was under way.

Chapter Twenty-Six
The Planet of the Quamernats

We sailed down to the Mare Nostrum, turned east, and dropped anchor at the southern island.

The mermaids and centaurs were flabbergasted to hear what had happened. They wasted no time in escorting us through the lava tube to the northern island, down into the volcano, and through the portal to the world of the quamernats.

We emerged onto the same green hillside where we had arrived during the last visit, and the two suns were high in the sky.

"What is this sorcery, Your Highness?" gasped Håkan, staring up at the sky.

I turned his head gently. "Don't look directly at the suns, Håkan, they will burn your eyes and you will go blind."

He looked into my eyes.

"What is this sorcery?" he repeated, a deeply concerned look on his face.

"Remember how we told you we were traveling to another land not on our world?" I asked.

He nodded, "I remember. I just ... I guess I did not realize it would be so different." He glanced around the hillside. "How is it that this world has two suns in the sky?"

"The binary stars in this solar system are just how this place developed. It is nothing to be concerned about Håkan," Khepri said, smiling.

"Okay, all right. It's just a little jarring," Håkan said.

"You get used to it," Caroline said.

"Okay, now," I said, looking around, my hands on my hips. "We know where we're headed. We'll proceed to the air pillow station, and borrow another flight."

"It should go smoothly. Hopefully," Tupu said, grinning.

We started down the hillside and veered off toward the hills.

We made it about a mile.

"HALT!" A dozen or so guards from the next hill ran toward us with spears and knives.

I just stared at them for a second, then, "Swords!" and drew my scimitar, and crouched in a fighting stance.

I glanced at Håkan. "These are the cave dwellers we told you about. Their society is disparate, and we spoke with both the haves and the have nots. Oh, and don't forget: They're cannibals."

"They're WHAT?" Håkan exclaimed.

"Don't let them take you to one of their mills," Khepri said.

"I wonder if they remember us?" Christianne said.

"Oh, I think they remember us, all right," I said.

The guards were rapidly approaching.

I glanced at my friends. Everyone was ready.

I nodded at Kym and she nodded back. We had earlier strategized that she was not to transform into the chimera, nor Jim into the djinn, until I gave the word.

I watched the guards' approach.

Looking at these guards, seeing their number and their weapons, I wondered why they acted so aggressively. We could easily best them in combat, so it wasn't clear why they were being so combative.

"Careful: Those spears may not look like much, but they are long and sharp. They can hurt us without getting into range of our swords," Tam cautioned.

The guards did not slow their headlong rush.

They were almost upon us.

POP!

POP!

POP!POP!POP!POP!POP!POP!POP!POP!

As the guards met us in a clang of steel and wood, their numbers quadrupled.

"WHAT?"

"HEY!"

"HOW DID THEY?"

"BE CAREFUL!"

"WATCH OUT!"

"HEY HEY! HEY!"

I whirled and struck again and again, and after a while, bodies started piling up at my feet.

Each one was rushing us with their spears and knives, lunging at us, but they didn't seem to have much skill, so it was relatively easy to deal with them ... at least individually.

But they did have a special talent.

They kept multiplying.

How are they doing this?

A tall guard rushed me, spear thrust out in front of her. I flipped it aside and brought my scimitar down on her spear, knocking it out of her hands. She turned suddenly, and jabbed a long, wicked looking knife at me.

I jumped aside, but she anticipated the move, and turned with me.

And suddenly there were three of her. Then nine of her.

I swung my sword at her arm, and made contact, slicing through skin, muscle, and bone. She cried out, falling to the ground.

But this gave her clones the chance to jump on me. They dog-piled on me, bringing me down with their sheer weight.

I tried to struggle, but there were simply too many of them. I got in several more blows, and drew plenty of blood, but in the end, three of them were sitting on me, a fourth was standing with her boot on my scimitar, and a fifth was tying my hands behind my back.

The rest of the troupe was similarly subdued.

What just happened?

As we were hustled over the hill and down to the opening of their underground city, I caught Khepri's eye and gave her a look of bewilderment.

How had these people multiplied? And so quickly?

Khepri looked at me and mouthed something, and I squinted, trying to make out what she was trying to communicate.

The guards were rough, shoving us and taunting us, and pulling us so violently along that several of us stumbled and fell.

"Get up, slave! GET UP!" One guard prodded Tupu with his spear. She gave him a dirty look and got to her feet.

I looked at Kym, and nodded. She nodded back. We would play along for a bit, out of curiosity.

I wanted to find out who these people were, and how they could duplicate themselves

It was hard to walk while being shoved, with hands tied.

"HEY! WATCH IT!" Inge yelled as he was shoved hard enough to stumble to his knee.

"You'll walk, slave, and you'll stay quiet, or you'll be dangling off the end of my spear!" The guard prodded him with the sharp spear tip on his arm, and a small drop of blood appeared.

I watched the exchange carefully.

If things get out of hand, if serious injuries are threatened ...

What would I do?

Hmmm.

I'll tell you what I'd do: I'd give Kym and Jim the signal, and they'd transform and all hell would break lose, that's what I'd do.

"Come on, COME ON, MOVE!" The guard behind me shoved me hard with his boot, and I pitched forward onto the ground.

"GET UP!"

This is getting old.

I looked over at Kym and saw she was again looking in my direction. Our eyes met, and she shook her head slightly.

What? What is up with her?

I got to my feet and continued walking.

Jim was behind me. I decided to turn and look to see exactly where he was.

I walked forward, then jumped and turned, scanning the group. I saw no sign of Jim.

Huh?

The guard next to me hit me on the side of the head with his spear, knocking me to the ground once more, and I saw stars.

"HEY!" Tam yelled, rushing to my side.

"Get back, slave!" A guard called, and I heard a scuffle break out.

I turned over and jumped to my feet, and saw several guards beating Tam, who crouched on the ground.

I had had enough.

"KYM!" I called out.

Within a second or two the chimera was there, swiping at guards with her paws, striking at guards with her snake head tail, and growling and roaring, flipping around and generally doing massive damage.

Suddenly, the djinn was there, too, slamming heads together, throwing guards high into the air to land hard and remain still, and causing general chaos.

He must've been waiting.

The original number of guards that had arrived to detain us had been about a dozen or so.

That number had tripled after the fight, even with the ones we'd subdued, to about forty.

Now, with the massive chimera fighting and smashing guards in twos and threes, and the djinn helping, and both of them knocking down a healthy number of guards, I noticed the guards were multiplying again.

Before long, they numbered nearly a hundred.

Oh, this cannot end well.

They were dog-piling on the chimera. There had to be at least several dozen climbing on her back, pulling on her mane and tail, and overwhelming her.

She fought valiantly, and the ground ran red with their blood.

Then the chimera began to grow, and where before she'd been ten feet at the shoulder, and twenty feet long, she was now thirty feet at the shoulder and at least sixty-five feet long.

The guards, no matter how many of them there were, simply could not best her. She simply shook them off.

"Back up, BACK UP!" I cried to the rest of the troupe.

We scrambled out of the way. The chimera was now larger than a whale.

She screamed and jumped up and pounced, over and over and over.

The guards had no chance.

We stayed out of the way and let her do her thing, which was very impressive to watch.

The djinn was zipping in and out of the fray, picking up guards by their legs and flinging them out over the horizon.

The chimera was sprayed with blood and smashed, dashed, clawed, bit, slapped, hacked, severed, sliced, and ripped her way through all of them.

At last, the guards were all dead.

Their bodies littered the hillside, and the grass ran red with their blood.

Every last one was dead, still, and unmoving.

And the air became silent.

I jumped up and trotted over to the thirty-foot chimera, who was trying to lick herself clean.

"Kym, don't. Ewww."

The chimera looked at me and wrinkled her nose.

The djinn landed next to us and transformed back to his human form.

I looked around. "We need a river or lake or something."

The rest of the troupe walked up to us then.

"Kym, that was so badass!"

"Why did they multiply like that?"

"HOW did they multiply like that?"

"Look at them, so much waste."

"It's silly."

"Why did they attack us?"

I held my hands, which were still tied together, out to the chimera, who used a claw to slice the rope in half. She cut through everyone's bonds, and we were all soon free.

"Jim, do you see any other guards coming out of that cave entrance?" I asked, rubbing my wrists.

"Uhhh," Jim looked for a minute, "I don't think so."

"Keep an eye on it. They are far more aggressive than they were the first time," I said.

"Kym, maybe if you transform, most of it will come off?" suggested Khepri, trying to wipe the blood off the chimera.

The chimera shivered and transformed back to Kym, the little six-year-old girl. She wrinkled her nose and looked over her arms and legs.

"Yuck," she said.

Khepri splashed water on Kym's hands. "Rub them together, sweetheart."

"Okay, well, we need this herb," I said. "It's here on this world someplace. But it's a big planet."

"I suggest asking the quamernats," said Caroline. "Remember their gardens? That's the likeliest place it might grow."

"I remember," I said, smiling.

"Well, let's hike fast, let's go catch a sky pillow," said Tupu. She turned and pointed, then started walking.

"Let's go, then," I said.

We all began to hike, moving uphill from the cave entrance to the underground city.

We were about five hundred yards from the bloody battlefield when I heard a faint sound, and turned.

My jaw fell open.

Dozens of people were pouring out of the cave entrance, and running to the fallen guards. They dragged each one back to the cave, running as fast as they could, then ran back out and grabbed another body.

It went on like this for quite some time.

"What do you think they're going to do with them?" Caroline asked.

"To tell you the truth," said Khepri. "I don't want to know."

"Let's go," I said, hazarding a final glance at the retrieval operation before I started to walk again. "I want to get the Nepenthes and get out of here."

Tam caught up to me and put his hand on my shoulder as he walked.

We all hurried over to where we remembered the air pillow launch pad was.

When we came over the hill, and looked, though, it was gone.

"What?" I felt exhausted and near tears.

Khepri studied the sight before us. "This looks like it's been deserted a long, long time."

The area was still flat; the plants and earth hadn't taken over yet, but there was no sign of anyone, no air pillows, no buildings, no nothing.

It was just flat grassland.

I felt like crying.

"Hold on," Jim said. "I'll do some reconnaissance." He stood back, and transformed into the djinn. Giving us a salute and a smile, he zoomed off to get a closer look at what had been our only hope for reaching the quamernat island.

We watched as he zipped over every square foot of the area, and then over the surrounding countryside. He was very fast.

He was back at my side in ten minutes.

"Nothing. Not a bit of anything other than nature," he said. "And no underground passageways or openings, either."

My shoulders fell.

The djinn looked thoughtful.

"I have another idea," he said.

I looked at him, hope in my heart.

"I could fly to the quamernat island myself, and see if they are still there, if they have the herb, or if they know where it can be found."

"That is an excellent idea, actually," said Khepri.

"Charlotte, this could work," Tam said, holding my shoulders and kissing my forehead.

I looked at the djinn; he was nearly ten feet tall, so I had to really crane my neck to see into his face.

He looked down at me with kind eyes and a smile on his face.

"Jim, the last time we wanted something from them, I was put through hell before they would give it to me," I said, looking into his face. "That could happen again."

"I'll risk it," the djinn said quickly. "We need that herb."

Such courage.

I nodded slowly.

Khepri opened her pack and withdrew a roll of parchment.

"Look here, Jim: Remember how we sketched this and noted all the details of the Nepenthes?

She unrolled the parchment and held it open with both hands.

It was the herb, drawn from several sides, and a list of its attributes, its location, what it smelled like, everything someone would need to identify and find it.

Khepri carefully rolled it back up and handed it to the djinn, who took it solemnly.

I hugged him and whispered, "Be careful."

He flew off in the direction of the quamernat island, gaining speed as he went, and was soon out of sight.

"Well, said Tam, "we might as well make camp here."

"I'll gather wood for a fire," Håkan said. "Come on, boys, lend a hand." He gestured for Inge and Olof to accompany him.

We all spread out a blanket around a circle, and Khepri broke out food.

I sat down and closed my eyes. My heart felt constricted. I was so worried, about my parents, about Merry, about the kidnapped townsfolk, and about Jim.

I looked off in the direction the djinn had flown.

"You look worried, Babe," said Tam, sitting down beside me.

"Last time, the quamernats – or their ancestors' spirits, I could never be sure – really put me through the wringer, to get *The Book of Mysteries*." I looked down as Håkan, and the boys returned, their arms full of firewood.

"I think it was better that I had no idea what they would put me through before it happened. It was that bad," I looked at Tam, feeling very worried.

He took me in his arms and held me, and we sat there, watching as Håkan built a fire.

Caroline and Khepri soon had a pot boiling, with delicious smells bubbling out of it.

We sat there and waited for Jim, long into the night.

Chapter Twenty-Seven

The Long and Short of It

We fell asleep around the fire, waiting for Jim, and woke up on the deck of *Pride of the Sea*, in the early morning.

"Oh, my goodness!" I exclaimed, opening my eyes and looking around.

"I will never get used to that," Caroline said.

I spotted Jim in a corner. Tupu had her arms around him. In his hands was a small burlap sack.

Tupu kissed Jim on his face, and I realized he was crying.

I hurried over and stood a few feet from them, not wanting to intrude.

Jim sniffed, and I handed him my handkerchief, and he blew his nose, looking at me gratefully.

"Khepri," Jim said quietly.

Khepri came forward, and he handed her the sack.

She opened it and looked inside. "OHHH!"

"It's the Nepenthes," he said.

Without a word, Khepri ran below decks to prepare the potion, motioning for Christianne to come with her.

I turned to Tam. "Ready all sails. We leave for Swerighe within the hour." He nodded and began barking orders to the crew.

I turned back to Jim, "Would you like to talk about it?"

Jim nodded.

Tupu held his hand tightly and would not let it go.

"I think I want to stay up here," he said. "The fresh air helps."

"I totally understand," I said, remembering my own trial with the aliens.

We moved to sit on the boxes on deck.

Jim took a deep breath and began to speak: "Well, first of all, the island was still there, although it looked a little different than last time. The quamernats told me it had been a very long time since we'd last been there."

"How long?" I asked gently.

Jim's brow furrowed. "They said it had been two centuries, which I didn't fully understand. They said time flows differently on their world than on ours. They said that 'after the supernova, it sped us up.' Before that event, they said, they had been going slower than we had," Jim looked up at me. "I am really not sure of what they meant by that, to be honest."

I nodded. They were very strange aliens.

"Did they say how the cave dwellers multiplied? I've been curious about that," I said.

"Oh, that. Yes. The explanation was alarming. They said the cave dwellers had stolen technology from their island a few decades before. They said the cave dwellers had all but died out: starved, they said. But that when there was only a few hundred of them left, they got desperate and snuck onto the island and stole a device that could 'replicate a person,' " Jim said this slowly, "and that they were using it to repopulate their city and also for 'use in the mills.' " He looked at me. "I think they were still practicing cannibalism." He looked nauseated.

"That would explain why they rushed out to take the bodies from the field," I said drily. "And why they were so cavalier about their great losses in battle."

"Ugh," said Jim. "But anyway, the quamernats were kind and friendly and helpful. They still remembered us, as a tribe."

"That's good," I said.

Jim continued, "They looked at the parchment, looked it over a long time. Then they asked me to come with them, and they led me back under the library, just like before. To that same small room." Jim got a faraway look in his eyes, remembering.

"They asked me if I wanted the herb, they called it the 'herb of truth' – I told them yes, all they had, please. I told them what had happened, how the wizard was hurting our planet with The Warming, and how he'd kidnapped the people and your baby," Jim looked at me and nodded.

"Go on," I said quietly.

"They said they had to test me, to see if I was worthy. Just between you and me, I found it just a little insulting."

I nodded in understanding. I had, too.

"Well, so the test started, and it was just me, in a black void, and a voice. The voice told me that if I agreed to ..." Jim blew his nose again. "Sorry."

"It's fine. I'm familiar with their tests," I said.

"They told me they would give me the Nepenthes, but I had to agree to ... to consign Tupu to a djinni bottle."

I felt an icy shock. I glanced at Tupu to make sure she was still there.

She's really here, right?

"I told them, no," said Jim. "They said I could not have the Nepenthes and I could not return without a sacrifice, and that it had to be Tupu, confined to the eternal slavery of the bottle."

Jim's voice had gotten very quiet.

"I told them no. No, I would not do that. They told me if I did not put Tupu in the bottle, I could not have the herb, and I would never be returned to our world, and neither would any of you. They asked me again and again, and I refused. They were quite insistent."

"Then I asked if they would take me, instead."

My eyes opened in shock, and my glance darted to Jim's wrists. I gave exhaled in relief when I confirmed his wrists did not have the band of djinni slavery on them.

"I told them I would agree to that. I pleaded with them. But they refused."

"Then they were silent for a long time, and I thought they had left me in the darkness, that I would stay there forever. It felt like days and days. I didn't sleep or eat or move. It was a long time to wait."

"I was ill with worry. I thought I had failed and that our world would suffer The Warming, and that I would spend forever in that dark place, just existing. I think they were trying to get me to see how awful eternity in a black void could be."

"But then they finally spoke again, and told me I had passed the test. I didn't understand, but they explained the test had been to see if I would ..." Jim's voice cracked, and he turned and put his face into Tupu's shoulder.

She held him for a long time.

Then he lifted his head and spoke again. "They said the test was to see if I would sacrifice the love of my life to get the Herb of Truth. But I couldn't. I just couldn't. Then they told me I had passed the real test. That my refusal to sacrifice Tupu was the successful end of the test."

Jim looked troubled.

"Charlotte, they tested my love for Tupu. I really resent that. You know?" He looked at me.

"Trust me, I know." I said dryly. "I think they have a voyeuristic attitude toward earthlings, to tell you the truth."

"I think you've nailed it," he whispered.

A week later, Khepri was practically dancing around with happiness. "I did it! I did it!" She twirled on the deck of the ship, her hair flying in all directions.

"Ha ha! What did you do?" I asked.

It was sunset on the deck, and I was at the rail with my face in the wind, mentally urging the giant manta rays to swim faster.

We'd been pampering them more than ever, feeding them black skipjacks and bluefin morning, noon, and night. All five were in perfect, tip-top condition, and performing admirably well.

It still wasn't fast enough.

"I finished the potion!" said Khepri. "Look! Look!" she held up a vial of swirling pearlescent purple liquid. "That ice wizard is goin' down!" she laughed.

I bent to look. I could see green, red and black specks floating in it.

"Are you sure it's stewed long enough?" I asked.

"Why," she turned to peer into the vial. "Oh, the flecks? Yes, those are supposed to be there."

"Do we have to make him drink it?"

"Yes, yes we do," said Khepri. "And the potion is absolutely correct, I tested it. The book is fabulous, just wonderful, Charlotte! It gives a test for every potion recipe it has. And this potion passed with flying colors. It fulfills ever description point in the recipe. It's perfect." She stared at the swirling liquid with a smile

"Does it have a potency shelf life?" I asked.

"It should be used within a month of concoction, well … within a month of the *completion* of the potion. It took several days to create. One of the requirements is that certain ingredients must be added during the full moon, which was two days ago. Another is that the order of ingredients must be unaltered. That means that of the twenty-seven different herbs and ointments called for, all of them had to be added in the correct order," said Khepri. She glanced at me, smiling. "It changed color with every ingredient I added. It was fascinating."

"I'll bet," I grinned. "And how did Christianne help?"

"Well, during the fourth day, the potion had to be stirred for seventeen hours, and every hour the direction of the movement had to change. Clockwise, counter-clockwise, back and forth, up and down, let me tell you, it was exhausting. Christianne helped a lot with that. Even Kym and Caroline took a turn."

"So much work!" I looked at the vial. "And this is the final product?"

"Sort of," said Khepri. "I made a tub full, actually. At least several gallons."

I raised my eyebrows in surprise.

"I didn't want to take any chances," she smiled. "So, with this bit," she looked into the vial," I filled this flask with potion out of the large tub, then added the final two ingredients, agitated it for a few minutes, and it changed from dark purple to this wonderful color."

"You'd done an incredible job, thank you," I hugged her for a long time.

The voyage back to Swerighe seemed to last forever. I was so impatient, I spent a lot of the journey pacing back and forth on the fo'c'sle deck, looking out to sea, willing the ship to fly faster.

As we approached the northlands, we spotted a small iceberg in the middle of the ocean. A lone polar bear was trapped on the floating ice, pacing slowly back and forth, agitated.

"Let's see what's going on with the bear," I said.

It will only take a short while.

We drew up alongside of the iceberg, which was about a hundred yards square.

As we approached, we could see the bear was very weak. And we could see why.

"Oh, my God," Kym said.

We were all lined up at the railing as *Pride of the Sea* reached the edge of the iceberg. The bear moved away from the ship, but we caught a glimpse of the poor thing before it retreated.

It was skin and bones.

The bodies of two cubs lay nearby; they looked like they'd been dead just a short while.

Christianne began to cry softly.

"We've seen this a bit in recent times," said Håkan quietly. "The ice is melting, the seals are moving away, or dying out, and polar bears like this one are left to starve. She can't make enough milk to feed her cubs, and they end up starving to death as her milk dries up. Then she starves to death, too." He looked sad.

I shook my head.

So much death, so much damage, all from The Warming spell.

"The fault for this death and suffering lies squarely on the shoulders of that ice wizard," Khepri said.

I gripped the railing of the ship tightly, and my knuckles went white.

"Tam," I called sharply over my shoulder. "Toss a bucketful of fish to that bear."

I knew it would only delay the inevitable, but maybe, just maybe, she could gain enough strength from the fish to swim to the mainland, or go fishing herself in these waters. I looked north. The weather was getting cooler and cooler. The north wasn't done releasing all the cold from its poles.

And maybe, just maybe, we can defeat the ice wizard, and reverse this monstrosity of climate cataclysm before it's too late.

Two days later, we sailed into port in Swerighe.

We had weeks to prepare for this day, and we'd made extensive plans. We knew exactly what would happen, because we were going on the offensive.

The ice wizard wouldn't know what hit him.

I was eager to get going.

The town looked much the same, and we wasted no time with pleasantries. We were on our steeds and galloping north to the realm of the ice wizard within an hour of dropping anchor.

Chapter Twenty-Eight
The Journey Back Begins

We made good time, until we got to the bog.

"It's flooded," Kym said, looking out over the expanse of water.

"What do we do now?" Christianne, asked dismounting.

I was already off Shêtân and crouching at the water's edge. "Håkan, what is the custom when the bog is flooded?" I asked.

I got no answer. I glanced back at the big man, who looked mildly dazed and confused. He snapped out of his reverie and turned to me. "I am not sure. The bog has never been flooded in my lifetime."

Great.

I stood up, brushing my hands off. "Well, we've got to get across. Let's think." I walked a few yards along the water's edge. The waves gently lapped against the peat at my feet.

"Can we go around?" Tupu asked. "Didn't Håkan say there was a small village to the northwest?"

"We could," Håkan said slowly. "It would add days to our journey, though."

I reached for a stick from the forest undergrowth nearby, and brought it to the water's edge. I stuck it in vertically: It sank a foot, then stuck.

"The moors get sticky when they get oversaturated," said Håkan. "In the springtime, the rains do this, although it doesn't flood. There's always runoff."

"I wonder ...," Tam said.

I turned to him, curious.

He looked at me. "I wonder if this is the ice wizard's doing." He turned to Håkan. "You mentioned a runoff?"

Håkan nodded, understanding. "Normally, the rainwater drains off."

"What is stopping this water from draining off?" Tupu said.

"You think someone's dammed up the river?" Caroline asked.

As we had left the moors, the hills had dropped into a valley, and there had been a small river feeding off the bogs, through the hills and out into the meadowland.

"Possibly," Håkan said slowly. There's just one way to find out."

"I'm on it," said Jim, transforming. "Make camp here. I'll be a while." The djinn zipped off.

"Good idea," I said. "Let's back up a few dozen feet, well back from the water's edge, though."

It was early afternoon, and we'd just ridden out of a sparse Nordic forest.

"I'm going hunting. Håkan? Inge? Olof? Want to join me?" Tam said.

"I'd like to come as well," Christianne said.

Olof looked up sharply.

I smiled.

Since we'd left the Mare Nostrum, Olof had taken a liking to Christianne. It was a puppy love, Olof was thirteen, and Christianne was sixteen. They were nearly the same height. Olof would be a tall man, I guessed.

"I'll gather firewood while you guys try for a rabbit or two," I said.

"Or a deer. I saw a few on the ride yesterday," Håkan said, winking.

"Or a deer." I smiled.

"If you do get a deer, I can salt the meat we don't eat, to preserve it for a long time," said Caroline. "Maybe even make rudimentary smoked jerky."

"Sounds good." Tam smiled, strapping his quiver onto his back.

They hiked off.

I turned to the forest.

"Okay. Wood," I said.

Tupu joined me, and we soon gathered a large pile of branches.

Khepri piled a pyramid atop the kindling she'd pulled out of a small bag of dry tinder; and with flint and steel, soon had a flame going.

I used the small ax the troupe carried, and made large branches into smaller, easily handled branches.

We were soon settled around the fire.

"It's been a few hours. I wonder if Tam's ventured very far?" I mused out loud.

As if on cue, I heard his voice.

"Ahoy hoy!" Tam called from maybe a hundred feet away. I looked. He and Håkan carried a yearling buck between their shoulders.

I gave a thumbs up, and Khepri and Caroline cheered.

"Whoop!" Kym called out, clapping.

Tam walked up and dropped the branch the deer was tied to.

"We were longer because, after we shot it, we strung it up and bled it out," he said, kissing the top of my head. "It took a while."

Olof and Inge were beaming. Håkan was in excellent spirits. Christianne had a small smile on her face.

Hmmmm.

Caroline, Khepri, and Håkan got to work skinning and butchering, while Tam rigged up a teepee smoker.

"This will smoke the meat all night, and we can preserve some of it with salt," Tam patted a large bag of coarse salt.

"It's a good thing we brought the donkey, huh Tam?" I winked at him.

Tam had been hesitant about the donkey, but it had been a real boon to the journey, carrying the heavy bag of salt, and several bags of oats, among other things.

I looked fondly over at the long-eared beast, strung next to the horses along the edge of camp. As if he knew we were talking about him, he raised his head from eating the grass at his feet, and made a loud, "HEE-HAW!"

"Ha ha ha!," laughed Kym. "I will never get tired of that!"

I motioned to Christianne to join me, patting the blanket next to me.

She sat, and made herself comfortable.

Khepri sat next to her.

Kym and Tupu joined us.

We looked at her, knowing smiles on our faces.

She grinned and looked over at Olof. He and Inge were helping with the butchering, which was hard work.

I nudged her. She looked back at me. I winked. She smiled and blushed.

I could hold it in no longer. "Christianne, WHAT HAPPENED?"

"He ..." she was blushing furiously. "He kissed me."

"HE DIDN'T!" cried Kym.

Olof looked over at us, then bent to his work again.

I heard Håkan talking, but couldn't make out the words. We bent close to Christianne.

"Okay, okay." She took a deep breath. "We were walking, trying to be quiet, you know, while searching for game. Then, Tam spotted movement and took aim. It was the deer. His first arrow got it high on the neck. He's really getting good, you know."

"Anyway, we were running to the deer, because it had run a dozen steps before falling. And I tripped. Olof heard me fall, and came back to help me. He asked me if I was okay. I told him I'd wrenched my ankle but that it was probably fine."

"He suggested I try to walk. So I tried to get up, and he put his hand out to help me. He pulled me up, and I stood on the ankle, which was sore but okay. He bent down and felt my leg to make sure it was okay, then stood back up and took a step closer. That's when ..."

Her face was scarlet, and she could not stop grinning.

"He ... he stepped close and looked into my eyes. You know how his hair falls over his eyes? Kind of a flop over his forehead?"

We nodded, holding our breaths.

"Well, he flipped his head so it would go back, and I moved ... I moved my face a tiny bit closer. His eyes went all crinkly-smiley, and he leaned over to ... kiss me. His mouth was just an inch away. I couldn't help it. I kissed him. Or he kissed me. We kissed."

We were all grinning from ear to ear.

Kym was trying to not scream in delight. "And? How did you like it?" she asked her friend.

"I liked it very much," Christianne smiled. "Right then, though, Håkan called him over to help. He stared into my eyes, then he took my hand and ..." Christianne raised her right hand and looked at it. "He kissed my hand. Then looked at me again with this ... this look in his eyes. I don't know. But it was wonderful." She pressed her hand to her cheek.

"OH! My God, that's so nice," Khepri said.

"Young love! How sweet!" Caroline said.

"Ohhhh, Chrissy, he likes you," I said.

"He sure does!" Kym said.

Tupu gave Christianne a long hug. "This is wonderful!"

"Do you think you're smitten?" Tupu grinned.

"All I know is, I really liked his kiss," Christianne grinned. "That's all I know." She sighed.

"Oh, you've got it baddddd," Kym said, clapping her hands in delight.

Later that evening, as the sun was setting, as Khepri and Caroline were salting the deer meat, and Tupu was cutting strips of meat and piercing them with sticks and laying them against the spit over the fire, the djinn returned.

We all gathered to hear what he had to say.

"Ho boy," he said. "That was interesting." He sat at the fire, transforming into his human form.

"What happened?" I asked.

"Well, Tam was definitely right. It was clearly sabotage," Jim said.

"Was it a dam?" Håkan asked.

Jim nodded, taking a long drink out from his water skin. "The mouth of the river was blocked by wall of mud eight feet high," he said. "It had been shucked up in haste, and hammered down."

"It was hard to move, but I eventually got it pulled down."

"Good job." Tam patted the man on his shoulder. Jim grinned.

"Have you looked at the moors lately?" Jim asked. "Go look."

We all got to our feet and hurried over.

My jaw dropped open. The water was almost gone. Draining away as we watched.

"Jim, this is fantastic," I kissed his cheek. "You're a hero."

The big man blushed.

"We'll start across at first light," I said. "We want to be sure of our footing." I stuck a foot over the line and pressed it into the bog. It squelched and went down a few inches.

"Hopefully, we'll find dry ground where we can stop along the way," Tam said.

"We could try to cross it in one day," suggested Håkan. "It would be a very long day, but we'd avoid the mists and whatever hides inside them."

I'd told the others what had transpired the last time we'd camped out on the moors. They'd been shocked.

"I think that's actually a grand idea, Håkan," I said, smiling at him. "I guess it will take around fifteen or sixteen hours to cross."

"Barring any mishaps," Jim raised his eyebrows.

"Barring any mishaps," I agreed.

We started across the soggy moor at dawn.

Riding Shêtân across the squelchy moors was an exercise in concentration. He didn't like the ground sucking on his hooves. He ended up lifting his legs high and prancing much of the way.

I patted his neck on the long journey. "If you keep doing that, you're going to tire yourself out much sooner."

"He is a magnificent beast, Your Highness," Håkan said, admiring the huge black stallion.

"Thank you, it has been an interesting journey for both of us." I petted Shêtân's neck again.

"Have you ever thought of breeding him?" asked Håkan. I think he'd be very valuable as a stud."

"Probably, but I've just been too busy to think of it," I said.

"Charlotte?" Tupu rode up on her horse. "We have trouble."

I clucked to Shêtân and followed Tupu, nodding goodbye to Håkan.

After we were out of earshot, I asked Tupu, "What's the problem?"

"The moors are filling up again," she said in a low voice.

I glanced down. The ground seemed okay.

Tupu pointed off to the northeast, toward the spring that fed the water table.

I squinted in the dying light.

Was that water? I couldn't tell.

"Jim transformed and went to check. What's-his-face had his gnomes start to rebuild the dam," Tupu said.

"Did he check the spring?" I asked.

Tupu nodded. "It's slowly filling. Jim says the water will be here soon."

"We need to ride fast," I said.

Tam came up then. "You heard?"

I nodded.

"Let's ride, then," he said.

I trotted back to the others. "We need to move fast. The wizard's mountain gnomes are rebuilding the dam."

We trotted the horses, watching carefully for problems on the ground as we rode.

The djinn flew back to the river and dam, so Tupu led his horse.

Kym's pony, Taimim, trotted rapidly next to me, his short legs working double time to keep up.

"Be careful! We don't want the horses to ..." I never got to finish my sentence.

Caroline's horse went down.

"AHHH!" she cried as her steed fell sideways. She landed on the went moor.

I circled back.

Khepri was already kneeling, examining the horse's leg.

He screamed in pain.

"Well?" I asked.

"It's not broken, but it is badly sprained," said Khepri. "He can't take another rider. We'll have to lead him behind."

I reached down and swung Caroline up behind me on Shêtân's back.

"Will he be okay?" I asked Khepri.

She shrugged. "Let's hope."

"Poor boy," murmured Caroline. "He's such a good horse, too."

I turned and trotted back to join the others.

Khepri followed on her horse, leading Caroline's horse behind her.

Night fell.

The djinn still was not back, which was worrying. He had a much shorter distance to travel, and should've returned by now.

Tupu, riding beside me, was lost in thought, a worried look on her face.

I slowed to walk as the light left the land.

This is not good.

The water hadn't risen any more, so I assumed the djinn had done *something*.

But riding after nightfall in a place that held such uncertain terrain was very worrisome.

We held lit torches, but they didn't do much for seeing the ground ahead of where our horses were stepping.

Inge's horse stumbled and went down, and he'd had to ride behind Olof on the boy's steed, and lead his behind them.

Both Inge's and Caroline's horses were limping more and more.

After Shêtân stumbled for a third time, almost going down, despite me studying the ground unblinkingly as we rode, I made a decision.

"Tam, Håkan, hold up," I called.

The men rode back to me.

"We're starting to straggle out," I pointed. Khepri and Christianne were about twenty yards to the right. "I want to scout out a dry bit of land to camp for the night. I fear more of the horses will be injured if we don't."

Tam and Håkan nodded.

"I want to find something close by, though." I looked out on the moors. "The mist is starting to rise." I looked back at them. "Can you venture out just a bit? And return soon? Say, in less than twenty minutes?"

"Sure, Babe," Tam said.

"We'll be back soon, Your Highness," Håkan said, nodding.

They swung their horses around and trotted away to search.

I watched them go, an uneasy feeling in the pit of my stomach.

Half an hour later, they had not returned.

We'd gathered our horses close together: Caroline, Khepri, Christianne, Kym, Tupu, Olof, and Inge. We'd dismounted to give them a rest.

I'd built a small fire out of peat and wood we'd packed on the donkey, and it sputtered fitfully.

"Add more wood?" Christianne suggested.

I tossed on another branch.

An owl hooted loudly somewhere.

"That's promising. Isn't it?" Inge said.

I frowned, puzzled.

Where did an owl come from?

"They fly over the moors to catch mice," said Olof. "Although with the flooding ..."

His voice tapered off, and he was silent again.

An hour passed, and they still had not returned.

I rose to my feet.

"I'm going to unsaddle and feed the horses, and tie them down for the night," I said. "Carrie, go ahead and start a stew or something."

She nodded.

I picked up a torch, grabbed some rope, and walked out half a dozen paces. I looked out over the night-shrouded moors. The mist was still low, and I wondered if the flood dampened the moor's abilities to grow mist at night.

I fixed the rope and strung the horses and mule out, wrapping the other end down near the campfire. After they each had hay and grain, and after I'd petted Shêtân, pressing my cheek to his warm neck, I walked back to the fire.

"Listen, I want us all to stay together tonight. Let's take three watches, two hours apart, and let's have three on each watch." I looked them over as they nodded. They relied on me as their leader, and I took that responsibility seriously. "Tupu, Inge, and Kym, take first watch. Start before midnight. Khepri and I will take second watch. Caroline, Olof, and Christianne, take third watch. Sound good?"

They all nodded.

"Listen," I looked at them seriously. "I don't care what you hear or see in the mist. I don't care if my mother appears in the mist and calls to you. You do not leave the fire. Not for anything. Understand?"

They all nodded solemnly.

I addressed Inge and Olof.

"You two? I know you're young, but I'm counting on you to use your heads and think. And follow my orders to a 'T.'"

The boys nodded. They would obey.

It's not that they aren't trustworthy, it's that they're just so darned young.

I sat down and accepted the bowl of venison stew Caroline handed me.

I sat eating and watching Inge, Kym, Christianne, and Olof interacting. "Caroline, was I ever that young?"

Caroline smiled. "Miss, you were younger."

Chapter Twenty-Nine
A Hard Night
and a New Plan

We all stayed awake until nearly midnight, unable to sleep, unable to relax, unable to stop eating toasted marshmallows.

"Okay," Khepri said, waving an empty bag, "That's it. I'm all out."

I held up my sticky fingers, and tried licking the stickiness off of them.

"Khepri, what?" Kym stared at the healer. Her mouth, ringed with marshmallow, dropped open.

"Out. As in I have no more," Khepri shrugged.

"Okay, okay, well," I used a drip of water out of my waterskin to try and scrub the stickiness off my hands, "We should be turning in, anyway."

"Rub your hands on the ground, the dirt will help scrub the marshmallow off, Miss," Caroline said.

It took me a while, but I was eventually somewhat successful in getting clean. Turning over in my blanket, I gave one more look at Tupu, who sat with Inge and Kym, on first watch. I gave her a thumbs up and said quietly, "Counting on you," then closed my eyes.

I hoped they heard me.

It was a long night.

I tossed and turned, and my brain just wouldn't let me rest too much.

I was worried about Tam most of all.

First my baby is stolen, then my mate goes missing. I've had just about enough of this.

It seemed to take a hundred hours for those two hours to pass, but eventually, I felt Tupu's hand on my shoulder.

"Charlotte, wake up. Time for second watch."

My brain, foggy and sleepy, slowly surfaced, and I sat up, blinking my eyes.

"I'm up. I'm up."

"Good. Here's some water," said Tupu, handing me a waterskin. "I need to go to sleep. First watch was bad."

"That's the understatement of the year," I heard Kym say nearby.

I opened my eyes, instantly awake.

"What happened," I said, looking from one to the other.

I glanced over at Inge, who was already slipping into his blanket next to Olof. His face was white.

"Oh, nothing much," said Tupu, ticking off fingers as she counted. "Just several moaning cries, the appearance of the queen, the sound of a newborn baby crying in the mist somewhere, the sight of Jim's face floating in the mist, red with blood, the sound of Tam's calls for help. You know, the usual." She looked at me, her eyebrows raised. "Have fun on second watch."

Khepri was already up, and stoking the fire with a stick. She glanced at me wryly, "I'll have some coffee in a few minutes. I suggest jumping around to fully wake up and get your blood circulating."

I nodded, pulling on my boots. I got to my feet, yawning and swinging my arms back and forth, then spent a minute running in place.

I decided to have a walk and check on the horses. Walking around the camp, everything was quiet and calm. Almost as if the moors were holding their breath in preparation for the second onslaught on the camp.

I visited Shêtân and fed him a wild carrot from my bag. He nuzzled me and nudged me with his head until I gave him a good scritch on the neck.

All the animals looked fine. All their traces were tight and secure.

I returned to the center of camp and took a deep breath, hands on my hips.

I had no clue where Tam, Jim, and Håkan had disappeared to, but I knew that whatever mischief might have befallen them, they were each very capable of handling it.

I sensed the ice wizard's evil was at work here, and I vowed to visit great harm upon the him.

And get back my baby. My Merry.

I looked out and saw the moors were as misty as always.

Sigh. I will not miss this place when I get back to the sea.

Khepri and I settled in next to the fire.

"Want some blackroot?" she offered.

I shrugged and took a twig, and stuck it in the corner of my mouth.

The first hour passed without incident.

The second hour began with a moaning cry, and a face appeared in the mist, bobbing up and down.

Without a word, I stood, picked up a rock, and threw it hard at the face.

It disappeared.

"Interesting tactic," Khepri smiled.

I nodded, "I decided to handle any more problems with violence. Rock throwing is especially satisfying."

"I like it," Khepri laughed.

"CHARLOTTE!" came Tam's voice from the mist.

I glanced out toward the voice, then returned my gaze to the fire. I could feel Khepri's gaze on me, then her shrug.

"Want more coffee?" she asked.

"Nah, if I drink too much, I won't be able to fall back to sleep when third watch comes along," I said.

"Very true, very true," Khepri said.

"There's something I was wondering about Merry," I said quietly.

"*woooo woooo woooo woooo woooo!*"

I sighed.

"What are you wondering about?" Khepri asked.

"Well," I said, "Do you think he'll have any lasting damage from the wizard's growing spell? I know I had unusual pain and bruised ribs, and I'm okay with that, those will eventually fade. I was just worried about him."

Khepri thought a minute. "Well, the main thing when a baby grows, aside from any genetic problems, is how the lungs mature. But he seemed to be breathing fine last time we saw him, even though it was just a few minutes, I mean. Once he started breathing, he seemed fine."

I stared into the fire. "I can't wait to see him again. To hold him again."

As if on cue, a baby's cry could be heard inside the mist.

wahhh wahhh wahhh WAHHH WAHHH WAHHH

"Whoever is doing that is cruel," Khepri said.

I shrugged. "I'm not going to let it bother me."

A baby appeared in the mist, floating and crying.

I sighed again.

It was going to be a long night.

Third watch relieved us, and we slept a few more hours. I warned them what to expect, and they nodded solemnly. Olof looked and acted more grown up, and stood taller in his boots.

I had assigned him to a watch with Christianne in the hope that it would sharpen his awareness, and I was heartened to see it working.

Caroline winked at me, "Get some sleep, Miss. Something tells me tomorrow is going to be a full day."

"You got that right, Carrie." I yawned. "Well, be strong. See you at dawn."

I crawled into my blanket and closed my eyes, and was asleep in seconds.

I slept very soundly, thank goodness.

I was awakened by sounds of the camp stirring. Caroline's quiet voice was calming, and familiar.

I opened my eyes.

Dawn was pinking the fog, and the Christianne had a pot of something delicious bubbling on the fire.

I yawned and sat up. Stretching, I asked, "So, how'd third watch go?"

Caroline shrugged. "It went."

I smiled.

"I think all three watches were similar, to tell you the truth," said Christianne. "After a while, it just got boring."

I laughed. "Yeah, they don't have much of a repertoire, do they?"

"Nope." She grinned.

"It was a bit spooky at first," said Olof. "But after a while you realize if you ignore it, it's not really dangerous. I think they want you to react."

I nodded. "That's it, exactly, Olof." I pulled on my boots and stood up.

"Well," I said, looking out at everything, the camp, the horses, the fire, "looks like everything came through the night without injury, huh?"

"Looks like it, Miss. Ready for some breakfast?" she handed me a bowl of stew, which I gratefully took.

It was delicious.

I ate, watching the troupe wake up and prepare to move out.

The light grew on the moor until it was bright and the mist began to burn off, although it was still quite early.

"Everyone, I want you to double check all your weapons," I said. "Sharpen every sword, every knife." I caught Olof's questioning eye. "Yes?"

"I just sharpened my knife yesterday; should I do it again today, Your Highness?" Olof asked.

"Yes, definitely. Sharpen it every day, Olof," I said. "A knife can be your best friend. It's your last line of defense. Keep it razor sharp, and it will always be there for you in a pinch."

"I sharpen my knife and my sword every morning," said Christianne. "The sharper they are, the easier they cut and chop, and slide into an enemy's gut."

Olof sat and got out his whetstone, and began drawing it carefully across the length of his blade.

"Your Highness," Inge said, "I have my new bow Tam was helping me make." He held up the bow. "But I don't have any arrows for it yet. Are there any to spare?"

"I've got the spares here," said Khepri, reaching for one of the bundles on the donkey. "Here you go. Remember to try and retrieve arrows, if you can."

"Yes, ma'am."

We packed up camp and prepared to head out.

I had one more thing to do.

"Everyone, Christianne, Kym: gather 'round. I want to do some strategy planning before we head out," I said.

They all sat in a circle around me.

"Christianne, about your wings?" I said.

"Hmmm?" Christianne said, spreading her wings out of her coat.

"I love those," I said. "Seriously love these wings." I smiled. "And I love the way your coat looks closed, but that it can let your wings out."

Christianne smiled.

"Now, I want to know, Christianne: when you propel yourself along the ground, can you do that while holding someone?" I asked.

"Yes, but I could use more practice," Christianne looked thoughtful.

"Let's stand up and try now." I got to my feet. "Kym, you, too." I motioned with my hand.

Both of them stood.

"Now, first let's try it with you alone," I motioned. "Run out about twenty feet, all the way to the horses, then turn and run back, okay? And go as fast as you can."

Christianne nodded, then turned and began whirring her wings. She took off running toward the horses. She was going so fast she was a blur. She was back in front of me in a few seconds.

"Okay, that was good," I smiled. "Can you try to go faster?"

She looked into my face.

"Lives may depend on it," I explained.

She nodded and turned, then disappeared.

In two seconds, she was back, puffing slightly.

"Wow. Okay. This is good. This is actually really good." I smiled at her and patted her shoulder.

Glancing around, I motioned the Kym.

"Stand right here, between Christianne and her path. There. Just like that. That's it." I moved Kym so that her back was up against Christianne's front.

"Now, Chrissy? Can you pick Kym up at all? Pick her up and run?" I asked.

"Let me try," Christianne said.

The first attempt she put her arms around Kym and tried to lift her a few inches off the ground and run. They fell after a few feet.

"Oww." Kym rubbed her nose.

"Sorry," Christianne grimaced.

"That's a good first try," I said. "Now, maybe lift her higher and let your momentum carry her. I think it might keep you from falling, if you get it just right."

Christianne nodded.

She looked along the path, and put her arms around Kym in a few different ways, trying out each one, before she tried to run again.

Finally, she grasped Kym, lifted her a foot off the ground, and took off. They were a blur. They zipped all the way to the horses, then back, in just a few seconds.

They didn't fall.

I felt ecstatic.

"Okay, that was great!" I beamed. "Now, Chrissy, try it a few more times until you can go really fast. Your top speed." I nodded.

The girls ran the course eight more times before they had it perfected.

Christianne ran a ninth time, picking Kym up, and disappearing, they were going so fast. They reappeared in less than two seconds.

"Okay, here's what we're going to do ..." We huddled, talking in low voices in case anything out on the moors was listening, for a long time.

"And don't talk about the plan at all," I whispered at them all. "From this moment on. Got that?"

Everyone nodded.

We mounted our steeds and rode out at a gallop.

Chapter Thirty
Hell to Pay

It took us two and a half days more to reach the wizard, far less time than it had the first time. But we knew the way, we knew the wizard's reach extended for hundreds of miles, and we were determined.

On the night of the third day, we crept into the cavern of the ice mage and hid.

We did not speak.

We barely breathed.

A low rumble filled the large cave.

I crept up, Christianne and Kym beside me, and peeked over the edge.

The wizard was snoring, stretched out on a bed of ice. Several mountain gnomes lay on the floor around him, curled up in the frozen dirt.

I wondered if one of them was Farryn.

Behind the sleeping wizard, the frozen ice encasing the abducted people of the village, and the queen and prince consort, looked dark.

That's not a good sign.

I worried the people were dying in the ice, but I knew I had to stay on task or all hope was lost.

The wizard's snores were loud, reverberating off the high walls of the cavern and emanating outward, like a summons.

I nodded to Christianne and Kym, and we crawled silently down the freezing rock, and closer to the evil creature.

I held my breath, listening.

I heard nothing, nothing at all.

It was quiet as a tomb inside the large cavern.

We crept closer.

And closer.

I looked behind me.

Caroline, Khepri, Tupu and Olof crawled in a line behind us, not making a sound.

We'd practiced this every evening on our way here.

It had become clear that Jim, Tam, and Håkan had very probably been snatched by the ice wizard's minions, so we knew we were on our own.

The wizard probably thought he was weakening us, chiseling away at our defenses and resources. He probably thought we'd run after the three had been caught.

I smiled a mirthless smile: The opposite was true.

I held up a finger, motioning for Kym and Christianne to stop, and just paused, watching the evil mage sleep.

I waited several minutes, until I was sure he was still fully asleep, fully relaxed.

It was utterly silent.

I knew the wizard very likely had multiple defenses in place. Sound enhancers, sound carriers, bringing every little noise directly to him. And motion sensors, triggers to alert him if anyone came close.

I crawled another foot along the ledge, silent and slow. The others followed me.

I paused every few steps to watch him. To listen for anything.

We drew close.

The ledge led downward; it was smooth, and had been cleared of all debris by multiple feet traversing it every waking hour. It was the second entrance to the wizard's lair.

After the ledge met the floor, it was maybe a hundred feet or so to the ice wizard.

I saw Christianne studying the area, just as we had practiced. She memorized every rock, every sleeping body, every ice chunk, every item on the floor.

Every square inch.

Finally, I decided we were close enough: not so close that we had triggered the wizard's sensors, but close enough.

I motioned to Christianne and Kym.

The element of surprise was a formidable weapon.

We stood, not making a sound.

Christianne got into position.

I had told both Christianne and Kym, days ago, *"This plan must anticipate every possible scenario. There will come a time, when all seems lost. That is when you must dig deep inside, and find the strength, the skill, the fortitude, that you will need."*

Kym stood in front of Christianne.

I held my breath.

The ice wizard snored.

I held up my hand and waited ... waited ...

NOW!

I dropped my hand, and Christianne and Kym disappeared.

The rest of us, Caroline, Khepri, Tupu, Olof, and I ran forward, drawing our swords.

Christianne and Kym appeared next to the ice wizard.

In the blink of an eye, Kym was gone and the chimera was there.

She grabbed the wizard with both paws, pinning his arms and hands to his body, and sinking her claws into his abdomen.

"AHHHHHHHHHHHHHHHHHHH!" He screamed, blinking his eyes.

Blood poured from his mouth.

He was so short the chimera's claws had hit a lung.

Dammit.

Tupu and Caroline swung their swords as they ran up, and the mountain gnomes squealed and ran off in terror.

Khepri and I reached the ice wizard first.

"Remember me?" I whispered, a deadly grin on my face. I brought my scimitar up and shoved it into his mouth, and pried.

The ice wizard's jaw cracked.

"RRRRRRRGGHHHHHH!"

"RRRRRRRGGHHHHHH!"

"RRRRRRRGGHHHHHH!"

He shrieked.

Careful, Charlotte. We need him alive.

I pried again, and his mouth opened.

I stuck my dagger in. The very same dagger he had tortured me with.

Khepri was beside me in an instant, unstoppering the vial she held and pouring it down his throat.

"GHGGHHHHHH!" The wizard screamed.

He spat out the potion. Every drop.

I shoved my dagger in farther, piercing his tongue.

"Hold the torch closer, Tupu," I said, and the warrior brought her torch, just lit, up to his face.

"AGAHHHHHHHHHHH!" The wizard's cheek smoked and turned black.

"Back a little," I murmured.

Tupu drew the torch back an inch or two.

I peered into his throat and moved my dagger around. It pierced his cheek, and sliced the side of his tongue.

Then it went down his throat a few inches and pierced the back of his throat.

"HHGHHHHAAAHHHH!" He screamed.

"Oh, trust me, you taught me well, little man," I whispered, my mouth close to his ear.

He tried to struggle, but the chimera squeezed, and fresh blood poured from his abdomen where her claws had gone in.

"AHHHHAHHHHHH!"

The tip of my dagger was about two or three inches down his throat. I pressed it downward, smashing his tongue.

Tears poured down the side of his face.

Khepri came forward with the second of twenty vials she had prepared. We'd assumed the wizard would fight. We'd assumed he would break a few vials. Khepri was well prepared.

She grinned as she carefully poured the potion down his throat. Blood mingled with the bright liquid in his mouth.

I didn't say a word. I just waited.

With his tongue held down, the potion slid easily down his throat and into his stomach.

It was supposed to act immediately.

I held him and waited.

And waited.

I glanced at Khepri, and she shrugged.

Nearly a minute after the potion had went down, the wizard went slack.

His eyes were unfocused, yet staring at me.

"This potion compels you to do our bidding, wizard," I whispered.

He nodded.

Fantastic!

"Free all the prisoners and perform the counter-spell to stop The Warming."

The ice wizard's eyes went wide and then closed.

"He can't do it unless you free his hands," Khepri said.

"If we free his hands, he could do anything," I answered.

"But you've given him an order," said Khepri. "He has to perform that order first."

I looked back at the wizard.

Have to do this right.

"Wizard, you will not cast any spell unless I tell you to act. You may breathe – that's it," I said.

Khepri nodded.

That should do it.

I hesitated.

What was I missing?

I took a deep breath.

I stepped back and nodded to the chimera. Christianne grabbed the ice mage from behind as he came loose and fell from the huge beast's grip.

He waved his hands, uttering a few words of magic that were forgotten as soon as we heard them. A heavy green mist dribbled out of his mouth, curling to the ground, and began drifting toward the ice wall encasing the prisoners.

We watched it travel.

After a minute, it reached the ice, and the second it touched the blue wall, it spread instantly to the entire surface.

The ice wall started to melt away, the water pouring from it and draining off the rock.

The villagers came into view, then my parents. Then Tam, Jim, and Håkan, last of all.

They looked as if they were waking up from a dream.

I held my breath, tears in my eyes.

"Charlotte?" my mother said weakly.

Tupu and Khepri ran to check on the prisoners.

I couldn't believe they were free.

A jubilant feeling ran through me, and I grinned.

The wizard began waving his hands again, in an even more intricate manner. The words that came out of his mouth were different, more guttural, more primal.

A purple cloud began to form over his head.

It was thick and billowing, emerging out of thin air directly over his head.

"The magic is coming directly from him," Khepri said.

He continued his chanting and spelling.

The counter-spell!

We watched him closely. The purple cloud began to grow.

The magic actually made a sound as it spread, an almost sizzling sound.

"Such strong magic," whispered Christianne.

The bewitching cloud spread out, growing exponentially.

Larger and larger.

Until it filled the cavern.

It touched the walls of the ice cave.

And they began to melt.

THANK GOD!

The walls of the icy cavern were melting.

And still the ice wizard continued to chant in that husky tone of voice that was almost like a primitive growl. His hands continued to wave in the air as he performed the intricate pattern of the counter-spell.

The purple cloud continued to grow.

At one point, it seemed to squeeze out of the cavern through multiple fissures and archways, escaping in every way possible.

And I knew. I knew the cloud was going outside.

Outside.

Out into the world.

Into the air, into the ground, into the oceans.

The Warming was being reversed.

I wanted to cry in relief and happiness.

I closed my eyes and took several deep breaths.

I felt a peace begin to flow through me.

Could it be happening? Finally?

The ice wizard continued for many, many minutes, until finally, the chanting came to the end.

His voice stopped, his hands dropped, and his entire body slouched in defeat.

"It's done," Jim said.

"The Warming is reversed?" Kym asked.

I nodded, sniffing. "I think so, Kymmy."

"Don't call me 'Kymmy'." She scowled.

Everyone laughed.

It was like a release.

We laughed in happiness.

The nightmare was over.

Finally.

Then everything happened at once, in slow motion.

Something caught my eye.

Movement.

The ice wizard grabbing my dagger from his mouth and swinging around.

I reached for him, catching his sleeve and pulling him back.

He lunged at the last minute, throwing all his weight in the opposite direction and thrusting the dagger...

... and plunging it into Christianne's side.

He cackled in glee, laughter sputtering from his swollen, bloody mouth.

I looked on, stunned, and caught Christianne as she fell, her wings fluttering weakly.

I heard a growl behind me.

The ice wizard moved to push the dagger into Christianne again.

Olof ran forward ...

and plunged his knife deep into the middle of the wizard's chest.

Chaos.

The wizard screamed weakly and fell to the ground.

I knelt, holding Christianne.

"Oh, God," I murmured. "Christianne ..." I turned my head up. "KHEPRI!"

She was still breathing. She looked up at me with surprised eyes.

Khepri was there in an instant, untying Christianne's leather armor.

"Lay her down," Khepri said in a quiet voice.

"Charlotte?" My mother's voice called.

I raised my head and sought out her face.

"Mother, I'm here. We have a warrior down." I glanced down at Christianne.

Olof was kneeling beside her. He kissed her forehead and held her hand.

"Charlotte," my father's voice rang out. "Let us know if we can help."

I nodded.

I felt a hand on my back. Tam.

"You did it, Babe. You rescued us," Tam smiled, tears in his eyes.

I looked close and gasped.

Tam had been badly beaten. He was covered in bruises, and his lip was split open.

"It looks worse than it is," he assured me.

I glanced down at Christianne.

Khepri was pulling her bag forward and opening Christianne's lower tunic, exposing the wound.

I released the breath I'd been holding.

The knife had pierced her side, not her middle.

I watched Khepri's shoulders and saw the tension leave them.

"You're going to be okay, Chrissy. The knife bounced off your ribs and went out the other side," she whispered.

Christianne grinned, then grimaced as Khepri cleaned the wound.

I looked.

Yep, a glancing blow. One chance in a million. I relaxed.

I heard the newly freed villagers talking, happy voices murmuring in the background.

I took a deep breath, closing my eyes as I held Christianne.

I was unwilling to let go of her.

So brave. Those wings of hers saved the day.

I opened my eyes and smiled down at Christianne.

"You did it. You saved us," I whispered.

She smiled up at me.

Olof remained where he was, unwilling to let go of Christianne's hand.

I understood how he felt.

I glanced to my side and saw the ice wizard splayed out in the dirt. His eyes were open and glassy.

Jim leaned over us and peered at the wizard. "Is he ...?"

"He's dead, Jim." Tam said, kneeling beside the body.

I leaned forward and kissed Tam.

Then I closed my eyes in relief.

Chapter Thirty-One
Opening a Can of Whoopass

Merry.

Christianne was sitting up, her side a neat, tan bandage Khepri was just finishing tying.

"Where's my baby?" I asked.

I looked around.

I stood up.

"Tupu, Tam, Caroline. EVERYONE." The murmured and hubbub of the crowd quieted and I turned to look at their faces.

"WHERE. IS. THE. BABY?" I said loudly.

Everyone looked around and shrugged.

"Look everywhere," called Tupu. "Search the cavern! GO!"

We lit torches and were soon spread out and searching every square inch of the huge ice cavern.

Merry was nowhere to be found.

"Charlotte!" called Jim. "I found something."

I ran to where he was waving, and my troupe followed me.

Christianne walked a little slower, holding Olof's hand, but with Khepri's help she was able to keep up.

Jim indicated the side of the cavern, icy moss glittering with melting snow. He pulled it aside to reveal a small tunnel.

It was about four feet high. We would have to crouch.

"Come on!" I called, darting in the tunnel.

The sides were rock and dirt, and I ran as fast as I could, my torch held high.

After a running for a few minutes along the passageway, the tunnel branched into two.

"Take that one, and I'll go this way," I said hurriedly.

Tam took Jim and Håkan and ran down the right-side tunnel, while I hurried down the left path, Tupu and Caroline fast on my heels.

I could hear others following us.

I got into a rhythm, bent over, my feet running forward. It worked great until I tripped and went sprawling forward.

"Oh! Miss, let me help you," Caroline lifted my arm and I got to my feet and began running again.

I soon arrived at a branching of four different tunnels: the one from which we'd just emerged, and three more.

"Okay," I said, "let's split up." I didn't wait for their response, I just started running down the middle tunnel.

It went on forever.

At one point, I stopped to rest and take a sip from my water skin.

It had been more than an hour, I guessed.

I took a deep breath and continued running down my tunnel. After ten more minutes, I came to a dead end.

"What?!" I said under my breath. I searched every square foot of the dead end, and found nothing. "Sheesh," I panted, turning back and running back the way I'd come.

I finally got to the spot where the tunnel had last branched off, picked the tunnel next to the one I'd gone down, and ran.

And ran.

And ran.

Crouched, running was making my back sore, but I didn't care. Until I was forced to stop and rest again.

I could see adult-sized bootprints in the dirt on the tunnel floor.

Tupu or Caroline must have gone this way.

I got up after just a few minutes and began to run again.

After a while, I came to another branch in the tunnel, and without thinking, picked one at random and began running down it.

Running.

Running.

After several hours I had to admit I was lost.

"HELLO?" I called.

I heard voices answer from far away, but I couldn't tell if they belonged to someone in my troupe or a villager or someone else.

I sat resting again, my head down, my eyes closed.

Everything was still and quiet for a few minutes.

It was then that I heard it, very faintly.

A baby crying.

My head snapped up.

I got up and started running again, calling out.

"DOES ANYBODY HEAR THAT TOO?"

I heard a faint voice in the distance. I kept running.

Twice I came to forks in the tunnel, with multiple shafts branching off in many directions. I stopped worrying about which one I should go through, and just kept picking one at random and running.

Always running.

The tunnels were cool, but no longer icy.

The mountain is thawing. The whole earth will cool now.

It ran against common sense, but Khepri suspected that the ice wizard had preferred his home chilly, so he'd kept this mountain and his cavern icy, while the rest of the world warmed at a dangerous rate.

Hopefully everything will go back to normal.

I kept running.

After another hour, hearing the baby's faint cry, then hearing it grow fainter, then doubling back and taking a different tunnel, and hearing it grow a bit less faint, I finally emerged into a larger section.

And there was Tam.

"Tam!" I ran to him. "Have you found anything?" I panted.

"Not yet, but I'm not giving up."

Khepri and Christianne emerged from a different tunnel.

I looked and saw a half dozen that emptied out on our location.

A few minutes later, Tupu ran out of another.

Then Caroline.

"The only one we haven't tried," Tam said, "is this one." He pointed to a smaller side tunnel that looked abandoned.

"We have no choice. We have to try it." I ran into the tunnel. I heard the others running after me.

It was a long time.

It felt like I was lost. I couldn't hear the baby crying any longer, but I kept running forward.

It was the only thing I could do.

An hour later I emerged, dripping with sweat, into a larger cave.

And I heard voices.

As the others emerged behind me, I held my finger to my lips.

We gathered behind a large rock and looked.

OH!

I spotted Tupu, Olof, and Kym hiding behind another boulder, off about fifty feet. Their tunnels had ended in this cave as well.

This is promising.

I decided to get a closer look at where the voices were coming from. They sounded strangely high-pitched.

I darted around the corner, and hid behind another boulder.

Then another.

Then I peeked and saw them.

They looked a bit like the mountain gnomes, only smaller.

And they were blue.

Why are they blue?

They were all huddled in one spot, and they were arguing.

A white-hot anger rose in my chest, and I decided to act.

I stomped over to them. They spotted me and squeaked in surprise, but held their ground.

One of them was taller than the others, who tried to hide behind him.

I walked right up to them, my scimitar drawn.

"WHO'S IN CHARGE?"

The little blue men pointed to the tallest one.

I looked at him, glowering.

"WHERE IS MY BABY?" I was yelling, I heard my voice echo off the cave walls behind me, but I didn't care.

The little man flinched.

I grabbed his sleeve and pulled him to me.

"What's your name? Where is the baby?"

He just squeaked in fear.

"Charlotte!" I turned, still holding on to the tiny blue man.

It was Jim.

He trotted up to me from an entirely different direction.

There must be dozens of tunnels in this mountain. It's a maze.

"Let me try," he said.

I shrugged, but kept hold of the creature's sleeve.

"You," said Jim. "You're ice goblins, aren't you?"

They nodded.

"Speak!" I said, tired of the slow pace of the conversation.

"Yes," the tall goblins squeaked out.

Now we're getting somewhere.

I leaned close to the leader's face, glowering. "WHERE. IS. THE. BABY?"

He blinked.

"We hid it. He told us to," the leader said. The other goblins nodded hurriedly.

"The ice wizard?" Jim asked.

"Well, of course the ice wizard," I said, exasperated. "Who else would it be?"

Jim patted my shoulder, then turned to the lead goblin.

"Was it the wizard?" he asked.

The leader nodded slowly.

Another ice goblin came forward then, pushing his way through the crowd. He was shorter and fatter than his companions, and dressed in blue robes, and carried a wooden staff with a crystal on the top. He smiled at us craftily.

"What? Do you know where the baby is?"

"Of course, I do. I helped hide it," the goblin mage said.

"Lead me to him! I demand it!" I said.

He just smiled and shook his head.

I lifted my sword and held it at the little man's throat.

He didn't flinch.

"I could run you through," I said.

"You would never find the baby if you did," he said softly.

ARGGGHHHHH!

"Listen, the ice wizard is dead," I said. "Olof killed him," I gestured to the young man beside me. "So you are free to tell us where the baby is hidden, understand?"

The other goblins seemed surprised, and turned to talk rapidly among themselves in their own tongue.

I waited.

A few minutes later, the tall one turned and whispered in the goblin mage's ear.

The mage turned to us. "We don't believe you."

My eyes opened wide in surprise, and I opened my mouth to say something.

But Jim held his hand up, and I closed it again. He knew what he was doing.

I waited.

Jim said, "Why don't you believe us?"

The goblin mage considered his question for a moment, then shrugged. "I guess it doesn't hurt to tell you," he said. "The wizard put us under a spell of compelling." He grinned evilly.

Tam reach out and grabbed the goblin mage, bringing his face close to him.

"Goblin, you are coming with me," he said. "Now point out the fastest route to the ice wizard's cavern, or I will run you through. And do not think I won't. There are a dozen more of you who can tell me how to find the baby. You're hardly special."

The goblin mage went white, and the grin fell off his face.

Tam nodded to Håkan, and they walked off with the goblin between them. I could hear the squeaky voice telling them which tunnel to enter.

I sat down to wait.

I had faith in Tam, so I tried to calm down.

Christianne sat next to me, and Olof on her other side.

I turned to her. "How're you feeling?"

"Oh, she answered, laughing, "much, much better. Khepri gave me something for the pain, and it doped me up good. I feel great!"

We waited.

And waited.

After what seemed like an hour, but turned out to be less than ten minutes, Tam reappeared, Håkan behind him, dragging the goblin mage.

Tam was carrying the ice wizard's head.

My eyebrows shot up.

Tam marched over to the other ice goblins, thrust the wizard's severed head at them, and yelled, "SEE?! DEAD!"

The tall goblin began babbling in terror, and the others cowered behind him.

Håkan came forward and threw the goblin mage to the ground at their feet, drew his sword, and put the point at the tall goblin's chest.

"Hi," he growled in a rough voice. "My name is Håkan. I'm not as nice as the princess. I'm not as loud as Tam. You know what I am?" Håkan wiggled his eyebrows. "I am ruthless. And I don't care."

And with that, he pushed and ran the tall ice goblin through with his sword.

The blade appeared on the other side of the goblin; whose eyes were opened wide in surprise.

Håkan put his boot on the goblin's chest and pushed, sliding him off his sword.

He turned to the goblin mage, "Who's next?"

The mage's mouth moved, but no sound came out.

He cleared his throat.

"Okay, okay, I'll show you where the baby is," he said. There was an enigmatic look on his face, and I felt a chilling horror at the man.

"Follow me," he said quietly.

He led us to a far tunnel, which emptied out on a small chamber.

And there was my baby.

I rushed to pick him up, and held him tightly to me, tears in my eyes.

"I will never let you go, never ever," I murmured to the newborn.

The goblin mage touched my elbow then.

"We fell in love with the baby," he said, and cryptic look on his face. "Is it your baby?"

I nodded, my tears falling.

"We love him, and we wanted to keep him and raise him as our goblin king," the mage said with a scowl.

I heard Håkan and Tam draw their swords again and saw them point the tips at this goblin mage.

The little man began to chant under his breath.

"What?" I said.

"What is he saying?" Tam said.

"STOP HIM!" Jim cried.

Håkan pushed the point of his sword into the goblin's neck. "STOP."

The goblin didn't stop.

He stared straight at me as he kept chanting the spell, then raised his voice to a call and said, "... *look straight into the eyes of death, and use it to create this last masterpiece ...*"

I shuddered, and felt an icy shiver descend over me as the curse took hold.

Håkan growled and pushed the sword in. It was a broad sword. The goblin mage was a tiny man. It took his head off.

The head rolled in the dirt where it fell, and I stared at it.

The eyes were still glowering, and the mouth still moving, whispering "... *look straight into the eyes of death, and use it to create this last masterpiece ...*"

Dear reader~

I'm so glad you read The Pirate Prince and I hope you loved it. I do hope you'll consider leaving a review. It means so very much to hear what you think.

Get book 5 of the series!

The Death of the Queen
On sale fall 2020!

Here ends The Pirate Prince, the fourth book of The Paladin Princess series. The fifth book will be called The Death of the Queen.

ABOUT THE AUTHOR

Samaire Wynne grew up in a lot of different places, and now happily resides on the East Coast, laboring away at writing stories every day. She is an animal lover with far too many pets, yet she still muses how she'd like to add even more. A lover of all things night and gothic, she also loves to read and reread her favorite books. Owned by a cat named Tyrion, she can be found haunting the shadows and mists that hang low over the hills of southern Virginia.